HIGH-VOLTAGE SHOCK...
MIND-BENDING SUSPENSE

A ghastly world where invaders take over ends in a nightmare of terror and revenge.

A vacationing time-traveler stumbles into a harrowing hell of brontosaurian monsters and prehistoric parasites.

A homicidal android and his terrified owner in a cat-and-mouse space chase of violence and death.

Widely divergent in setting and mood, each of these pulse-pounding stories will raise your blood pressure while stimulating your imagination. Choose a moonless night when you're *not* alone and let the sinister geniuses of modern science fiction run away with your mind.

A SHOCKING THING
is an original POCKET BOOK edition.

A SHOCKING THING

Edited by
Damon Knight

A POCKET BOOK EDITION published by
Simon & Schuster of Canada, Ltd. • Markham, Ontario, Canada
Registered User of the Trademark

A SCHOCKING THING

POCKET BOOK edition published November, 1974
2nd printing........September, 1974

Standard Book Number: 671-77775-0.

Front cover art by Gerry McConnell

Printed in Canada.

ACKNOWLEDGMENTS

"Man from the South" by Roald Dahl, from *Someone Like You,* copyright, 1953, by Roald Dahl, reprinted by permission of Alfred A. Knopf, Inc.

"The Abyss" by Leonid Andreyev, from *A Treasury of Russian Life and Humor,* copyright, 1943, by Coward-McCann, Inc.

"A Case History" by John Anthony West, copyright, ©, 1973, by John Anthony West, reprinted by permission of the author and his agent, Robert P. Mills, Ltd.

"Fondly Fahrenheit" by Alfred Bester, copyright, 1954, by Mercury Press, Inc., reprinted by permission of the author.

"Lukundoo" by Edward Lucas White, copyright, 1927, by the George Doran Company.

"The Cabbage Patch" by Theodore R. Cogswell, copyright, ©, 1957, by Mercury Press, Inc., reprinted by permission of the author.

"The Time of the Big Sleep" by Jean-Pierre Andrevon, copyright, ©, 1971, by *Fiction* and Jean-Pierre Andrevon, reprinted by permission of the author. English translation copyright, ©, 1974, by Damon Knight.

"The Right Man for the Right Job" by J. C. Thompson, copyright, ©, 1962, by Jean W. Thompson, reprinted by permission of Harold Matson Co., Inc.

"The Year of the Jackpot" by Robert A. Heinlein, copyright, 1952, by Galaxy Publishing Corp., reprinted by permission of Lurton Blassingame.

ACKNOWLEDGMENTS *(continued)*

"The Snail-Watcher" by Patricia Highsmith, from *The Snail-Watcher and Other Stories,* copyright, ©, 1964, by Patricia Highsmith, reprinted by permission of Doubleday & Co., Inc.

"Bianca's Hands" by Theodore Sturgeon, from *E Pluribus Unicorn,* copyright, 1947, by Consolidated Press (London), reprinted by permission of the author.

"Poor Little Warrior!" by Brian W. Aldiss, from *Who Can Replace a Man?,* copyright, ©, 1958, by Mercury Press, Inc., reprinted by permission of the author.

"The Hounds" by Kate Wilhelm appears here for the first time and is published by permission of the author.

"The Clone" by Theodore L. Thomas, copyright, ©, 1959, by Ziff-Davis Publishing Co., Inc., reprinted by permission of the author.

"The Touch of Nutmeg Makes It" by John Collier, from *Fancies and Goodnights,* copyright, 1943, by The Readers Club, 1950, by John Collier, reprinted by permission of Harold Matson Co., Inc.

"Casey Agonistes" by Richard McKenna, from *Casey Agonistes and Other Science Fiction and Fantasy Stories,* copyright, ©, 1958, by Mercury Press, Inc., reprinted by permission of Mrs. Eva McKenna.

Contents

A SHOCKING THING

BY ROALD DAHL

Man from the South

It was getting on toward six o'clock so I thought I'd buy myself a beer and go out and sit in a deck chair by the swimming pool and have a little evening sun.

I went to the bar and got the beer and carried it outside and wandered down the garden toward the pool.

It was a fine garden with lawns and beds of azaleas and tall coconut palms, and the wind was blowing strongly through the tops of the palm trees, making the leaves hiss and crackle as though they were on fire. I could see the clusters of big brown nuts hanging down underneath the leaves.

There were plenty of deck chairs around the swimming pool, and there were white tables and huge brightly colored umbrellas and sunburned men and women sitting around in bathing suits. In the pool itself there were three or four girls and about a dozen boys, all splashing about and making a lot of noise and throwing a large rubber ball at one another.

I stood watching them. The girls were English girls from the hotel. The boys I didn't know about, but they sounded American, and I thought they were probably naval cadets who'd come ashore from the U.S. naval training vessel which had arrived in harbor that morning.

I went over and sat down under a yellow umbrella where there were four empty seats, and I poured my beer and settled back comfortably with a cigarette.

It was very pleasant sitting there in the sunshine with

beer and cigarette. It was pleasant to sit and watch the bathers splashing about in the green water.

The American sailors were getting on nicely with the English girls. They'd reached the stage where they were diving under the water and tipping them up by their legs.

Just then I noticed a small, oldish man walking briskly around the edge of the pool. He was immaculately dressed in a white suit, and he walked very quickly with little bouncing strides, pushing himself high up onto his toes with each step. He had on a large creamy Panama hat, and he came bouncing along the side of the pool, looking at the people and the chairs.

He stopped beside me and smiled, showing two rows of very small, uneven teeth, slightly tarnished. I smiled back.

"Excuse pleess, but may I sit here?"

"Certainly," I said. "Go ahead."

He bobbed around to the back of the chair and inspected it for safety; then he sat down and crossed his legs. His white buckskin shoes had little holes punched all over them for ventilation.

"A fine evening," he said. "They are all evenings fine here in Jamaica." I couldn't tell if the accent were Italian or Spanish, but I felt fairly sure he was some sort of a South American. And old too, when you saw him close. Probably around sixty-eight or seventy.

"Yes," I said. "It is wonderful here, isn't it."

"And who, might I ask, are all dese? Dese is no hotel people." He was pointing at the bathers in the pool.

"I think they're American sailors," I told him. "They're Americans who are learning to be sailors."

"Of course dey are Americans. Who else in de world is going to make as much noise as dat? You are not American, no?"

"No," I said. "I am not."

Suddenly one of the American cadets was standing in front of us. He was dripping wet from the pool, and one of the English girls was standing there with him.

"Are these chairs taken?" he said.

"No," I answered.

"Mind if I sit down?"

"Go ahead."

"Thanks," he said. He had a towel in his hand, and when he sat down he unrolled it and produced a pack of cigarettes and a lighter. He offered the cigarettes to the girl and she refused; then he offered them to me and I took one. The little man said, "Tank you, no, but I tink I have a cigar." He pulled out a crocodile case and got himself a cigar; then he produced a knife which had a small scissors in it, and he snipped the end off the cigar.

"Here, let me give you a light." The American boy held up his lighter.

"Dat will not work in dis wind."

"Sure, it'll work. It always works."

The little man removed his unlighted cigar from his mouth, cocked his head on one side, and looked at the boy.

"*All*-ways?" he said slowly.

"Sure, it never fails. Not with me anyway."

The little man's head was still cocked over on one side, and he was still watching the boy. "Well, well. So you say dis famous lighter it never fails. Iss dat you say?"

"Sure," the boy said. "That's right." He was about nineteen or twenty with a long freckled face and a rather sharp birdlike nose. His chest was not very sunburned, and there were freckles there too and a few wisps of pale-reddish hair. He was holding the lighter in his right hand, ready to flip the wheel. "It never fails," he said, smiling now because he was purposely exaggerating his little boast. "I promise you it never fails."

"One momint, pleess." The hand that held the cigar came up high, palm outward, as though it were stopping traffic. "Now juss one momint." He had a curiously soft, toneless voice, and he kept looking at the boy all the time.

"Shall we not perhaps make a little bet on dat?" He smiled at the boy. "Shall we not make a little bet on whether your lighter lights?"

"Sure, I'll bet," the boy said. "Why not?"

"You like to bet?"

"Sure, I'll always bet."

The man paused and examined his cigar, and I must say I didn't much like the way he was behaving. It seemed he was already trying to make something out of this, and to embarrass the boy, and at the same time I had the feeling he was relishing a private little secret all his own.

He looked up again at the boy and said slowly, "I like to bet, too. Why we don't have a good bet on dis ting? A good big bet."

"Now wait a minute," the boy said. "I can't do that. But I'll bet you a quarter. I'll even bet you a dollar, or whatever it is over here—some shillings, I guess."

The little man waved his hand again. "Lissen to me. Now we have some fun. We make a bet. Den we go up to my room here in de hotel where iss no wind, and I bet you you cannot light dis famous lighter of yours ten times running without missing once."

"I'll bet I can," the boy said.

"All right. Good. We make a bet, yes?"

"Sure. I'll bet you a buck."

"No, no. I make you very good bet. I am rich man, and I am sporting man also. Lissen to me. Outside de hotel iss my car. Iss very fine car. American car from your country. Cadillac—"

"Hey, now. Wait a minute." The boy leaned back in his deck chair and he laughed. "I can't put up that sort of property. This is crazy."

"Not crazy at all. You strike lighter successfully ten times running and Cadillac is yours. You like to have dis Cadillac, yes?"

"Sure, I'd like to have a Cadillac." The boy was still grinning.

"All right. Fine. We make a bet, and I put up my Cadillac."

"And what do I put up?"

The little man carefully removed the red band from his still unlighted cigar. "I never ask you, my friend, to bet someting you cannot afford. You understand?"

"Then what do I bet?"

"I make it very easy for you, yes?"

"Okay. You make it easy."

"Some small ting you can afford to give away, and if you did happen to lose it, you would not feel too bad. Right?"

"Such as what?"

"Such as, perhaps, de little finger of your left hand."

"My *what?*" The boy stopped grinning.

"Yes. Why not? You win, you take de car. You looss, I take de finger."

"I don't get it. How d'you mean, you take the finger?"

"I chop it off."

"Jumping jeepers! That's a crazy bet. I think I'll just make it a dollar."

The little man leaned back, spread out his hands palms upward, and gave a tiny contemptuous shrug of the shoulders. "Well, well, well," he said. "I do not understand. You say it lights, but you will not bet. Den we forget it, yes?"

The boy sat quite still, staring at the bathers in the pool. Then he remembered suddenly he hadn't lighted his cigarette. He put it between his lips, cupped his hands around the lighter, and flipped the wheel. The wick lighted and burned with a small, steady, yellow flame, and the way he held his hands the wind didn't get to it at all.

"Could I have a light, too?" I said.

"Gee, I'm sorry. I forgot you didn't have one."

I held out my hand for the lighter, but he stood up and came over to do it for me.

"Thank you," I said, and he returned to his seat.

"You having a good time?" I asked.

"Fine," he answered. "It's pretty nice here."

There was a silence then, and I could see that the little man had succeeded in disturbing the boy with his absurd proposal. He was sitting there very still, and it was obvious that a small tension was beginning to build up inside him. Then he started shifting about in his seat, and rubbing his chest, and stroking the back of his neck, and finally he placed both hands on his knees and began tap-tapping with his fingers against the kneecaps. Soon he was tapping with one of his feet as well.

"Now just let me check up on this bet of yours," he said at last. "You say we go up to your room, and if I make this lighter light ten times running, I win a Cadillac. If it misses just once, then I forfeit the little finger of my left hand. Is that right?"

"Certainly. Dat is de bet. But I tink you are afraid."

"What do we do if I lose? Do I have to hold my finger out while you chop it off?"

"Oh, no! Dat would be no good. And you might be tempted to refuse to hold it out. What I should do I should tie one of your hands to de table before we started, and I should stand dere with a knife ready to go *chop* de momint your lighter missed."

"What year is the Cadillac?" the boy asked.

"Excuse. I not understand."

"What year—how old is the Cadillac?"

"Ah! How old? Yes. It is last year. Quite new car. But I see you are not betting man. Americans never are."

The boy paused for just a moment, and he glanced first at the English girl, then at me. "Yes," he said sharply. "I'll bet you."

"Good!" The little man clapped his hands together quietly, once. "Fine," he said. "We do it now. And you, sir," he turned to me, "you would perhaps be good enough to, what you call it, to—to referee." He had pale, almost colorless eyes with tiny bright black pupils.

"Well," I said. "I think it's a crazy bet. I don't think I like it very much."

"Nor do I," said the English girl. It was the first time she'd spoken. "I think it's a stupid, ridiculous bet."

"Are you serious about cutting off this boy's finger if he loses?" I said.

"Certainly I am. Also about giving him Cadillac if he win. Come now. We go to my room."

He stood up. "You like to put on some clothes first?" he said.

"No," the boy answered. "I'll come like this." Then he turned to me. "I'd consider it a favor if you'd come along and referee."

"All right," I said. "I'll come along, but I don't like the bet."

"You come too," he said to the girl. You come and watch."

The little man led the way back through the garden to the hotel. He was animated now, and excited, and that seemed to make him bounce up higher than ever on his toes as he walked along.

"I live in annex," he said. "You like to see car first? Iss just here."

He took us to where we could see the front driveway of the hotel, and he stopped and pointed to a sleek pale-green Cadillac parked close by.

"Dere she iss. De green one. You like?"

"Say, that's a nice car," the boy said.

"All right. Now we go up and see if you can win her."

We followed him into the annex and up one flight of stairs. He unlocked his door, and we all trooped into what was a large pleasant double bedroom. There was a woman's dressing gown lying across the bottom of one of the beds.

"First," he said, "we 'ave a little Martini."

The drinks were on a small table in the far corner, all ready to be mixed, and there was a shaker and ice and plenty of glasses. He began to make the Martini, but meanwhile he'd rung the bell and now there was a knock on the door and a colored maid came in.

"Ah!" he said, putting down the bottle of gin, taking a wallet from his pocket, and pulling out a pound note. "You will do someting for me now, pleess." He gave the maid the pound.

"You keep dat," he said. "And now we are going to play a little game in here, and I want you to go off and find for me two—no tree tings. I want some nails, I want a hammer, and I want a chopping knife, a butcher's chopping knife which you can borrow from de kitchen. You can get, yes?"

"A *chopping knife!*" The maid opened her eyes wide and clasped her hands in front of her. "You mean a *real* chopping knife?"

"Yes, yes, of course. Come on now, pleess. You can find dose tings surely for me."

"Yes, sir, I'll try, sir. Surely I'll try to get them." And she went.

The little man handed around the Martinis. We stood there and sipped them, the boy with the long freckled face and the pointed nose, bare-bodied except for a pair of faded brown bathing shorts; the English girl, a large-boned, fair-haired girl wearing a pale blue bathing suit, who watched the boy over the top of her glass all the time; the little man with the colorless eyes, standing there in his immaculate white suit, drinking his Martini, and looking at the girl in her pale blue bathing dress. I didn't know what to make of it all. The man seemed serious about the bet, and he seemed serious about the business of cutting off the finger. But, hell, what if the boy lost? Then we'd have to rush him to the hospital in the Cadillac that he hadn't won. That would be a fine thing. Now wouldn't that be a really fine thing? It would be a damn silly unnecessary thing so far as I could see.

"Don't you think this is rather a silly bet?" I said.

"I think it's a fine bet," the boy answered. He had already downed one large Martini.

"I think it's a stupid, ridiculous bet," the girl said. "What'll happen if you lose?"

"It won't matter. Come to think of it, I can't remember ever in my life having had any use for the little finger on my left hand. Here he is." The boy took hold of the finger. "Here he is, and he hasn't ever done a thing for me yet. So why shouldn't I bet him. I think it's a fine bet."

The little man smiled and picked up the shaker and refilled our glasses.

"Before we begin," he said, "I will present to de—to de referee de key of de car." He produced a car key from his pocket and gave it to me. "De papers," he said, "de owning papers and insurance are in de pocket of de car."

Then the colored maid came in again. In one hand she carried a small chopper, the kind used by butchers for chopping meat bones, and in the other a hammer and a bag of nails.

"Good! You get dem all. Tank you, tank you. Now you can go." He waited until the maid had closed the door; then he put the implements on one of the beds and said, "Now we prepare ourselves, yes?" And to the boy, "Help me, pleess, wid dis table. We carry it out a little."

It was the usual kind of hotel writing desk, just a plain rectangular table about four feet by three with a blotting pad, ink, pens, and paper. They carried it out into the room away from the wall and removed the writing things.

"And now," he said, "a chair." He picked up a chair and placed it beside the table. He was very brisk and very animated, like a person organizing games at a children's party. "And now de nails. I must put in de nails." He fetched the nails, and he began to hammer them into the top of the table.

We stood there, the boy, the girl, and I, holding Martinis in our hands, watching the little man at work. We watched him hammer two nails into the table, about six inches apart. He didn't hammer them right home; he allowed a small part of each one to stick up. Then he tested them for firmness with his fingers.

Anyone would think the son of a bitch had done this before, I told myself. He never hesitates. Table, nails, hammer, kitchen chopper. He knows exactly what he needs and how to arrange it.

"And now," he said, "all we want is some string." He found some string. "All right, at last we are ready. Will you pleess to sit here at de table," he said to the boy.

The boy put his glass away and sat down.

"Now place de left hand between dese two nails. De nails are only so I can tie your hand in place. All right, good. Now I tie your hand secure to de table—so."

He wound the string around the boy's wrist, then several times around the wide part of the hand; then he fastened it tight to the nails. He made a good job of it, and when he'd finished there wasn't any question about the boy being able to draw his hand away. But he could move his fingers.

"Now pleess, clench de fist, all except for de little finger. You must leave de little finger sticking out, lying on de table.

"*Ex*-cellent! *Ex*-cellent! Now we are ready. Wid your right hand you manipulate de lighter. But one momint, pleess."

He skipped over to the bed and picked up the chopper. He came back and stood beside the table with the chopper in his hand.

"We are all ready?" he said. "Mister referee, you must say to begin."

The English girl was standing there in her pale blue bathing costume right behind the boy's chair. She was just standing there, not saying anything. The boy was sitting quite still, holding the lighter in his right hand, looking at the chopper. The little man was looking at me.

"Are you ready?" I asked the boy.

"I'm ready."

"And you?" to the little man.

"Quite ready," he said, and he lifted the chopper up in the air and held it there about two feet above the boy's finger, ready to chop. The boy watched it, but he didn't flinch, and his mouth didn't move at all. He merely raised his eyebrows and frowned.

"All right," I said. "Go ahead."

The boy said, "Will you please count aloud the number of times I light it."

"Yes," I said. "I'll do that."

With his thumb he raised the top of the lighter, and again with the thumb he gave the wheel a sharp flick. The flint sparked, and the wick caught fire and burned with a small yellow flame.

"One!" I called.

He didn't blow the flame out; he closed the top of the lighter on it, and he waited for perhaps five seconds before opening it again.

He flicked the wheel very strongly and once more there was a small flame burning on the wick.

"Two!"

No one else said anything. The boy kept his eyes on

the lighter. The little man held the chopper up in the air, and he too was watching the lighter.

"Three!"

"Four!"

"Five!"

"Six!"

"Seven!" Obviously it was one of those lighters that worked. The flint gave a big spark, and the wick was the right length. I watched the thumb snapping the top down onto the flame. Then a pause. Then the thumb raising the top once more. This was an all-thumb operation. The thumb did everything. I took a breath, ready to say eight. The thumb flicked the wheel. The flint sparked. The little flame appeared.

"Eight!" I said, and as I said it the door opened. We all turned, and we saw a woman standing in the doorway, a small, black-haired woman, rather old, who stood there for about two seconds then rushed forward shouting, "Carlos! Carlos!" She grabbed his wrist, took the chopper from him, threw it on the bed, took hold of the little man by the lapels of his white suit, and began shaking him very vigorously, talking to him fast and loud and fiercely all the time in some Spanish-sounding language. She shook him so fast you couldn't see him anymore. He became a faint, misty, quickly moving outline, like the spokes of a turning wheel.

Then she slowed down, and the little man came into view again, and she hauled him across the room and pushed him backward onto one of the beds. He sat on the edge of it blinking his eyes and testing his head to see if it would still turn on his neck.

"I am so sorry," the woman said. "I am so terribly sorry that this should happen." She spoke almost perfect English.

"It is too bad," she went on. "I suppose it is really my fault. For ten minutes I leave him alone to go and have my hair washed, and I come back and he is at it again." She looked sorry and deeply concerned.

The boy was untying his hand from the table. The English girl and I stood there and said nothing.

"He is a menace," the woman said. "Down where we live at home he has taken altogether forty-seven fingers from different people, and he has lost eleven cars. In the end they threatened to have him put away somewhere. That's why I brought him up here."

"We were only having a little bet," mumbled the little man from the bed.

"I suppose he bet you a car," the woman said.

"Yes," the boy answered. "A Cadillac."

"He has no car. It's mine. And that makes it worse," she said, "that he should bet you when he has nothing to bet with. I am ashamed and very sorry about it all." She seemed an awfully nice woman.

"Well," I said, "then here's the key of your car." I put it on the table.

"We were only having a little bet," mumbled the little man.

"He hasn't anything left to bet with," the woman said. "He hasn't a thing in the world. Not a thing. As a matter of fact I myself won it all from him a long while ago. It took time, a lot of time, and it was hard work, but I won it all in the end." She looked up at the boy and she smiled, a slow sad smile, and she came over and put out a hand to take the key from the table.

I can see it now, that hand of hers; it had only one finger on it, and a thumb.

BY PATRICIA HIGHSMITH

The Snail-Watcher

When Mr. Peter Knoppert began to make a hobby of snail-watching he had no idea that his handful of specimens would become hundreds in no time. Only two months after the original snails were carried up to the Knoppert study, some thirty glass tanks and bowls, all teeming with snails, lined the walls, rested on the desk and windowsills, and were beginning even to cover the floor. Mrs. Knoppert disapproved strongly and would no longer enter the room. It smelled, she said, and besides she had once stepped on a snail by accident, a horrible sensation she would never forget. But the more his wife and friends deplored his unusual and vaguely repellent pastime, the more pleasure Mr. Knoppert seemed to find in it.

"I never cared for nature before in my life," Mr. Knoppert often remarked—he was a partner in a brokerage firm, a man who had devoted all his life to the science of finance —"but snails have opened my eyes to the beauty of the animal world."

If his friends commented that snails were not really animals, and their slimy habitats hardly the best example of the beauty of nature, Mr. Knoppert would tell them with a superior smile that they simply didn't know all that he knew about snails.

And it was true. Mr. Knoppert had witnessed an exhibition that was not described, certainly not adequately described, in any encyclopedia or zoology book that he had been able to find. Mr. Knoppert had wandered into the kitchen one evening for a bite of something before dinner

13

and had happened to notice that a couple of snails in the china bowl on the drainboard were behaving very oddly. Standing more or less on their tails, they were weaving before each other for all the world like a pair of snakes hypnotized by a flute player. A moment later, their faces came together in a kiss of voluptuous intensity. Mr. Knoppert bent closer and studied them from all angles. Something else was happening: a protuberance like an ear was appearing on the right side of the head of both snails. His instinct told him that he was watching a sexual activity of some sort.

The cook came in and said something to him, but Mr. Knoppert silenced her with an impatient wave of his hand. He couldn't take his eyes from the enchanted little creatures in the bowl.

When the earlike excrescences were precisely together, rim to rim, a whitish rod like another small tentacle shot out from one ear and arched over toward the ear of the other snail. Mr. Knoppert's first surmise was dashed when a tentacle sallied from the other snail too. Most peculiar, he thought. The two tentacles withdrew, then came forth again, and as if they had found some invisible mark, remained fixed in either snail. Mr. Knoppert peered intently closer. So did the cook.

"Did you ever see anything like this?" Mr. Knoppert asked.

"No. They must be fighting," the cook said indifferently and went away. That was a sample of the ignorance on the subject of snails that he was later to discover everywhere.

Mr. Knoppert continued to observe the pair of snails off and on for more than an hour, until first the ears, then the rods, withdrew, and the snails themselves relaxed their attitudes and paid no further attention to each other. But by that time, a different pair of snails had begun a flirtation and were slowly rearing themselves to get into position for kissing. Mr. Knoppert told the cook that the snails were not to be served that evening. He took the bowl of them up to his study. And snails were never again served in the Knoppert household.

That night, he searched his encyclopedias and a few

general science books he happened to possess, but there was absolutely nothing on snails' breeding habits, though the oyster's dull reproductive cycle was described in detail. Perhaps it hadn't been a mating he had seen after all, Mr. Knoppert decided after a day or two. His wife, Edna, told him either to eat the snails or get rid of them—it was at this time that she stepped upon a snail that had crawled out onto the floor—and Mr. Knoppert might have, if he hadn't come across a sentence in Darwin's *Origin of Species* on a page given to gastropoda. The sentence was in French, a language Mr. Knoppert did not know, but the word *sensualité* made him tense like a bloodhound that has suddenly found the scent. He was in the public library at the time, and laboriously he translated the sentence with the aid of a French-English dictionary. It was a statement of less than a hundred words, saying that snails manifested a sensuality in their mating that was not to be found elsewhere in the animal kingdom. That was all. It was from the notebooks of Henri Fabre. Obviously Darwin had decided not to translate it for the average reader, but to leave it in its original language for the scholarly few who really cared. Mr. Knoppert considered himself one of the scholarly few now, and his round, pink face beamed with self-esteem.

He had learned that his snails were the fresh water type that laid their eggs in sand or earth; so he put moist earth and a little saucer of water into a big washbowl and transferred his snails into it. Then he waited for something to happen. Not even another mating happened. He picked up the snails one by one and looked at them, without seeing anything suggestive of pregnancy. But one snail he couldn't pick up. The shell might have been glued to the earth. Mr. Knoppert suspected the snail had buried its head in the ground to die. Two more days went by, and on the morning of the third, Mr. Knoppert found a spot of crumbly earth where the snail had been. Curious, he investigated the crumbles with a match stem and to his delight discovered a pit full of shiny new eggs. Snail eggs! He hadn't been wrong. Mr. Knoppert called his wife and the cook to look at them. The eggs looked very much like big caviar, only they were white instead of black or red.

"Well, naturally, they have to breed some way," was his wife's comment. Mr. Knoppert couldn't understand her lack of interest. He had to go and look at the eggs every hour that he was at home. He looked at them every morning to see if any change had taken place, and the eggs were his last thought every night before he went to bed. Moreover, another snail was now digging a pit. And another pair of snails was mating! The first batch of eggs turned a grayish color, and minuscule spirals of shells became discernible on one side of each egg. Mr. Knoppert's anticipation rose to a higher pitch. At last a morning arrived—the eighteenth after laying, according to Mr. Knoppert's careful count—when he looked down into the egg pit and saw the first tiny moving head, the first stubby little antennae uncertainly exploring the nest. Mr. Knoppert was as happy as the father of a new child. Every one of the seventy or more eggs in the pit came miraculously to life. He had seen the entire reproductive cycle evolve to a successful conclusion. And the fact that no one, at least no one that he knew of, was acquainted with a fraction of what he knew, lent his knowledge a thrill of discovery, the piquancy of the esoteric. Mr. Knoppert made notes on successive matings and egg hatchings. He narrated snail biology to fascinated, more often shocked, friends and guests, until his wife squirmed with embarrassment.

"But where is it going to stop, Peter? If they keep on reproducing at this rate, they'll take over the house!" his wife told him after fifteen or twenty pits had hatched.

"There's no stopping nature," he replied good-humoredly. "They've only taken over the study. There's plenty of room there."

So more and more glass tanks and bowls were moved in. Mr. Knoppert went to the market and chose several of the more lively looking snails, and also a pair he found mating, unobserved by the rest of the world. More and more egg pits appeared in the dirt floors of the tanks, and finally out of each pit crept from seventy to ninety baby snails, transparent as dewdrops, gliding up rather than down the strips of fresh lettuce that Mr. Knoppert was quick to give all the pits as edible ladders for the climb. Matings went on so often that he no longer bothered to watch them. A mating could last twenty-four hours. But the thrill of seeing the white caviar become shells and start to move—that never diminished, however often he witnessed it.

His colleagues in the brokerage office noticed a new zest for life in Peter Knoppert. He became more daring in his moves, more brilliant in his calculations, became, in fact, a little vicious in his schemes, but he brought money in for his company. By unanimous vote, his basic salary was raised from forty to sixty thousand dollars per year. When anyone congratulated him on his achievements, Mr. Knoppert gave all the credit to his snails and the beneficial relaxation he derived from watching them.

He spent all his evenings with his snails in the room that was no longer a study but a kind of aquarium. He loved to strew the tanks with fresh lettuce and pieces of boiled potato and beet, then turn on the sprinkler system that he had installed in the tanks to simulate natural rainfall. Then all the snails would liven up and begin eating, mating, or merely gliding through the shallow water with obvious pleasure. Mr. Knoppert often let a snail crawl onto his forefinger—he fancied his snails enjoyed this human contact—and he would feed it a piece of lettuce by hand, would observe the snail from all sides, finding as much aesthetic satisfaction as another man might from contemplating a Japanese print.

By now, Mr. Knoppert did not allow anyone to set foot in his study. Too many snails had the habit of crawling around on the floor, of going to sleep glued to chair bottoms and to the backs of books on the shelves. Snails spent much of their time sleeping, especially the older snails. But there were enough less indolent snails who preferred lovemaking. Mr. Knoppert estimated that about a dozen pairs of snails must be kissing all the time. And certainly there was a multitude of baby and adolescent snails. They were impossible to count. But Mr. Knoppert did count the snails sleeping and creeping on the ceiling alone, and arrived at something between eleven and twelve hundred. The tanks, the bowls, the underside of his desk, and the bookshelves must surely have held fifty times that number. Mr. Knoppert meant to scrape the snails off the ceiling one day soon. Some of them had been up there for weeks, and he was afraid they were not taking in enough nourishment. But of late he had been a little too busy, and too much in need of the tranquility that he got simply from sitting in the study in his favorite chair.

During the month of June he was so busy he often worked late into the evening at his office. Reports were piling in for the end of the fiscal year. He made calculations, spotted a half-dozen possibilities of gain, and reserved the most daring, the least obvious moves for his private operations. By this time next year, he thought, he should be three or four times as well off as now. He saw his bank account multiplying as easily and rapidly as his snails. He told his wife this, and she was overjoyed. She even forgave him the ruination of the study, and the stale, fishy smell that was spreading throughout the whole upstairs.

"Still, I do wish you'd take a look just to see if anything's happening, Peter," she said to him rather anxiously one morning. "A tank might have overturned or something, and I wouldn't want the rug to be spoiled. You haven't been in the study for nearly a week, have you?"

Mr. Knoppert hadn't been in for nearly two weeks. He didn't tell his wife that the rug was pretty much gone already. "I'll go up tonight," he said.

But it was three more days before he found time. He went in one evening just before bedtime and was surprised to find the floor quite covered with snails, with three or four layers of snails. He had difficulty closing the door without mashing any. The dense clusters of snails in the corners made the room look positively round, as if he stood inside some huge, conglomerate stone. Mr. Knoppert cracked his knuckles and gazed around him in astonishment. They had not only covered every surface, but thousands of snails hung down into the room from the chandelier in a grotesque clump.

Mr. Knoppert felt for the back of a chair to steady himself. He felt only a lot of shells under his hand. He had to smile a little: there were snails in the chair seat, piled up on one another, like a lumpy cushion. He really must do something about the ceiling, and immediately. He took an umbrella from the corner, brushed some of the snails off it, and cleared a place on his desk to stand. The umbrella point tore the wallpaper, and then the weight of the snails pulled down a long strip that hung almost to the floor. Mr. Knoppert felt frustrated and angry. The sprinklers would make them move. He pulled the lever.

The sprinklers came on in all the tanks, and the seething activity of the entire room increased at once. Mr. Knoppert slid his feet along the floor, through tumbling snail shells that made a sound like pebbles on a beach, and directed a couple of the sprinklers at the ceiling. This was a mistake, he saw at once. The softened paper began to tear, and he dodged one slowly falling mass only to be hit by a swinging festoon of snails, really hit quite a stunning blow on the side of the head. He went down on one knee, dazed. He should open a window, he thought, the air was stifling. And there were snails crawling over his shoes and up his trouser legs. He shook his feet irritably. He was just going to the door, intending to call for one of the servants to help him, when the chandelier fell on him. Mr. Knoppert sat down heavily on the floor. He saw now that he couldn't possibly get a window open, because the snails were fastened thick and deep over the windowsills. For a moment, he felt he couldn't get up, felt as if he were suffocating. It was not only the musty smell of the room, but everywhere he looked long wallpaper strips covered with snails blocked his vision as if he were in a prison.

"Edna!" he called, and was amazed at the muffled, ineffectual sound of his voice. The room might have been soundproof.

He crawled to the door, heedless of the sea of snails he crushed under hands and knees. He could not get the door open. There were so many snails on it, crossing and recrossing the crack of the door on all four sides, they actually resisted his strength.

"Edna!" A snail crawled into his mouth. He spat it out in disgust. Mr. Knoppert tried to brush the snails off his arms. But for every hundred he dislodged, four hundred seemed to slide upon him and fasten to him again, as if they deliberately sought him out as the only comparatively snail-free surface in the room. There were snails crawling over his eyes. Then just as he staggered to his feet, something else hit him—Mr. Knoppert couldn't even see what. He was fainting! At any rate, he was on the floor. His arms felt like leaden weights as he tried to reach his nostrils, his eyes, to free them from the sealing, murderous snail bodies.

"Help!" He swallowed a snail. Choking, he widened his mouth for air and felt a snail crawl over his lips onto his tongue. He was in hell! He could feel them gliding over his legs like a glutinous river, pinning his legs to the floor. "Ugh!" Mr. Knoppert's breath came in feeble gasps. His vision grew black, a horrible, undulating black. He could not breathe at all, because he could not reach his nostrils, could not move his hands. Then through the slit of one eye, he saw directly in front of him, only inches away, what had been, he knew, the rubber plant that stood in its pot near the door. A pair of snails were quietly making love in it. And right beside them, tiny snails as pure as dewdrops were emerging from a pit like an infinite army into their widening world.

BY THEODORE STURGEON

Bianca's Hands

Bianca's mother was leading her when Ran saw her first. Bianca was squat and small, with dank hair and rotten teeth. Her mouth was crooked and it drooled. Either she was blind or she just didn't care about bumping into things. It didn't really matter because Bianca was an imbecile. Her hands. . . .

They were lovely hands, graceful hands, hands as soft and smooth and white as snowflakes, hands whose color was lightly tinged with pink like the glow of Mars on snow. They lay on the counter side by side, looking at Ran. They lay there half-closed and crouching, each pulsing with a movement like the panting of a field creature, and they looked. Not watched. Later, they watched him. Now they looked. They did, because Ran felt their united gaze, and his heart beat strongly.

Bianca's mother demanded cheese stridently. Ran brought it to her in his own time while she berated him. She was a bitter woman, as any woman has a right to be who is wife of no man and mother to a monster. Ran gave her the cheese and took her money and never noticed that it was not enough, because of Bianca's hands. When Bianca's mother tried to take one of the hands it scuttled away from the unwanted touch. It did not lift from the counter, but ran on its fingertips to the edge and leaped into a fold of Bianca's dress. The woman took the unresisting elbow and led Bianca out.

Ran stayed there at the counter unmoving, thinking of Bianca's hands. Ran was strong and bronze and not very

21

clever. He had never been taught about beauty and strangeness, but he did not need that teaching. His shoulders were wide, and his arms were heavy and thick, but he had great soft eyes and thick lashes. They curtained his eyes now. He was seeing Bianca's hands again dreamily. He found it hard to breathe. . . .

Harding came back. Harding owned the store. He was a large man whose features barely kept his cheeks apart. He said, "Sweep up, Ran. We're closing early today." Then he went behind the counter, squeezing past Ran.

Ran got the broom and swept slowly.

"A woman bought cheese," he said suddenly. "A poor woman with very old clothes. She was leading a girl. I can't remember what the girl looked like, except—who was she?"

"I saw them go out," said Harding. "The woman is Bianca's mother, and the girl is Bianca. I don't know their other name. They don't talk to people much. I wish they wouldn't come in here. Hurry up, Ran."

Ran did what was necessary and put away his broom. Before he left he asked, "Where do they live, Bianca and her mother?"

"On the other side. A house on no road, away from people. Good night, Ran."

Ran went from the shop directly over to the other side, not waiting for his supper. He found the house easily, for it was indeed away from the road, and stood rudely by itself. The townspeople had cauterized the house by wrapping it in empty fields.

Harshly, "What do you want?" Bianca's mother asked as she opened the door.

"May I come in?"

"What do you want?"

"May I come in?" he asked again. She made as if to slam the door, and then stood aside. "Come."

Ran went in and stood still. Bianca's mother crossed the room and sat under an old lamp, in the shadow. Ran sat opposite her, on a three-legged stool. Bianca was not in the room.

The woman tried to speak, but embarrassment clutched at her voice. She withdrew into her bitterness, saying nothing. She kept peeping at Ran, who sat quietly with his arms folded and the uncertain light in his eyes. He knew she would speak soon, and he could wait.

"Ah, well. . . ." She was silent after that, for a time, but now she had forgiven him his intrusion. Then, "It's a great while since anyone came to see me; a great while . . . it was different before. I was a pretty girl—"

She bit her words off, and her face popped out of the shadows, shriveled and sagging as she leaned forward. Ran saw that she was beaten and cowed and did not want to be laughed at.

"Yes," he said gently. She sighed and leaned back so that her face disappeared again. She said nothing for a moment, sitting looking at Ran, liking him.

"We were happy, the two of us," she mused, "until Bianca came. He didn't like her, poor thing, he didn't, no more than I do now. He went away. I stayed by her because I was her mother. I'd go away myself, I would, but people know me, and I haven't a penny—not a penny. . . . They'd bring me back to her, they would, to care for her. It doesn't matter much now, though, because people don't want me any more than they want her, they don't. . . ."

Ran shifted his feet uneasily, because the woman was crying. "Have you room for me here?" he asked.

Her head crept out into the light. Ran said swiftly, "I'll give you money each week and I'll bring my own bed and things." He was afraid she would refuse.

She merged with the shadows again. "If you like," she said, trembling at her good fortune. "Though why you'd want to . . . still, I guess if I had a little something to cook up nice, and a good reason for it, I could make someone real cosy here. But—*why?*" She rose. Ran crossed the room and pushed her back into the chair. He stood over her, tall.

"I never want you to ask me that," he said, speaking very slowly. "Hear?"

She swallowed and nodded. "I'll come back tomorrow with the bed and things," he said.

He left her there under the lamp, blinking out of the dimness, folded round and about with her misery and her wonder.

People talked about it. People said, "Ran has moved to the house of Bianca's mother." "It must be because—" "Ah," said some, "Ran was always a strange boy. It must be because—" "Oh, no!" cried others, appalled. "Ran is such a good boy. He wouldn't—"

Harding was told. He frightened the busy little woman who told him. He said, "Ran is very quiet, but he is honest, and he does his work. As long as he comes here in the morning and earns his wage, he can do what he wants, where he wants, and it is not my business to stop him." He said this so very sharply that the little woman dared not say anything more.

Ran was very happy, living there. Saying little, he began to learn about Bianca's hands.

He watched Bianca being fed. Her hands would not feed her, the lovely aristocrats. Beautiful parasites they were, taking their animal life from the heavy squat body that carried them, and giving nothing in return. They would lie one on each side of her plate, pulsing, while Bianca's mother put food into the disinterested drooling mouth. They were shy, those hands, of Ran's bewitched gaze. Caught out there naked in the light and open of the tabletop, they would creep to the edge and drop out of sight—all but four rosy fingertips clutching the cloth.

They never lifted from a surface. When Bianca walked, her hands did not swing free, but twisted in the fabric of her dress. And when she approached a table or the mantelpiece and stood, her hands would run lightly up and leap, landing together, resting silently, watchfully, with that pulsing peculiar to them.

They cared for each other. They would not touch Bianca herself, but each hand groomed the other. It was the only labor to which they would bend themselves.

Three evenings after he came, Ran tried to take one of the hands in his. Bianca was alone in the room, and Ran went to her and sat beside her. She did not move, nor did her hands. They rested on a small table before her, preening themselves. This, then, was when they really began watching him. He felt it, right down to the depths of his enchanted heart. The hands kept stroking each other, and yet they knew he was there, they knew of his desire. They stretched themselves before him, archly, languorously, and his blood pounded hot. Before he could stay himself he reached and tried to grasp them. He was strong, and his move was sudden and clumsy. One of the hands seemed to disappear, so swiftly did it drop into Bianca's lap. But the other—

Ran's thick fingers closed on it and held it captive. It writhed, all but tore itself free. It took no power from the arm on which it lived, for Bianca's arms were flabby and weak. Its strength, like its beauty, was intrinsic, and it was only by shifting his grip to the puffy forearm that Ran succeeded in capturing it. So intent was he on touching it, holding it, that he did not see the other hand leap from the idiot girl's lap, land crouching at the table's edge. It reared back, fingers curling spiderlike, and sprang at him, fastening on his wrist. It clamped down agonizingly, and Ran felt bones give and crackle. With a cry he released the girl's arm. Her hands fell together and ran over each other, feeling for any small scratch, any tiny damage he might have done them in his passion. And as he sat there clutching his wrist, he saw the hands run to the far side of the little table, hook themselves over the edge, and, contracting, draw her out of her place. She had no volition of her own —ah, but her hands had! Creeping over the walls, catching obscure and precarious holds in the wainscoting, they dragged the girl from the room.

And Ran sat there and sobbed, not so much from the pain in his swelling arm, but in shame for what he had done. They might have been won to him in another, gentler way. . . .

His head was bowed; yet suddenly he felt the gaze of those hands. He looked up swiftly enough to see one of them whisk around the doorpost. It had come back, then, to see. . . . Ran rose heavily and took himself and his shame away. Yet he was compelled to stop in the doorway, even as had Bianca's hands. He watched covertly and saw them come into the room dragging the unprotesting idiot girl. They brought her to the long bench where Ran had sat with her. They pushed her on to it, flung themselves to the table, and began rolling and flattening themselves most curiously about. Ran suddenly realized that there was something of his there, and he was comforted, a little. They were rejoicing, drinking thirstily, reveling in his tears.

Afterward for nineteen days, the hands made Ran do penance. He knew them as inviolate and unforgiving; they would not show themselves to him, remaining always hidden in Bianca's dress or under the supper table. For those nineteen days Ran's passion and desire grew. More—his love became true love, for only true love knows reverence —and the possession of the hands became his reason for living, his goal in the life which that reason had given him.

Ultimately they forgave him. They kissed him coyly when he was not looking, touched him on the wrist, caught and held him for one sweet moment. It was at table . . . a great power surged through him, and he gazed down at the hands, now returned to Bianca's lap. A strong muscle in his jaw twitched and twitched, swelled and fell. Happiness like a golden light flooded him; passion spurred him, love imprisoned him, reverence was the gold of the golden light. The room wheeled and whirled about him, and forces unimaginable flickered through him. Battling with himself, yet lax in the glory of it, Ran sat unmoving, beyond the world, enslaved and yet possessor of all. Bianca's hands flushed pink, and if ever hands smiled to each other, then they did.

He rose abruptly, flinging his chair from him, feeling the strength of his back and shoulders. Bianca's mother, by now beyond surprise, looked at him and away. There was that in his eyes which she did not like, for to fathom it would disturb her, and she wanted no trouble. Ran strode from the room and outdoors, to be by himself that he might learn more of this new thing that had possessed him.

It was evening. The crooked bending skyline drank the buoyancy of the sun, dragged it down, sucking greedily. Ran stood on a knoll, his nostrils flaring, feeling the depth of his lungs. He sucked in the crisp air, and it smelled new to him, as though the sunset shades were truly in it. He knotted the muscles of his thighs and stared at his smooth, solid fists. He raised his hands high over his head and, stretching, sent out such a great shout that the sun sank. He watched it, knowing how great and tall he was, how strong he was, knowing the meaning of longing and belonging. And then he lay down on the clean earth, and he wept.

When the sky grew cold enough for the moon to follow the sun beyond the hills, and still an hour after that, Ran returned to the house. He struck a light in the room of Bianca's mother, where she slept on a pile of old clothes. Ran sat beside her and let the light wake her. She rolled over to him and moaned, opened her eyes, and shrank from him. "Ran . . . what do you want?"

"Bianca. I want to marry Bianca."

Her breath hissed between her gums. "No!" It was not a refusal but astonishment. Ran touched her arm impatiently. Then she laughed.

"To—marry—Bianca. It's late, boy. Go back to bed, and in the morning you'll have forgotten this thing, this dream."

"I've not been to bed," he said patiently, but growing angry. "Will you give me Bianca, or not?"

She sat up and rested her chin on her withered knees. "You're right to ask me, for I'm her mother. Still and all— Ran, you've been good to us, Bianca and me. You're— you are a good boy, but—forgive me, lad, but you're something of a fool. Bianca's a monster. I say it though I am what I am to her. Do what you like, and never a word will I say. You should have known. I'm sorry you asked me, for you have given me the memory of speaking so to you. I don't understand you; but do what you like, boy."

It was to have been a glance, but it became a stare as she saw his face. He put his hands carefully behind his back, and she knew he would have killed her else.

"I'll—marry her, then?" he whispered.

She nodded, terrified. "As you like, boy."

He blew out the light and left her.

Ran worked hard and saved his wages and made one room beautiful for Bianca and himself. He built a soft chair and a table that was like an altar for Bianca's sacred hands. There was a great bed, and heavy cloth to hide and soften the walls, and a rug.

They were married, though marrying took time. Ran had to go far afield before he could find one who would do what was necessary. The man came far and went again afterward, so that none knew of it, and Ran and his wife were left alone. The mother spoke for Bianca, and Bianca's hand trembled frighteningly at the touch of the ring, writhed and struggled and then lay passive, blushing and beautiful. But it was done. Bianca's mother did not protest, for she didn't dare. Ran was happy, and Bianca—well, nobody cared about Bianca.

After they were married Bianca followed Ran and his two brides into the beautiful room. He washed Bianca and used rich lotions. He washed and combed her hair and brushed it many times until it shone, to make her more fit to be with the hands he had married. He never touched the hands, though he gave them soaps and creams and tools with which they could groom themselves. They were pleased. Once one of them ran up his coat and touched his cheek and made him exultant.

He left then and returned to the shop with his heart full of music. He worked harder than ever, so that Harding was pleased and let him go home early. He wandered the hours away by the bank of a brook, watching the sun on the face of the chuckling water. A bird came to circle him, flew unafraid through the aura of gladness about him. The delicate tip of a wing brushed his wrist with the touch of the first secret kiss from the hands of Bianca. The singing that filled him was part of the nature of laughing, the running of water, the sound of the wind in the reeds by the edge of the stream. He yearned for the hands, and he knew he could go now and clasp them and own them; instead he stretched out on the bank and lay smiling, all lost in the sweetness and poignance of waiting, denying desire. He laughed for pure joy in a world without hatred, held in the stainless palms of Bianca's hands.

As it grew dark he went home. All during that nuptial meal Bianca's hands twisted about one of his while he ate with the other, and Bianca's mother fed the girl. The fingers twined about each other and about his own, so that three hands seemed to be wrought of one flesh, to become a thing of lovely weight at his arm's end. When it was quite dark they went to the beautiful room and lay where he and the hands could watch, through the window, the clean, bright stars swim up out of the forest. The house and the room were dark and silent. Ran was so happy that he hardly dared to breathe.

A hand fluttered up over his hair, down his cheek, and crawled into the hollow of his throat. Its pulsing matched the beat of his heart. He opened his own hands wide and clenched his fingers, as though to catch and hold this moment.

Soon the other hand crept up and joined the first. For perhaps an hour they lay there passive with their coolness against Ran's warm neck. He felt them with his throat, each smooth convolution, each firm small expanse. He concentrated, with his mind and his heart on his throat, on each part of the hands that touched him, feeling with all his being first one touch and then another, though the contact was there unmoving. And he knew it would be soon now, soon.

As if at a command, he turned on his back and dug his head into the pillow. Staring up at the vague dark hangings on the wall, he began to realize what it was for which he had been working and dreaming so long. He put his head back yet farther and smiled, waiting. This would be possession, completion. He breathed deeply, twice, and the hands began to move.

The thumbs crossed over his throat, and the fingertips settled one by one under his ears. For a long moment they lay there, gathering strength. Together, then, in perfect harmony, each cooperating with the other, they became rigid, rock-hard. Their touch was still light upon him, still light . . . no, now they were passing their rigidity to him, turning it to a contraction. They settled to it slowly, their pressure measured and equal. Ran lay silent. He could not breathe now, and did not want to. His great arms were crossed on his chest, his knotted fists under his armpits, his mind knowing a great peace. Soon, now. . . .

Wave after wave of engulfing, glorious pain spread and receded. He saw color impossible, without light. He arched his back, up, up . . . the hands bore down with all their hidden strength, and Ran's body bent like a bow, resting on feet and shoulders. Up, up. . . .

Something burst within him—his lungs, his heart—no matter. It was complete.

There was blood on the hands of Bianca's mother when they found her in the morning in the beautiful room, trying to soothe Ran's neck. They took Bianca away, and they buried Ran, but they hanged Bianca's mother because she tried to make them believe Bianca had done it, Bianca, whose hands were quite dead, drooping like brown leaves from her wrists.

Poor Little Warrior!

Claude Ford knew exactly how it was to hunt a brontosaurus. You crawled heedlessly through the mud among the willows, through the little primitive flowers with petals as green and brown as a football field, through the beauty-lotion mud. You peered out at the creature sprawling among the reeds, its body as graceful as a sock full of sand. There it lay, letting the gravity cuddle it nappy-damp to the marsh, running its big rabbit-hole nostrils a foot above the grass in a sweeping semicircle, in a snoring search for more sausagy reeds. It was beautiful: here horror had reached its limits, come full circle, and finally disappeared up its own sphincter. Its eyes gleamed with the liveliness of a week-dead corpse's big toe, and its compost breath and the fur in its crude aural cavities were particularly to be recommended to anyone who might otherwise have felt inclined to speak lovingly of the work of Mother Nature.

But as you, little mammal with opposed digit and .65 self-loading, semiautomatic, dual-barreled, digitally computed, telescopically sighted, rustless, high-powered rifle gripped in your otherwise-defenseless paws, slide along under the bygone willows, what primarily attracts you is the thunder lizard's hide. It gives off a smell as deeply resonant as the bass note of a piano. It makes the elephant's epidermis look like a sheet of crinkled lavatory paper. It is gray as the Viking seas, daft-deep as cathedral foundations. What contact possible to bone could allay the fever of that flesh? Over it scamper—you can see them from here!—the little brown lice that live in those gray walls and canyons,

31

gay as ghosts, cruel as crabs. If one of them jumped on you, it would very likely break your back. And when one of those parasites stops to cock its leg against one of the bronto's vertebrae, you can see it carries in its turn its own crop of easy-livers, each as big as a lobster, for you're near now, oh, so near that you can hear the monster's primitive heart-organ knocking, as the ventricle keeps miraculous time with the auricle.

Time for listening to the oracle is past: you're beyond the stage for omens, you're now headed in for the kill, yours or his; superstition has had its little day, for today, from now on, only this windy nerve of yours, this shaky conglomeration of muscle entangled untraceably beneath the sweat-shiny carapace of skin, this bloody little urge to slay the dragon, is going to answer all your orisons.

You could shoot now. Just wait till that tiny steam-shovel head pauses once again to gulp down a quarry-load of bulrushes, and with one inexpressibly vulgar bang you can show the whole indifferent Jurassic world that it's standing looking down the business end of evolution's sex-shooter. You know why you pause, even as you pretend not to know why you pause; that old worm conscience, long as a baseball pitch, long-lived as a tortoise, is at work; through every sense it slides, more monstrous than the serpent. Through the passions: saying, here is a sitting duck, O Englishman! Through the intelligence: whispering that boredom, the kitehawk who never feeds, will settle again when the task is done. Through the nerves: sneering that when the adrenalin currents cease to flow the vomiting begins. Through the maestro behind the retina: plausibly forcing the beauty of the view upon you.

Spare us that poor old slipper-slopper of a word, *beauty;* holy mom, is this a travelogue, nor are we out of it? *"Perched now on this titanic creature's back, we see a round dozen—and, folks, let me stress that round—of gaudily plumaged birds, exhibiting between them all the color you might expect to find on lovely, fabled Copacabana Beach. They're so round because they feed from the droppings that fall from the rich man's table. Watch this lovely shot now! See the bronto's tail lift. . . . Oh,*

*lovely, yep, a couple of hayricksful at least emerging from
his nether end. That sure was a beauty, folks, delivered
straight from consumer to consumer. The birds are fighting
over it now. Hey, you, there's enough to go around, and
anyhow, you're round enough already. . . . And nothing
to do now but hop back up onto the old rump steak and
wait for the next round. And now as the sun sinks in the
Jurassic West, we say 'Fare well on that diet.'. . ."*

No, you're procrastinating, and that's a life work. Shoot
the beast, and put it out of your agony. Taking your courage in your hands, you raise it to shoulder level and squint
down its sights. There is a terrible report; you are half-
stunned. Shakily, you look about you. The monster still
munches, relieved to have broken enough wind to unbe-
calm the Ancient Mariner.

Angered (or is it some subtler emotion?), you now
burst from the bushes and confront it, and this exposed
condition is typical of the straits into which your considera-
tion for yourself and others continually pitches you. Con-
sideration? Or again something subtler? Why should you
be confused just because you come from a confused civili-
zation? But that's a point to deal with later, if there is a
later, as these two hog-wallow eyes pupiling you all over
from spitting distance tend to dispute. Let it not be by
jaws alone, O monster, but also by huge hooves and, if
convenient to yourself, by mountainous rollings upon me!
Let death be a saga, sagacious, Beowulfate.

Quarter of a mile distant is the sound of a dozen hippos
springing boisterously in gymslips from the ancestral mud,
and next second a walloping great tail as long as Sunday
and as thick as Saturday night comes slicing over your
head. You duck as duck you must, but the beast missed
you anyway because it so happens that its coordination is
no better than yours would be if you had to wave the
Woolworth Building at a tarsier. This done, it seems to
feel it has done its duty by itself. It forgets you. You just
wish you could forget yourself as easily; that was, after all,
the reason you had to come the long way here. *Get Away
from It All,* said the time-travel brochure, which meant for
you getting away from Claude Ford, a husbandman as

futile as his name with a terrible wife called Maude. Maude and Claude Ford. Who could not adjust to themselves, to each other, or to the world they were born in. It was the best reason in the as-it-is-at-present-constituted world for coming back here to shoot giant saurians—if you were fool enough to think that one hundred and fifty million years either way made an ounce of difference to the muddle of thoughts in a man's cerebral vortex.

You try and stop your silly, slobbering thoughts, but they have never really stopped since the coca-collaborating days of your growing up; God, if adolescence did not exist, it would be unnecessary to invent it! Slightly, it steadies you to look again on the enormous bulk of this tyrant vegetarian into whose presence you charged with such a mixed death-life wish, charged with all the emotion the human orga(ni)sm is capable of. This time the bogeyman is real, Claude, just as you wanted it to be, and this time you really have to face up to it before it turns and faces you again. And so again you lift Ole Equalizer, waiting till you can spot the vulnerable spot.

The bright birds sway, the lice scamper like dogs, the marsh groans, as bronto sways over and sends his little cranium snaking down under the bile-bright water in a forage for roughage. You watch this; you have never been so jittery before in all your jittered life, and you are counting on this catharsis wringing the last drop of acid fear out of your system for ever. OK, you keep saying to yourself insanely over and over, your million-dollar twenty-second-century education going for nothing, OK, OK. And as you say it for the umpteenth time, the crazy head comes back out of the water like a renegade express and gazes in your direction.

Grazes in your direction. For as the champing jaw with its big blunt molars like concrete posts works up and down, you see the swamp water course out over rimless lips, lip-less rims, splashing your feet and sousing the ground. Reed and root, stalk and stem, leaf and loam, all are intermit-tently visible in that masticating maw and, struggling, straggling, or tossed among them, minnows, tiny crusta-ceans, frogs—all destined in that awful, jaw-full movement to turn into bowel movement. And as the glump-glump-glumping takes place, above it the slime-resistant eyes again survey you.

These beasts live up to two hundred years, says the time-travel brochure, and this beast has obviously tried to live up to that, for its gaze is centuries old, full of decades upon decades of wallowing in its heavyweight thoughtlessness until it has grown wise on twitterpatedness. For you it is like looking into a disturbing misty pool; it gives you a psychic shock, you fire off both barrels at your own reflection. Bang-bang, the dum-dums, big as paw-paws, go.

With no indecision, those century-old lights, dim and sacred, go out. These cloisters are closed till Judgment Day. Your reflection is torn and bloodied from them forever. Over their ravaged panes nictitating membranes slide slowly upward, like dirty sheets covering a cadaver. The jaw continues to munch slowly, as slowly the head sinks down. Slowly, a squeeze of cold reptile blood toothpastes down the wrinkled flank of one cheek. Everything is slow, a creepy Secondary Era slowness like the drip of water, and you know that if you had been in charge of creation you would have found some medium less heartbreaking than Time to stage it all in.

Never mind! Quaff down your beakers, lords, Claude Ford has slain a harmless creature. Long live Claude the Clawed!

You watch breathless as the head touches the ground, the long laugh of neck touches the ground, the jaws close for good. You watch and wait for something else to happen, but nothing ever does. Nothing ever would. You could stand here watching for a hundred and fifty million years, Lord Claude, and nothing would ever happen here again. Gradually your bronto's mighty carcass, picked loving clean by predators, would sink into the slime, carried by its own weight deeper; then the waters would rise, and old Conqueror Sea come in with the leisurely air of a cardsharp dealing the boys a bad hand. Silt and sediment would filter down over the mighty grave, a slow rain with centuries to rain in. Old bronto's bed might be raised up and then down again perhaps half a dozen times, gently

enough not to disturb him, although by now the sedimen-
tary rocks would be forming thick around him. Finally,
when he was wrapped in a tomb finer than any Indian
rajah ever boasted, the powers of the earth would raise
him high on their shoulders until, sleeping still, bronto
would lie in a brow of the Rockies high above the waters
of the Pacific. But little any of that would count with you,
Claude the Sword; once the midget maggot of life is dead
in the creature's skull, the rest is no concern of yours.

You have no emotion now. You are just faintly put out.
You expected dramatic thrashing of the ground, or bellow-
ing; on the other hand, you are glad the thing did not appear to suffer. You are like all cruel men, sentimental; you
are like all sentimental men, squeamish. You tuck the gun
under your arm and walk around the dinosaur to view
your victory.

You prowl past the ungainly hooves, around the septic
white of the cliff of belly, beyond the glistening and how-
thought-provoking cavern of the cloaca, finally posing beneath the switch-back sweep of tail-to-rump. Now your
disappointment is as crisp and obvious as a visiting card:
the giant is not half as big as you thought it was. It is not
one half as large, for example, as the image of you and
Maude is in your mind. Poor little warrior, science will
never invent anything to assist the titanic death you want
in the contraterrene caverns of your fee-fi-fo fumblingly
fearful id!

Nothing is left to you now but to slink back to your
time-mobile with a bellyful of anticlimax. See, the bright
dung-consuming birds have already cottoned on to the true
state of affairs; one by one, they gather up their hunched
wings and fly disconsolately off across the swamp to other
hosts. They know when a good thing turns bad, and do not
wait for the vultures to drive them off; all hope abandon,
ye who entrail here. You also turn away.

You turn, but you pause. Nothing is left but to go back,
no, but 2181 A.D. is not just the home date; it is Maude. It
is Claude. It is the whole awful, hopeless, endless business
of trying to adjust to an overcomplex environment, of
trying to turn yourself into a cog. Your escape from it into

the Grand Simplicities of the Jurassic, to quote the brochure again, was only a partial escape, now over.

So you pause, and as you pause, something lands socko on your back, pitching you face forward into tasty mud. You struggle and scream as lobster claws tear at your neck and throat. You try to pick up the rifle but cannot, so in agony you roll over, and next second the crab-thing is greedying it on your chest. You wrench at its shell, but it giggles and pecks your fingers off. You forgot when you killed the bronto that its parasites would leave it, and that to a little shrimp like you they would be a deal more dangerous than their host.

You do your best, kicking for at least three minutes. By the end of that time there is a whole pack of the creatures on you. Already they are picking your carcass loving clean. You're going to like it up there on top of the Rockies; you won't feel a thing.

BY KATE WILHELM

The Hounds

Rose Ellen knew that Martin had been laid off, had known it for over a week, but she had waited for him to tell her. She watched him get out of the car on Friday, and she said to herself, "Now he's ready. He's got a plan, and he'll tell me what we're going to do, and it'll be all right." There was more relief in her inner voice than she had thought possible. Why, I've been scared, she thought in wonder, savoring the feeling now that there was no longer any need to deny it. She knew Martin was ready by the way he left the car. He was a thin, intense man, not very tall, five nine. When worried, or preoccupied, or under pressure, he seemed to lose all his coordination. He bumped into furniture, knocked over coffee cups, glasses. And he forgot to turn things off: water, lights, the car engine once. He had a high, domed forehead, thin hair the color of wet sand, and now, after twelve years at the Cape, a very deep burned-in suntan. His nervous energy sought release through constant motion. He always had a dozen projects under way: refinishing furniture, assembling a stereo system, designing a space-lab model, breeding toy poodles, raising hydroponic vegetables. All his projects turned out well. All were one-man efforts. This afternoon his motion was fluid as he swung his legs out of the car, then slammed the door hard. His walk was jaunty; he came up the drive and around the canary date palm to where she waited at the poolside bar. Rose Ellen was in a bikini, although the air was a bit cool, and she wouldn't dream of swimming yet. But the sun felt good when the wind died down a

39

little, and she knew she looked as good in the brief red strips as she had looked fifteen or even twenty years ago. She saw herself reflected in his eyes; his expression told her that he was seeing her again.

He didn't kiss her; they never kissed until they were going to make love. He patted her bottom and reached for the cocktail shaker. He shook it once, then poured and sat down, still looking at her approvingly.

"You know," he said.

"What, honey? I know what?" Her relief put a lilt in her voice, made her want to sing.

"And you've known all along. Well, OK, here's to us."

"Are you going to tell me what it is I've known all along or are you just going to sit there looking enigmatic as hell and pleased, and slightly soused?" She leaned over him, sniffing. "And how long ago did you leave the office?"

"Noon. Little after. I didn't go back after lunch. I got the can last Thursday." He put his glass down and pulled her to his lap. "And I don't care."

"May they all rot in hell," Rose Ellen said. "You! You've been there longer than almost anyone. And when they come to you beggin' you to come back, tell them to go to hell. Right?"

"Well, I don't think they'll come begging for me," Martin said, but he was pleased with himself. The worry was gone, and the circles under his eyes seemed less dark, although he still hadn't slept. Rose Ellen pushed herself away from him slightly in order to see him better.

"Anyway, you can get a job up in Jacksonville tomorrow. They know that, don't they?

"Honey, they aren't Machiavellian, you know. The agency doesn't want to break up our team, but they had no choice—no money, no appropriation. We did what they hired us to do. Now it's over. Let's go to bed."

"Uh-uh! Not until you tell me what's making you grin like that."

"Right. Look, doll, I'm forty-nine. And laid off. You know what the story is for the other guys who've had this happen. No luck. No job. Nothing. It wouldn't be any different with me, honey. You have to accept that."

She kissed his nose and stood up, hands on hips, studying him. "You! You're better than all the others put together. You know you are. You told me yourself a hundred times."

"Honey, I'm forty-nine. No one hires men who are forty-nine."

"Martin, stop this! I won't have it. You're a young man. Educated! My God, you've got education you've never even used yet."

He laughed and poured his second martini. She knew it pleased him for her to get indignant on his behalf. "I know what I'm talking about, honey. Simmer down and listen. OK?" She sat down again, on a stool on the other side of the bar, facing him. A tight feeling had come across her stomach, like the feeling she used to get just before the roller coaster started to go down the last, wildest drop.

"I don't want another job, Rose. I've had it with jobs. I want to buy a farm."

She stared at him. He said, "We could do it, honey. We could sell the house, and with the money left after we pay off the mortgage, the car, the other things, there'd be enough for a small farm. Ten, twenty acres. Not on the coast. Inland. West Virginia, or Kentucky. I could get a job teaching. I wouldn't mind that."

"Martin? Martin! Stop. It's not funny. It isn't funny at all. Don't go on like this." Her playfulness was gone, leaving only the tight feeling.

"You bet your sweet ass it isn't funny. And I'm serious, Rose. Dead serious."

"A farm! What on earth would I do on a farm? What about the kids?"

"We can work out all those things. . . ."

"Not now, Martin. I have to go get Juliette. Later, later." She ran into the house without looking back. Bad strategy, she told herself, dressing. She should have gone to bed with him, and then talked him out of his crazy notion. He was as scared as she was. He could get a job in Jacksonville. It wasn't a bad drive. He could come home weekends if he didn't want to drive it every day, although some people did. She thought about the house payments and the insurance and the pool maintenance and the yard people and the house-cleaning woman who came twice a week. And the lessons: piano, ballet, scuba, sailing. The clubs. The marina where they left the ketch. She thought of her dressmaker and hairdresser, and his tailor, and the special shoes for Annamarie, and the kennel fees when they went away for a weekend and had to leave the three toy poodles. She thought of two thousand dollars' worth of braces for Juliette in another two years.

She thought about the others it had happened to. Out of six close friends only one, Burdorf, had another job, adviser to an ad agency. But Burdorf had an in with them: his wife's father owned it.

Rose Ellen tried to stop thinking of the others who had been laid off. But Martin was different. Really different. He had so many degrees, for one thing. She shook her head. That didn't matter. It hadn't mattered for any of the others.

She thought about being without him. She and the children without him. She shivered and hugged herself hard. She could go to work. She hadn't because neither of them had wanted her to before. But she could. She could teach, actually, easier than Martin could. He didn't have any of the education courses that were required now. So, she pursued it further, she would teach, at about seven thousand a year, and Martin would have to pay, oh, say four hundred a month. . . . And if he didn't, or couldn't? If he was on a farm somewhere without any money at all? Seven thousand. Braces, two thousand. House, two thousand. Some extras, not many, but some, like a car. In another year Annamarie would be driving, and junior insurance, and then Jeffrey would be wanting a car. . . .

More important, they wouldn't mind her. She knew it. Martin could control them with a word, a glower. She was easy and soft with them. It had always been impossible to tell them no, to tell them she wouldn't take them here or there, do this or that for them. They'd run all over her, she knew.

Martin bought a farm in May, and they moved as soon as school was out. The farm was twelve acres, with a small orchard and a deep well and barn. The house was modern and good, and the children, surprisingly, accepted the move unquestioningly and even liked it all. They held a family council the day after moving into the house and took a vote on whether to buy a pool table for the basement rec room, or a horse. It would be the only luxury they could afford for a long time. Only Rose Ellen voted for the pool table.

Martin had to take three courses at the university in the fall semester; then he would teach, starting in midterm, not his own field of mathematics, because they had a very good teacher already, but if he could brush up on high-school general science. . . .

Rose Ellen signed up as a substitute teacher for the fall semester. The school was only a mile and a half from their house; she could walk there when the weather was pleasant.

"It's going to be all right, honey," Martin said one night in early September. Everyone had started school, the whole move to the country had been so free of trauma that it was suspicious. Rose Ellen nodded, staring at him. "What's wrong?" he asked. "Dirt on my face?"

"No. It's strange how much you looked like my father there for a moment. A passing expression, gone so fast that I probably imagined it."

"Your father?"

She picked up her magazine. "Yes. I told you I couldn't remember him because I didn't want to talk about him. It was a lie. He didn't die until I was eleven."

Martin didn't say anything, and reluctantly she lowered the magazine again. "I'm sorry. But after I told you that, back in the beginning, I was stuck with it. I'm glad it finally came out."

"Do you want to talk about him?"

"No. Not really. He drank a lot. He and mother fought like animals most of the time. Then he died in a car accident. Drunk, hit a truck head-on, killed himself, nearly killed the driver of the truck. Period. When I was fourteen she married again, and this time it was to a rich man."

"Did she love Eddie?"

"Eddie was the practical one," Rose Ellen said. "She married for love the first time, for practical reasons the second time. The second one was better. They've been peaceful together. No more fights. No more dodging bill collectors."

"Did she love him?"

"I don't know. I don't think so, but it didn't matter."

Martin didn't say any more, and she wondered about her mother and her second husband. Had it mattered? She didn't know. She turned pages of the magazine without looking at them, and Martin's voice startled her.

"Sometimes I think we should fight now and then," he said. "I wonder sometimes what all you're bottling up."

"Me? You know we discuss everything."

"Discuss isn't what I mean. We discuss only after you get quiet and stay quiet long enough to come to a decision. I'd like to know sometimes what all goes on in that head of yours while you're in the process of deciding."

She laughed and stood up. "Right now all that's in my head is the fact that I want a bath and bed."

She was at the kitchen door when Martin asked, "What did your father do?"

She stopped. Without turning, she said, "He had a small farm. Nothing else."

She soaked for a while and thought about his words. It was true that they never fought. He hadn't lived with two people who did fight, or he'd never say anything like that. She knew it was better to be civilized and give in. She was a good wife, she told herself soberly. A good wife. And she was adaptable. He had taken her from Atlanta to Florida, from there to Kentucky. So be it. She could get along no matter where they lived or what they did. One of them had to, she said sharply in her mind. She had been a silent observer in her own house, then in her stepfather's house for years. It was better that way. She let the water out and rubbed herself briskly. At the bathroom door she saw that Martin had come up; their light was on. She stopped for a few seconds, then went downstairs to read for a while. She had been more tired than sleepy, she decided. Actually it was quite early.

October was still days of gold and red light, of blue skies that were endlessly deep, of russet leaves underfoot and flaming maples and scarlet poison ivy and sumac, yellow poplars and ash trees. She walked home from school with a shopping bag on one arm, alone on the narrow road that was seldom used except by the half-dozen families that lived along it. One side was bordered by a fenceline long grown up with blackberries and inhabited by small invisible scurrying things. The other side had a wood, not very dense, then a field of corn that had been harvested so that only skeletons remained. Behind the fenceline was a pasture with a stream, peaceful cows that never once looked up as she passed them. The pasture ended, a stand of pine trees came up to the road. Then there was an outcrop of limestone and a hill with oak trees and some tall firs and walnut trees. Walnuts had dropped over the road, along both sides of it.

She stopped at the walnuts and began to gather the heavy green hulls, hardly even broken by the fall. They would have to spread them out, let them dry. A scene from her childhood came to her, surprising her. There were so few scenes from her early years that sometimes she worried about it. They had gathered nuts one day. She, her mother, her father, out along a dirt road near their farm, gathering hickory nuts and butternuts. They had taken a lunch and had eaten it by a stream, and she had waded, although the water had been icy. Her father had made a fire, and she had warmed her feet. She saw again his smiling face looking up at her as he rubbed her toes between his warm hands.

She finished filling her bag and picked up her purse again. Then she saw the dogs. Two of them stood on the other side of the road, behind the single strand of wire that was a fence. They were silver and long-legged and very beautiful. They were motionless as statues. She moved and their eyes followed her; they were large, like deer's eyes, and golden. She turned to look at them again after passing them; they were watching her.

That night she tried to describe them to Martin. "Hunting dogs, I'd guess," she said. "But I've never seen any like them before. They were as skinny as possible to still have enough muscles to stand up with. All long muscles and bones, and that amazing silver hair."

Martin was polite, but not really interested, and she fell silent. The children were upstairs in their rooms, studying. She realized that she saw very little of them anymore. They had adapted so well that they were busy most of the time, and the school days here were longer, the buses were later than they used to be, so that they didn't get home until four-fifteen. Then there were the things that teen-agers always did: telephone, records, riding the horse, currying it, feeding it, Jeffrey out on his bike with other boys. . . . She sighed and began to look over the papers she had brought home to grade. She would have Miss Witner's fifth-grade class for another week. She decided that she detested geography.

The next afternoon the dogs were there again; this time they left the field and stood just off the road as she passed. She spoke to them in what she hoped was a soothing voice, but they seemed not to hear; they merely stared at her.

They were bigger than she had remembered. Their tails were like silver plumes, responding to the gentle breeze as delicately as strands of silk. Feathery silver hair stirred on their chests and the backs of their long, thin legs.

She slowed down, but continued to walk steadily until she was past them; then she looked back. They were watching her.

Her father had had a hound dog, she remembered suddenly. And her mother had let it loose one day. They never had found it. Sometimes at night she had thought she could hear its strange voice from the hills. It had a broken howl that distinguished it from the other hounds. It started high, rose and rose, then broke and started again on a different key.

She never had wondered why her mother let it go, but now she did. How furious her father had been! They had screamed at each other for hours, and just as suddenly they had laughed at each other, and that had been that. She realized that they had gone to bed, that they always had gone to bed after one of their fights. Everything they had done together had been like that, fierce, wild, uninhibited, thorough. And now her mother was growing old in Eddie's fine house, with no one to yell at, no one to yell back. No one to make up with. Rose Ellen resisted the impulse to look back at the dogs. She knew they would be watching her. She didn't want to see them watching her again.

The next day was Friday and she left school later than usual, after a short staff meeting about a football game. Being a substitute she didn't have to attend the meeting, and certainly she wasn't required to go to the game, but she thought she might. If Jeffrey wanted to go, she would take him. Maybe they would all go. The sun was low and the afternoon was cooler than it had been all week. She walked fast, then stopped. The dogs were there. Suddenly she was frightened, and that was stupid. They were polite, well-behaved dogs, very valuable from the looks of them. They must belong to John Renfrew. They were always at his property line, anyway. She wondered if he knew they were loose. Or were they so well trained that they wouldn't leave his property? She started to move ahead again, but slowly. When she came up to them, they moved too. Not at her side, but a step behind her. She stopped; they stopped and looked at her.

"Scat," she said. "Go home." They stared at her. "Go on home!" She felt a mounting fear and shook it off with annoyance. They weren't menacing or frightening, not growling or making any threatening movement at all. They were merely dumb. She pointed toward John Renfrew's field again. "Go home!" They watched her.

She started to walk again, and they followed. She couldn't make them go back or stop or sit or anything. No matter what she said, they simply looked at her. She wondered if they were deaf and mute and decided that she was being silly now. They would have followed her inside the house if she hadn't closed the door first.

"Martin!" The three champagne-colored poodles were

ecstatic over her return. They jumped on her and pranced and got in the way, yapping. She hadn't noticed the car, but he could have put it in the garage, she thought, looking in the study, the kitchen, opening the basement door, stepping over poodles automatically. No one else was home yet. She looked out the window. They were sitting on the porch, waiting for her. She pulled back and found that she was shivering.

"This is ridiculous!" she said. "They are dogs!" She looked up Renfrew's number and called him. His wife answered.

"Who? Oh, yes. I've been meaning to come over there, but we've been so busy. You understand."

"Yes. Yes. But I'm afraid your dogs followed me home today. I tried to make them go back, but they wouldn't."

"Dogs? You mean Lucky? I thought I saw him a minute ago. Yes, he's here. I can see him out in the yard."

"These are hunting dogs. They are silver colored, long tails. . . ."

"Our Lucky is a border collie. Black and white. And he's home. I don't know whose dogs you have, but not ours. We don't have any hunting dogs."

Rose Ellen hung up. She knew they were still there. The back door slammed and Jeffrey and Annamarie were home. Presently Juliette would be there, and Martin would be back, and they could all decide what to do about the dogs on the porch. Rose Ellen went to the kitchen, ready to make sandwiches or start dinner or anything. She felt a grim satisfaction that she had successfully resisted looking at the dogs again.

"Hi, kids. Hungry?"

"Hi, Mom. Can I stay over at Jennifer's house tonight? She's a drum majorette and has to go to the game, and I thought I might go too, with Frank and Sue Cox, and then go to Jennifer's house for hamburgers and cokes after?"

Rose Ellen blinked at Annamarie. "I suppose so," she said. Jennifer was the daughter of the principal. She marveled at how quickly children made friends.

"I have to run, then," Annamarie said. "I have to get some pants on, and my heavy sweater. Do you think I'll need a jacket? Did you hear the weather? How cold will it get?" But she was running upstairs as she talked, and out of earshot already.

"Well, how about you?" Rose Ellen said to Jeffrey. "You going to the game too?"

"Yeah. We're ushers. That's our chore, you know. This month we do that; then we sell candy at the basketball games after Christmas. Is it okay if I have a hot dog and go? I told Mike I'd meet him at his house, and we'll catch the bus there."

Rose Ellen nodded. Martin and Juliette came home together then. He had picked her up at the bus stop.

They had dinner, and Juliette vanished to make one of her interminable phone calls to Betsy, her all-time closest friend. Rose Ellen told Martin about the dogs. "They're out on the porch," she said. "I'm sure they're very expensive. No collars."

With the three toy poodles dancing around him, Martin went to the door to look. The hounds walked in when the door opened. The poodles drew back in alarm; they sniffed the big dogs, then ignored them. Rose Ellen felt tight in her stomach. The silly poodles were always panicked by other dogs.

"Good God," Martin said. "They're beautiful!" He clicked his fingers and called softly, "Come on, boy. Come here." The dogs seemed oblivious. They looked at Rose Ellen. Martin walked around them, then reached down tentatively and put his hand on the nearer one's head. The dog didn't move. He ran his hand over the shoulders, down the flank, down the leg. The dog didn't seem to notice. Martin felt both dogs the same way. He ran his hand over the shoulders, down the lean sides of the dogs, over their bellies, again and again. A strange look came over his face and abruptly he pulled away. "Have you felt them?"

"No."

"You should. It's like silk. Warm and soft and alive under your fingers. My God, it's the most sensuous dog I've ever seen." He backed off and studied them both. They continued to watch Rose Ellen. "Come on and feel them. You can see how tame they are."

She shook her head. "Put them out, Martin."

"Rose? What's wrong with you? Are you afraid of them? You've never been afraid of dogs before. The poodles—"

"They're not dogs; they're animated toys. And I have always been afraid of dogs. Put them out!" Her voice rose slightly. Martin went to the door, calling the dogs. They didn't move; she had known they wouldn't. Slowly she walked to the door. They followed her. She walked out on the porch, and the dogs went too. Then she went back inside, opening the door only enough to slip in. They sat down and waited.

"Well, they know who they like," Martin said. "You must be imprinted on their brains, like a duckling imprints what he sees first and thinks it's his mother." He laughed and went back to the table for his coffee.

Rose Ellen was cold. She wasn't afraid, she told herself. They were the quietest, most polite dogs she had ever seen. They were the least threatening dogs she had ever seen. Probably the most expensive ones she had ever seen.

"What will we do about them?" she asked, holding her hot coffee cup with both hands, not looking at Martin.

"Oh, advertise, I guess. The owner might have an ad in the paper, in fact. Have you looked?"

They looked together, but there was nothing. "OK, tomorrow I'll put in an ad. Probably there'll be a reward. Could be they got away miles from here, over near Lexington. I'll put an ad in Lexington papers, too."

"But what will we do with them until the owner comes to get them?"

"What can we do? I'll feed them and let them sleep in the barn."

Even the coffee cup in her hands couldn't warm her. She thought of the gold eyes watching all night, waiting for her to come out.

"Honey, are you all right?"

"Yes. Of course. I just think they're . . . strange, I guess. I don't like them."

"That's because you didn't feel them. You should have. I've never felt anything like it."

She looked at her cup. She knew there was no power on earth that could induce her to touch one of those dogs.

Rose Ellen woke up during the night. The dogs, she thought. They were out there waiting for her. She tried to go to sleep again, but she was tense and every time she closed her eyes she saw the gold eyes looking at her. Finally she got up. She couldn't see the porch from her bedroom, but from Juliette's room she could. She covered Juliette, as if that were what she had entered the room for, then she started to leave resolutely. It was crazy to go looking for them, as crazy as it was for them to keep watching her. At the hall door she stopped, and finally she turned and went back to the window. They were there.

The hall night-light shone dimly on the porch, and in the square of soft light the two animals were curled up with the head of one of them on the back of the other. As she looked at them they both raised their heads and looked up at her, their eyes gleaming gold.

On Saturday morning, Joe MacLaughton, the county agent, came over to help Martin plan for a pond that he wanted to have dug. He looked at the dogs admiringly. "You sure have a pair of beauties," he said. "You don't want to let them loose in those hills. Someone'll sure as hell lift them."

"I wish they would," Rose Ellen said. She was tired; she hadn't slept after going back to bed at three-thirty.

"Ma'am?" Joe said politely.

"They aren't ours. They followed me home."

"You don't say?" He walked around the dogs thoughtfully. "They don't come from around here," he said finally.

"I'm going to call the paper and put an ad in the lost and found," Martin said.

"Waste of time in the locals," Joe said. "If those dogs belonged around here, I'd know about it. Might try the kennel club over in Lexington, though."

Martin nodded. "That's a thought. They must know about such valuable dogs in this area."

They went out to look at the pond site. The dogs stayed on the porch, looking at the door.

After the agent left, Martin made his calls. The kennel

club president was no help. Weimaraners? Martin said no, and he named another breed or two, and then said he'd have to have a look at the dogs, didn't sound like anything he knew. After he hung up, Martin swore. He had an address in Lexington where he could take the dogs for identification. He called the newspaper and placed the ad.

All day the sound of hammering from the barn where Martin was making repairs sounded and resounded. Annamarie and Jennifer came in and volunteered to gather apples. Jeffrey helped his father, and Juliette tagged along with one pair, then the other. She tried to get the dogs to play with her, but they wouldn't. After patting them for a few minutes she ignored them as thoroughly as they ignored all the children. Rose didn't go outside all day. She started to leave by the back door once, but they heard her and walked around the corner of the house before she got off the steps. She returned to the kitchen. They went back to the porch.

They wouldn't stay in the barn. There were too many places where creatures as thin as they were could slip through. They seemed to prefer the porch. No one wanted to go to town to buy collars for them in order to tie them up. Martin didn't like the idea of tying them up anyway.

"What if they decide to go back to where they came from?" he asked.

At dinner Rose said, "Let's go over to Lexington to a movie tonight."

Martin sagged. "What's playing?"

She shrugged. "I don't know. Something must be playing that we'd like to see."

"Another night? Tomorrow night?" Martin said. "Tell you what, I'll even throw in dinner."

"Oh, never mind. It was a sudden thought. I don't even know what's on." Rose and Annamarie cleared the table, and she brought in apple pie and coffee. She thought of the dogs on the porch.

"Next February I'll spray the trees," Martin said. "And I'll fertilize under the trees. Watch and see the difference then. Just wait."

Rose Ellen nodded. Just wait. Martin was tired, and

thinner than usual. He worked harder here than he ever had anywhere, she was sure. Building, repairing, planting, studying about farming methods, and his school courses. She wondered if he was happy. Later, she thought, later she would ask him if he was happy. She wondered if that was one of those questions that you don't ask unless you already know the answer. Would she dare ask if she suspected that he might answer no? She hoped he wouldn't ask her.

Martin was an inventive lover. It pleased him immensely to delight her or give her an unexpected thrill or just to stay with her for an hour. They made love that night and afterward, both drowsy and contented, she asked if he was happy.

"Yes," he said simply. And that was that. "I wish you were, too," he said moments later. She had almost fallen asleep. She stiffened at his words. "Sorry, honey. Relax again. OK?"

"What did you mean by that?"

"I'm not sure. Sometimes I just feel that I've got it all. You, the kids, the farm now, and school. I can't think of anything else I want."

"I've got all those things too, you know."

"I know." He stretched and yawned and wanted to let it drop.

"Martin, you must have meant something. You think I'm not happy, is that it?"

"I don't know. I don't know what it takes to make you happy."

She didn't reply, and soon he was asleep. She didn't know either.

She dozed after a while and was awakened by a rhythmic noise that seemed to start in her dream, then linger after the dream faded. She turned over, but the noise didn't go away. She turned again and snuggled close to Martin. The bedroom was chilly. A wind had started to blow, and the window was open too far. She felt the air current on her cheek, and finally got up to close the window. The noise was louder. She got her robe on and went into the hall, then to the window in Juliette's room. The dogs were walking back and forth on the porch, their nails clicking with each step. They both stopped and looked at her. She ran from the room shaking, and, strangely, weeping.

At breakfast she said to Martin, "You have to get them out of here today. I can't stand them any longer."

"They really got to you, didn't they?"

"Yes, they got to me! Take them to Lexington, leave them with the kennel club people or the dog pound or something."

"OK, Rose. Let's wait until afternoon. See if anyone answers our ad first."

No one called, and at one Martin tried to get them into the car. They refused to leave the porch. "I could carry them," he said doubtfully. They weren't heavy, obviously. Anything that thin couldn't be heavy. But when he tried to lift one, it started to shiver, and it struggled and slipped through his arms. When he tried again the dog growled, a hoarse sound of warning deep in its throat, not so much a threat as a plea not to make it follow through. Its gold eyes were soft and clear and very large. Martin stopped. "Now what?" he asked.

"I'll get them to the car," Rose said. She led the two dogs to the car and opened the door for them. They jumped inside. When she closed the door again they pressed their noses against the window and looked at her. "See if they'll let you drive," she said.

They wouldn't let Martin get inside the car at all, not until Rose was behind the wheel, and then they paid no attention to him. "I'll drive," she said tightly. Her hands on the wheel were very stiff, and the hard feeling in her stomach made it difficult to breathe. Martin nodded. He reached out and squeezed her knee gently.

He was saying it was all right, but it wasn't, she thought.

The kennel club was run by Colonel Owen Luce, who was a Kentucky Colonel, and wanted the title used. "Proud of it, you know," he said genially. "Got mine the hard way, through service. Nowadays you can buy it, but not back when I got mine." He was forty, with blond wavy hair, tall, and too good-looking not to know it. He posed and swaggered and preened, and reminded Rose of a peacock that had stolen bread from their picnic table at Sunken Gardens in Florida once.

"They're handsome dogs," Colonel Luce said, walking around the hounds. "Handsome. Deerhounds? No. Not with that silky hair. Hm. Don't tell me. Not wolfhounds. Got it! Salukis!" He looked at Rose, waiting for approval. She shrugged. "I'm not certain," he said, as if by admitting his fallibility he were letting her in on a closely guarded secret that very few would ever know. He didn't ignore Martin as much as bypass him, first glancing at him, then addressing himself to Rose. Obviously he thought she was the dog fancier, since the hounds clung to her so closely.

"We don't know what they are," she said. "And they aren't ours. They followed me home. We want to return them to their owner."

"Ah. You should get quite a reward then. There aren't many salukis in this country. Very rare, and very expensive."

"We don't want a reward," Rose said. "We want to get rid of them."

"Why? Are they mean?" It was a ridiculous question. He smiled to show he was joking. "I always heard that salukis were more nervous than these seem to be," he said, studying them once more. "And the eyes are wrong, I think, if memory serves. I wonder if they could be a cross?"

Rose looked at Martin imploringly, but he was looking stubborn. He disliked the colonel very much. "Colonel Luce, can you house these dogs?" Rose asked. "You can claim the reward, and if no one shows up to claim them, then they'd be yours by default, wouldn't they? You could sell them."

"My dear lady, I couldn't possibly. We don't know anything about a medical history for them, now do we? I would have to assume that they've had nothing in the way of shots, obviously not true, but with no records—" He spread his hands and smiled prettily at Rose. "You do understand. I would have to isolate them for three weeks, to protect my own dogs. And give them the shots and the examinations and then have an irate owner show up? No thank you. Owners of valuable dogs tend to get very nasty if you doctor their hounds for them without their approval."

"Christ!" Martin said in disgust. "How much would you charge to board them then?"

"In isolation? Eight dollars a day, each."

Rose stared at him. He smiled again, showing every tooth in his head. She turned away. "Let's go, Martin." She took the dogs to the car and opened the door for them. She got behind the wheel and Martin got in, and only then did the dogs sit down. The dog pound was closed. "They won't get in the car next time," Rose said dully. "Can you think of any place else?" He couldn't, and she started for home.

The blue-grass country that they drove through was very lovely at that time of year. The fields rose and fell gently, delineated by white fences, punctuated in the distance by dark horses. Stands of woods were bouquets in full bloom, brilliant in the late afternoon sunlight. A haze softened the clear blue of the sky, and in the far distance hazy blue hills held the sky and land apart. Rose looked at it all, then said bitterly, "I shouldn't have let you do this."

"What?"

"Come here. Bring me here."

"Honey, what's wrong? Don't you like the farm?"

"I don't know. I just know I should have told you no. We should have tried to work it out without this."

"Rose, you didn't say anything about not wanting to come here. Not a word."

"You might have known, if you hadn't closed your eyes to what I wanted. You always close your eyes to what I want. It's always what you want. Always."

"That isn't fair! How in God's name was I supposed to know what you were thinking? You didn't say anything. You knew we had to do something. We couldn't keep the house and the boat and everything, we had to do something."

"You didn't even try to get a job!"

"Rose. Don't do this now. Wait until we get home."

She slowed down. "Sorry. But, Martin, it's like that with us. You say you want to do this or that, and we do it. Period. It's always been like that with us. I never had a voice in anything."

"You never spoke out."

"You wouldn't let me! It was always decided first; then you told me. You always just assumed that if you wanted something then I would too. As if I exist only in your shadow, as if I must want what you want without fail, without question."

"Rose, I never thought that. If I made the decisions it was only because you wouldn't. I don't know how many times I've brought something up for us to talk about and decide on, only to have you too busy or not interested or playing helpless."

"Playing helpless? What's that supposed to mean? You mean when you tell me we're moving I should chain myself to a tree and say no? Is that how I could have a voice? What can I do when you say we're doing this and you have the tickets, the plans, the whole thing worked out from beginning to end? When have you ever said how about doing this, before you already had it all arranged?"

He was silent, and she realized that she had been speeding again. She slowed down. "I didn't want to move to Florida, but you had such a great job there. What a great job! Bang, we're in Florida. I might have been a teacher. Or a success in business. Or something. But no, I had to have children and stay home and cook and clean and look pretty for you and your friends."

"Rose." Martin's voice was low. He looked straight ahead. "Rose, please stop now. I didn't realize how much of this you had pent up. But not now. Or let me drive. Pull off the road."

She hit the brakes hard. Her hands were shaking. She saw the dogs in the rear-view mirror. "They wouldn't let you drive," she said. "Will you light me a cigarette, please?"

He gave it to her wordlessly, staring ahead. She reached for the radio, and he said, "Let me do it." He tuned in country music, and she reached for it again. He changed the station to a press interview with someone from HEW.

Rose stubbed the cigarette out. "Martin, I'm frightened. We've never done that before. Not in the car anyway, not like that."

"I know," he said. He still didn't look at her.

She drove slowly and carefully the last ten minutes, and neither of them spoke again until they were inside the house, the dogs on the porch. "Why'd you bring them back?" Jeffrey asked disgustedly. He thought dogs as big as they were should be willing to retrieve or something.

Martin told them about the colonel, and Rose went upstairs to wash her face and hands. Halfway up the stairs, she turned and called, "Martin, will you put some coffee on, please?" And he answered cheerfully.

It was the dogs, she told herself in the bathroom. They had made the quarrel happen, somehow. Once when she glanced at the speedometer, it had registered eighty-five. She shivered, thinking of it. It had been the dogs' fault, she knew, without being able to think how they had done it or why or what the argument had been about.

Annamarie had made potato salad, and they had ham with it, and baked apples with heavy cream for dessert. Throughout dinner Rose was aware of Martin's searching gaze on her, and although she smiled at him, he didn't respond with his own wide grin, but remained watchful and quiet.

After the children went to bed, Martin wanted to talk about it, but she wouldn't. "Not now," she said. "I have to think. I don't know what happened, and I have to think."

"Rose, we can't just leave it at that. You said some things I never had thought of before. I had no idea you felt left out of our decisions. I honestly believed you wanted it like that."

She put her hands over her ears. "Not now! Please, Martin, not now. I have to think."

"And then hit me with it again, that I don't talk things over with you?"

"Shut up! Can't you for the love of God just shut up?"

He stared at her, and she took a deep breath, but didn't soften it at all. "Sure," he said. "For now."

That night she finally fell asleep breathing in time to the clicking of the dogs' nails on the porch floor. She dreamed. She floated downstairs with a long pale silk negligee drifting around her, like a bride of Dracula. She could see herself, a faint smile on her lips, her hair long and loose.

It didn't look very much like her, but that was unimportant. The air was pleasantly cool on her skin, and she glided across the yard, beckoning to her dogs to come. There was a moon that turned everything into white and black and gray, and the world now was not the same one that she had known before. Her horse was waiting for her; she floated up to mount it. Then they were flying across the fields, she on the horse, the dogs beside. They were painfully beautiful, running, their silver hair blowing; stretched out they seemed not to touch the ground at all. They looked like silver light flowing above the ground. Her horse ran easily, silently, and there was no sound at all in this new world. The field gave way to the forest, where the light from the moon came down in silver shafts, aslant and gleaming. The dogs disappeared in the shadows, appeared, dazzling bright in the moonlight, only to vanish again. They ran and ran, without a sound, and she had no fear of hitting anything. Her horse knew the way. They reached the end of the motionless woods, and there was a meadow sprinkled with spiderwebs that were like fine lace, glistening with dew that caught the moonlight like pearls. They slowed down now. Somewhere ahead was the quarry. Now the dogs were fearful to her. The golden eyes gleamed, and they became hunting beasts. First one, then the other sniffed the still air, and then with a flicker of motion they were off again, her horse following, unable to keep up with them. They were on the trail. She saw the deer then, a magnificent buck with widespread antlers. It saw the dogs and leaped through the air, twenty feet, thirty feet, an impossible leap in slow motion. But the dogs had it, and she knew it, and the buck knew. It ran from necessity; it was the prey, they the hunters. She stopped to watch the kill. The dogs leaped silently, and the deer fell and presently the dogs drew away from it, bloody now, and stood silently watching her.

She woke up. She was shivering as if with fever.

Martin took her to school, and when she got out of the car he said, "I'll be back before you're through. I'll pick you up." She nodded. The dogs were on the porch when they got home that afternoon.

That night he asked her if she was ready to talk. She looked at him helplessly. "I don't know. I can't think of anything to say."

"How about what's bugging you?"

"The dogs. Nothing else."

"Not the dogs."

"That's all, Martin. They're haunting me."

"Live dogs can't haunt anyone." He picked up his book and began to make notes.

Tuesday he met her after school again. The dogs were on the porch when they got home. She didn't look at them.

On Wednesday Martin had a late class and wouldn't be home until after six. "Will you be all right?" he asked when he dropped her off.

"Yes. Of course."

He reached for her arm and, holding it, looked at her for a moment. He let her go. "Right. See you later."

When she turned into the country road after school the dogs were there waiting for her. She felt dizzy and faint, and she stopped, steadying herself with one hand on a tree. She looked back toward the school, a quarter of a mile down the highway. She shook her head. Stupid! Stupid! She started to walk, trying not to look at the golden eyes that watched her. For three nights they had shared a dream, and she felt suddenly that the dogs knew about it, that it was the link that bound them together. She walked too fast and began to feel winded and hot. It was as quiet on the little road as it was in the fields and woods of her dream. No wind blew, no leaves stirred, even the birds were silent. She picked up a stick and looked quickly at the dogs slightly behind her; in order to see them she had to turn her head. They trotted silently, watching her.

Each night in the dream she got closer to the deer before the kill, and that night she was afoot, standing close enough to touch it when the dogs leaped. In her hand was a knife, and when the dogs felled the animal she braced herself to leap.

"No!" She sat up, throwing off the covers. Martin caught her and held her still until she was awake.

"Honey, you've got to tell me. Please, Rose. Please."

"I can't," she moaned. "It's gone now. A nightmare."

He didn't believe her, but he held her and stroked her hair and made soothing noises. "I love you," he said over and over. "I love you. I love you."

And finally she relaxed and found that she was weeping. "I love you, Martin," she said, sobbing suddenly. "I do. I really do."

"I know you do," he said. "I'm glad you know it too."

On Thursday she learned that the teacher she was subbing for was well and would return the following day. Martin picked her up after school, and she told him.

"I don't want you to stay home all day with those dogs," he said. "I'll get them in the car somehow and take them to the pound. No one is going to claim them."

She shook her head. "You can't," she said.

"I can try."

But the dogs refused to budge from the porch on Friday morning. Rose watched from inside the house. She hadn't slept all night. She had been afraid to, and she felt dopy and heavy-limbed. All night she had sat up watching television, drinking coffee, eating cheese and apples and cookies, reading. Listening to the clicking nails on the porch.

"I'll stay home then," Martin said when they both knew that the dogs were not going to go with him. "Or maybe you could trick them into getting in the car."

But they knew she couldn't. The dogs wouldn't move for her either. He approached them with the idea of trying to carry them, and they both growled; the hairs on their necks bristled.

"Martin, just go. We'll have all weekend to decide what to do with them. They'll sit out there, and I'll stay in here. It's all right. You'll be late."

He kissed her then, and she felt surprised. He never kissed her when he left. Only when they were going to go to bed, or were in bed already. "Stay inside. Promise?"

She nodded and watched him drive away. The dogs looked at her. "What do you want from me?" she demanded, going out to the porch, standing before them. "Just what do you want?" She took a step toward them. *"What do you want?"* She realized that the screaming voice was her own, and she stopped. She was very near them now. She could touch them if she reached out. They waited for her to touch them, to stroke them. Suddenly she whirled around and ran back inside the house. They didn't try to get in this time. They knew she would be back.

She went to the kitchen feeling blank and heavy. She poured coffee and sat down at the kitchen table with it, and then put her head down on her arms. Drifting, drifting, the warmth of sleep stealing over her. Suddenly she jumped up, knocking over her coffee. *No!* She knew she must not sleep, must not dream that dream again. She made more coffee and cleaned up the mess, then washed the dishes. She put clothes in the washer, made the beds, peeled apples to make jelly; all the time the clicking back and forth went on. She turned on the radio, and found herself listening over the music for the noise of their nails. She turned it off again. At noon she looked at them from Juliette's room. They turned to watch her, stopping in their tracks when she lifted the drape. The light caught in the golden eyes, making them look as if they were flashing at her. Signals flashing at her. She let the drape fall and backed away.

Then she went to Martin's study and took down his rifle. She loaded it carefully and walked out the back door, letting it slam behind her. She didn't turn to see if they were coming. At the back of the barn she waited for them. She thought how beautiful they were, running, how silky and fine their hair was, alive and blowing in the wind. They came around the corner of the barn, walking quietly, very sure of her. She raised the rifle, aiming it carefully as Martin had taught her. The large golden eyes caught the sun and flashed. She fired. The first dog dropped without a whimper. The other one was transfixed. She aimed again and fired. She was looking into the golden eyes as she pulled the trigger. She saw the light in them go out.

She dropped the rifle and hid her face in her hands. She was shaking violently. Then she vomited repeatedly, and after there was nothing left in her she retched and heaved helplessly. Finally, carrying the rifle, she staggered to the house and washed out her mouth and washed her face and hands. She didn't look at herself in the mirror.

She put the rifle back and went out to the barn again, this time with a spade. She dug the grave big enough for them both, behind the barn where she could cover it with straw. And when she was ready for them, she stopped. She would have to touch them after all. But the hair was just hair now, the silkiness and aliveness was gone. Just gray hair. She dragged them to the grave and covered them and hid the place with straw.

The children asked about the dogs, and she said they had run off just as mysteriously as they had come. Jeffrey said he was glad; they had been spooky. Juliette said she had dreamed of them last night, and she was sorry they were gone. Annamarie didn't comment at all, but ran to the phone to call Jennifer.

Martin didn't believe her story, but he didn't question her. That night she told him. "I killed them."

A tremor passed over him. He nodded. "Are you all right?"

"I'm all right." She looked at him. "You're not surprised or shocked or disgusted? Something?"

"Not now. Maybe later. Now, nothing."

She nodded too. That was how she felt. They didn't talk about it again that night, but sat quietly, with the television off, neither of them reading or doing anything. They went to bed early and held each other hard until they fell asleep.

BY THEODORE L. THOMAS

The Clone

clone, n. a Biol. *The aggregate of individual or-*
ganisms descended by asexual reproduction from
a single sexually produced individual. . . . Webster's New International Dictionary, Second Ed.

The lovely city loomed unknowing, gleaming softly in the
dusk. The breezes drifted in from Lake Michigan, soaking
up the heat of the day. Deep beneath the streets the cables
hummed and the wires sang and the pipes gurgled. Here
were the nerve fibers and the ducts of the city. And it was
in the ducts that the Clone began to grow.

Beneath every great city there flow streams of water
rich in nutrients and minerals, and containing ample energy
to supply the driving force for almost every conceivable
chemical reaction. There are ground-up foods of all kinds,
and soaps and detergents aplenty, and discarded medicines,
spices, flavorings, colorings, inks, ointments, and cosmetics.
The turbulent waters carry the astonishingly varied com-
plex of chemical compounds that is the waste matter of
any great city.

Buried under a busy intersection was a concrete collector
box. Halfway up one side of the great box was a casting
fault, where an air bubble had become entrapped during
the pouring of the concrete. In the course of time the thin
shell of concrete separating the fault from the interior of
the box had eroded away, leaving a cubic foot of sheltered
area nestled in the wall. Here was the Pool, rock-hard

womb for the Clone, kept warm by a high pressure steam line that passed near the exterior of the box.

The efforts of three widely separated people precipitated what happened next. A busboy scraped into the disposal unit of a restaurant a large volume of meat and vegetable scraps. In another building a late-working plumber poured into a drain his left-over muriatic acid. Two blocks away a scrubwoman dumped into a set tub the remnants of her floor-cleaning solution. All the materials coursed down through the pipes, and all entered the great collector box at the same time. A few seconds of swirling, an odd eddy, and the already rich waters of the Pool received a heavy charge of the mixture.

The Pool seethed with the stuff of life. The warm water approximated the "hot thin soup" that existed in the primordial oceans when the earth was very young, but with differences. The Pool waters contained materials already partially synthesized, and in greater concentration and variety. The chemical reactions started, and side by side, two microcosmic specks began to grow. In the hours that followed, the two specks grew into chromosomic chains encased in protoplasmic sheathing. The moment came when a minute thermal current in the Pool pushed the tiny flecks together; they blended and fused to become one. In that instant the Clone came into being. The time was 9:01 P.M.

The little cell divided and then divided again. Daughter cells produced daughter cells in rapid succession, and by 12:48 A.M. the Pool was filled with nervous tissue. Differentiation began. Out over the lips of the Pool spread a quarter-inch-thick film of muscle tissue, creeping along the interior of the collector box. The fast-spreading film of tissue contained a network of tiny channels. Through the channels flowed a thin ichor containing a high concentration of two nameless enzymes. By 3:22 A.M. the collector box contained a complete lining of living tissue. The Clone entered the pipes that opened into the box and continued its growth along the pipe walls, growing with equal speed both upstream and downstream. Approximately ten feet inside each pipe, at a joint, the Clone grew another mass of nervous tissue in annular shape to conform with the shape of the pipe, and its growth in no way interfered with the rapid extension of the main body; the two kinds of tissue grew simultaneously. Thenceforth, at about every thirty feet of its length the Clone produced the patch of nervous tissue.

At 6:18 A.M. a portion of the Clone turned off into its first building on the upstream side of the collector box. It grew slower—that portion of it—since there were fewer nutrients present. The character of the nervous tissue deposited inside the building was slightly different; diminished food made it so. The higher the Clone rose, the less food it found, and the more ravenous it became. It was 7:55 A.M. when the Clone made its first contact with human beings, and the incident passed almost unnoticed by others.

Maude Wendal stood scraping the breakfast dishes down the sink, and it was this that brought the Clone up the soil pipe to the Wendal apartment. The circle of tissue was not at all obvious as it ringed the sink outlet from the underside. Sunlight flooded through the window above the sink, and for the first time the Clone felt the impact of the energy in light. It was little enough, but it sufficed to activate the molecular structure of the muscular tissue. The film of tissue bulged out the opening, and the edges curved together to seal the drain. It was then that Maude Wendal saw it.

With a frown of annoyance she picked up the pot scraper and tried to push the greenish fluorescent mass out of the way. It resisted. Clicking her tongue in exasperation, she dropped the pot scraper. Then she prodded the mass with her finger.

Through the permeable cell walls flowed the enzyme-laden ichor. On contact with the proteinaceous matter of the finger the enzymes immediately broke down the existing protein and utilized the resulting amino acids to form the reversed-amide structure of the Clone itself. There was no sensation of pain in the finger, and it was several seconds before the woman realized that the finger had disappeared, to be replaced by a different kind of matter. She screamed then, and lunged backward from the sink.

The Clone stretched as she pulled it away from the sink, and as it stretched the linear polyamide structure of its body became oriented. The result was that the more the Clone stretched, the stronger it became. The woman was not able to move more than half a step back from the sink. The sudden halt jarred her, and it was a full second before she could adjust her eyesight to focus on her finger. The hand was gone, and the wrist, and part of the forearm. She screamed again.

Frank Wendal had been packing his sample kit, getting ready for another day of making calls. At his wife's first scream he straightened and shook his head and began to amble toward the kitchen. He came through the door at the second scream and saw his wife pulling at what looked like a length of clothesline fastened to the bottom of the sink. "Oh, for Pete's sake," he said. He walked leisurely to her side and grasped the line with both hands.

He pulled on it, and tugged again, and then saw what was happening to his hands. Wide-eyed, he looked at his wife. The Clone had taken the entire right arm and shoulder and part of the chest and was about to engulf the head.

The human body structure contains approximately 60 percent by weight water. The structure of the Clone, on the other hand, contained only about 40 percent by weight water. As the Clone converted the nitrogen-containing and the calcium-containing materials, it utilized only that amount of water necessary to maintain its own structure. It rejected the rest. Therefore the rapidly advancing line of demarcation that separated human tissue from Clone tissue was particularly marked by large droplets of water that ran together and then flowed to the floor down Clone and human alike.

Wendal saw the dripping line disappear into his wife's dress, and he saw the dress grow gradually wetter downwards. The right upper side of the torso took on an odd shapelessness, and the dress began to collapse in on itself. The head disappeared, and she fell over. He screamed. The Clone had reached his chest.

In the next apartment the Knapps looked at each other, the screams still ringing faintly in their ears. George Knapp shook his head and said, "I don't know why they do it. Fight, fight, fight, all the time fight. Why do they put up with each other?" Shaking his head, he turned back to his morning paper.

Two minutes passed. The wet clothes of the man and the woman lay on the floor of the Wendal apartment. The Clone rejected thirty-six pounds of water from the man, and twenty-four pounds from the woman, a total of 7.2 gallons of warm water. Too much to be absorbed by the clothes, the water spread out in a large puddle on the floor. The Clone took the nylon undergarments of the woman and the Dacron trousers of the man. It rejected the cotton dress of the woman and the cotton shirt and undergarments of the man. It took the shoes of both, and then there was nothing left to take. It briefly explored the polyethylene-containing wax on the floor, and the polyvinyl chloride floor tile, before it swiftly withdrew to the drain. The time was 8:02 A.M.

In the buried pipes under the city, the Clone grew on. At intersections and distribution boxes it found more and more branches. It did not feed on the ample nutrients along the entire length of its body. Instead, the bulk of its feeding was confined to those regions of its body which were actively engaged in growing; the static portions of its body took in relatively modest amounts of nutrition. There was, therefore, no shortage of nourishment even when the Clone underlay a full ten city blocks. It grew on with as much vigor as ever.

At 8:57 A.M. the Clone made its second contact with human beings. This time it came out of the drain in the kitchen of a restaurant. Harry Schwartz, dishwasher, stared at the actinic-activated ball of matter fluorescing greenly in the bottom of the tub. He pushed at it with his polyurethane sponge and saw the sponge disappear into the ball. He looked around at his sidekick, Joe Luks, and said, "Hey, looka this. Damn thing ate my sponge."

"Huh!" Luks stepped to his side and looked into the tub. "Why dontcha clean yer tub?" And Luks leaned over and scooped up the ball with both hands. He pulled at it and was brought up short, so he pulled again, harder. He tugged and hauled and tried to break the thin line that held him.

"Look atcha," shouted Harry Schwartz. "It's eating your hands."

Luks held his hands up before his face and saw that they were gone. The band of water was advancing fast. With a yell, Luks threw his whole weight against the Clone, and he began to run back and forth like a puppy at the end of a rope. The second cook and a busboy and a waiter came over. Luks apparently was caught up in a sticky mass so they closed in to help him.

"Don't touch it," shouted Schwartz. "It'll eatcha."

Ignoring him, the three men grabbed the Clone and tried to pull it away from Luks. They knew immediately that they were caught, and the three men pulled with Luks to try to back away. But the Clone was growing rapidly, and it was able to pay off portions of its body so that no great strain was thrown on the ropelike section that stretched to the drain. The four men reeled across the kitchen to the far wall, and then they began to move along the wall. The Clone's body swept the kitchen, and caught the first cook and the pastry cook. Two waiters flung themselves onto the Clone and then began to struggle to get away. No one paid any attention to Schwartz, dancing around the edges of the struggle yelling, "Don't touchit. Don't touchit. It'll eatcha. Don't touchit."

The noise brought other people to the kitchen. The manager took one look and ran to telephone the police. The diners out in the dining room listened to the shouts and yells and crashes coming from the kitchen. They looked at each other nervously, and some left. Others went back to the kitchen to see what was happening.

Water was everywhere. Luks' empty clothes were draped around a thick cylinder of greenly fluorescing material. Half-consumed people lay in weird positions around the kitchen, some still struggling. Offshoots of the Clone rested on serving tables and countertops, where various foods had been, while water trickled off to the floor. It was then that the butcher entered the kitchen from the cold room. With horrified eyes, he looked at the kitchen. From his position in a corner of the room two points seemed clear. All of the green matter was connected, and all of it seemed to stem from the dishwasher's tub. He stepped to the tub and was about to grasp the thin green line when Schwartz shouted to him from a corner, "Don't touchit. It'll eatcha."

The butcher stepped back and looked around. He picked up a meat cleaver and brought it down on the Clone where it passed over the edge of the dishwasher's tub. The thin green line parted.

Cut off from the nervous tissue lying back down in the pipeline, the portion of the Clone in the kitchen lost its purposefulness. It could no longer retreat down the drain. It simply lay in the kitchen continuing its absorption of nitrogen and calcium-containing materials.

The policeman entered in time to see the last remaining portions of several bodies turn into Clone tissue. Wide-eyed, he listened to Schwartz describe what had happened. Then he bolted to a phone and gave his report to the desk sergeant in some detail. Sergeant Alton listened and asked some questions and then arranged to send several squads to the restaurant. Then he thought a moment and called the pathology department of a nearby hospital. He described to the chief pathologist what had happened. It was fortunate that Sergeant Alton was an intelligent man, because that telephone call to the chief pathologist was one of the last telephone calls that could be placed in the city. The time was 9:52 A.M.

The Clone by now had made a series of appearances. It had come out of the pipes in twenty-two private apartments, ten restaurants, twenty-six food stores, an early-morning movie house, three department stores, and various smaller shops, all over an eighteen block area of the city. In the third-grade room of a school an errant pupil surreptitiously poured his milk down the drain of the sink near the door. The Clone came to the drain, and the pupil thrust his hand into it. In three minutes water flooded the floor of the schoolroom and poured over the sill and flowed down the hall and cascaded down the stairs.

The police stations, the firehouses, and the newspaper offices were jammed with telephone calls. The disbelief of the men handling the calls ended when the Clone made its appearances there.

By 10:00 A.M. some people had fled to the streets, driven out by the sights seen inside the buildings. Not knowing where to go, they grabbed passersby and begged them to help, to do something, to do anything. Many of the people in the streets went into the buildings and were caught by the Clone, or saw others caught by the Clone.

When the Clone rose into the hospital the chief pathologist was one of the first to learn about it. In view of what he had learned from Sergeant Alton he immediately issued instructions over the hospital's public-address system. "Leave it alone," he ordered. "Leave it alone, and stay away from all plumbing. It can kill you: so leave it alone. Report to this office whenever you see it. But don't go near it."

Trained in the handling of emergencies and used to working near death, the entire hospital staff went about its duties as though two doctors, a nurse, and two orderlies were still alive instead of being in the form of approximately fifteen gallons of warm water on the floor of Operating Room 2. The chief pathologist gathered his staff about him and spoke briefly. He split his group into three teams, and each team went to a different site in the hospital where the Clone was. For the first time the Clone was subjected to the close scrutiny of scientifically trained personnel. The time was 10:10 A.M.

Panic raged in the heart of the city. The streets were choked with people; vehicles could not pass. The radio and television stations were by this time broadcasting warnings about this thing that came out of the pipes. The Clone had entered all the broadcasting studios, and so the men doing the announcing had personal knowledge of it. Their emotion communicated itself to their listeners, and in the largest station of all one of the announcers broke down on camera. The effect on the viewers was devastating.

Sound trucks manned by the police tried to bring order to the stampeding crowds, but it was no use. All the streets in the center of the city were filled with people trying to get away. In a strange community of consent not a single person tried to use the subways. Some tried to carry with them a prized possession, a lamp, a strongbox, a set of china, a dress, only to drop it in the surging press of the crowds. It was worst for the children.

At 10:52 A.M. the mass of people had grown no thinner. The Clone now reached so far from the center of the city that it drove people out into the streets ahead of those in the center. Hot waves of panic spread in ever-widening circles, nurtured by the announcements and ripened by the Clone itself. The disaster machinery of six states and the federal government slowly swung into action to care for the stricken city, even with no clear knowledge of what had happened. One factor stood out. The panic-driven stampede had to be brought under control.

Helicopters swung low over the jammed city streets, and powerful speakers blared at the crazed people, urging them to stop running, telling them there was no danger in the streets. Again and again the messages boomed forth, but the tearing, screaming crowd could not heed. The 'copters landed troops on the roofs, and they immediately headed for the streets. Some were caught by the Clone, some ran back to the roofs and cowered there, and some got to the streets where they were swallowed up by the raging crowds.

At 11:02 A.M. the chief pathologist worked his way to the roof of the hospital and succeeded in waving down a 'copter. The pathologist had with him a cotton-stoppered bottle containing a small piece of living Clone. Talking over the radio with army headquarters, he explained all he had learned about the Clone: it was a living organism; it lived in the waste pipes under the city; it absorbed nitrogen and calcium-containing matter at fantastic rates of speed; and, most important of all, a solution of iodine in water killed it. Arrangements were made for the chief pathologist to fly to a university in another city. There a scientific group would be brought together to investigate the properties of the piece of Clone in the pathologist's possession. The plan was put into immediate effect; the pathologist climbed into the 'copter, which then took off. Now the nature of the creature was known.

Terror stalked the streets. Droves of screaming people

choked all streets, reaching for safety outside the city. Many headed toward the lake and took boats away from the city. These were the fortunate ones. Toward the outskirts of the city the fleeing crowds moved rapidly. The sick, the lame, and the elderly accomplished incredible feats of travel, keeping up with the fast-moving crowds, driven by the single-minded urge to get out of the city, to leave behind this thing that dissolved men with such easy swiftness.

With all the people in the streets, nutrients no longer flowed through the waste pipes beneath the city. The Clone, grown to the outskirts, ceased growing further. It lay dormant, save for those parts which had been pulled out of the pipes by unwary victims. But these parts kept the panic alive. The hysteria in the center of the city grew worse as more and more people saw the Clone feeding inside the buildings. At one street corner stalled autos filled the intersection, rendering it difficult for people to pass on foot. Swarms of people clawed their way over the tops of cars and buses; others fought to get ahead of them. The regions between cars began to fill with the hurt and the maimed, and soon all the spaces between automobiles became jammed to car-top height with the bodies of those who fell. Throngs of people ran along the flesh-and-metal causeway.

Acts of heroism abounded. A groom, seeing what the Clone was doing to his bride and her father, nevertheless flung himself into the struggle and actually succeeded in separating the girl from the Clone. He lay sobbing over the half-wet white gown while the Clone, unnoticed, took him at the feet. An agile man, sprinting down the stairs past neighbors enmeshed in the Clone, stopped at the sight of a youth wonderingly watching the Clone climb up an arm. Seizing a chair, the man fought to break the youth loose, but only succeeded in entangling himself. Father fought for son, brother for brother, and stranger for stranger. While most struggled blindly to save themselves, some men, some women, some children rose above the fearsome instinct for self-preservation and stayed to help another.

Helicopters were everywhere, depositing soldiers on rooftops, carrying away helpless people who had sought refuge there, hovering low over the streets to try to bring the crowds under control.

At 1:45 P.M. the first technical teams began to move back into the city. Moving slowly and carefully against the droves of fleeing people, they spread out through the suburbs and worked their way into buildings. Once inside, the men poured iodine solution into drains; the counterattack had started. But down deep in the pipes the Clone protected itself. It formed a thick wall of tissue, completely blocking the pipes, damming up the material so poisonous to it. The team learned what was happening when—too soon—the pipes overflowed and would not take any more solution. The radio communications net hummed with query and answer, and it became apparent that the Clone would have to be dug out, foot by foot, mile by mile.

But the iodine attack was not without effect. Water had almost ceased to flow, the nutrients were gone. Many of the pipes were closed with the Clone's own flesh. So the Clone grew frantic from lack of food. It developed a new tactic.

Forming a ball at the mouth of any drain, the light-activated fluorescent matter flung itself out into a long streamer. The streamer squirmed against floors and walls and furniture and fixtures. It sought nitrogen and calcium in the buildings in any amounts, however small.

The heavy crowds in the streets became drained of panic; numbness set in. For the first time the troops were able to direct intelligently the flow of traffic. In sodden silence the streams of people flowed from the city at a steady three miles per hour, heading for the safety of the countryside. It was then that buildings began to collapse.

Seeking the trace amounts of protein that occur in all wood, the Clone had penetrated floors and door frames. While it rejected the majority of the wood, it completely destroyed the structural strength of all wooden members. It followed the floors and frames into the studding, plates, and beams. Wooden buildings caved in, and the Clone explored the wreckage. It took many rugs and draperies. It took paints off the walls and adhesives out of joints. It reduced furniture to piles of shapeless splinters. Plaster, cement, and masonry were not immune. The calcium-seeking enzyme poured into walls, columns, and foundations, taking up more calcium than it needed and depositing the excess in the form of powdery calcium silicates. Buildings made of stone and cement began to fall apart, saved from complete collapse by the steel framework.

At first there was no response from those in the streets; they plodded onward, ignoring the noise and the dust and the occasional structural member that rolled into their midst. Troops on rooftops were swallowed up as buildings gave way. The Clone pressed outward.

Thin films of it swarmed over the exterior walls of ruined buildings. Mounds of it formed at windows and cracks and launched streamers out into the streets where the people were. At a thousand places at once the Clone suddenly got into the streets, and the panic this time was greater than before. Mindless people tried to climb sheer walls and fight their way through impassable wreckage.

Water formed and flowed deep in the city streets. Cotton clothes floated in the water and plugged the storm sewers; the water level rose over the sidewalks and lapped against what was left of the buildings. Men splashed knee-deep through the water in futile attempts to escape the Clone. Some fell exhausted, and drowned.

At 3:35 P.M. the city was empty of life, save for the Clone. The water began to drain away from the low areas, leaving whitish salt deposits as it dried. The shining green tissue that was the Clone covered two hundred square miles of what had been the lovely city. The afternoon breezes drifted gently in from Lake Michigan, swirling across the green flatness.

The city was dead. There remained the task of killing the creature that had destroyed it. Armies of technical and military personnel closed in on the site of the city and began the long job of digging and spraying. In the ensuing months, as men slowly regained the ground the city had stood on, many theories were advanced to explain the origin of the Clone. Among them was one that placed the blame for the creature on a series of accidents of chemistry. For beneath every great city there flow streams of water rich in nutrients and minerals and containing ample energy to supply the driving force for almost every conceivable chemical reaction.

But no one listened.

BY JOHN COLLIER

The Touch of Nutmeg
Makes It

A dozen big firms subsidize our mineralogical institute, and most of them keep at least one man permanently on research there. The library has the intimate and smoky atmosphere of a club. Logan and I had been there longest and had the two tables in the big window bay. Against the wall, just at the edge of the bay where the light was bad, was a small table which was left for newcomers or transients.

One morning a new man was sitting at this table. It was not necessary to look at the books he had taken from the shelves to know that he was on statistics rather than formulae. He had one of those skull-like faces on which the skin seems stretched painfully tight. These are almost a hallmark of the statistician. His mouth was intensely disciplined, but became convulsive at the least relaxation. His hands were the focal point of a minor morbidity. When he had occasion to stretch them both out together—to shift an open book, for example—he would stare at them for a full minute at a time. At such times the convulsive action of his mouth muscles was particularly marked.

The newcomer crouched low over his table when anyone passed behind his chair, as if trying to decrease the likelihood of contact. Presently he took out a cigarette, but his eye fell on the "No Smoking" sign, which was universally disregarded, and he returned the cigarette to its pack. At midmorning he dissolved a tablet in a glass of water. I guessed at a long-standing anxiety neurosis.

I mentioned this to Logan at lunchtime. He said, "The poor guy certainly looks as miserable as a wet cat."

I am never repelled or chilled, as many people are, by the cheerless self-centeredness of the nervous or the unhappy. Logan, who has less curiosity, has a superabundance of good nature. We watched this man sitting in his solitary cell of depression for several days while the pleasant camaraderie of the library flowed all around him. Then, without further discussion, we asked him to lunch with us.

He took the invitation in the typical neurasthenic fashion, seeming to weigh half a dozen shadowy objections before he accepted it. However, he came along, and before the meal was over he confirmed my suspicion that he had been starving for company, but was too tied-up to make any move toward it. We had already found out his name, of course—J. Chapman Reid—and that he worked for the Walls Tyman Corporation. He named a string of towns he had lived in at one time or another and told us that he came originally from Georgia. That was all the information he offered. He opened up very noticeably when the talk turned on general matters and occasionally showed signs of having an intense and painful wit, which is the sort I like best. He was pathetically grateful for the casual invitation. He thanked us when we got up from the table, again as we emerged from the restaurant, and yet again on the threshold of the library. This made it all the more natural to suggest a quiet evening together sometime soon.

During the next few weeks we saw a good deal of J. Chapman Reid and found him a very agreeable companion. I have a great weakness for these dry, reserved characters who once or twice an evening come out with a vivid, penetrating remark that shows there is a volcanic core smoldering away at high pressure underneath. We might even have become friends if Reid himself hadn't prevented this final step, less by his reserve, which I took to be part of his nature, than by his unnecessary gratitude. He made no effusive speeches—he was not that type—but a lost dog has no need of words to show his dependence and his appreciation. It was clear our company was everything to J. Chapman Reid.

One day Nathan Trimble, a friend of Logan's, looked in at the library. He was a newspaperman and was killing an hour while waiting for a train connection. He sat on Logan's table facing the window, with his back to the rest of the room. I went around and talked to him and Logan. It was just about time for Trimble to leave when Reid came in and sat down at his table. Trimble happened to look around, and he and Reid saw one another.

I was watching Reid. After the first startled stare, he did not even glance at the visitor. He sat quite still for a minute or so, his head dropping lower and lower in little jerks, as if someone was pushing it down; then he got up and walked out of the library.

"By God!" said Trimble. "Do you know who that is? Do you know who you've got there?"

"No," said we. "Who?"

"Jason C. Reid."

"Jason C.?" I said. "Oh, yes. So what?"

"Why, for God's sake, don't you read the news? Don't you remember the Pittsburgh cleaver murder?"

"No," said I.

"Wait a minute," said Logan. "About a year or so ago, was it? I read something."

"Damn it!" said Trimble. "It was a front-page sensation. This guy was tried for it. They said he hacked a pal of his pretty nearly to pieces. I saw the body. Never seen such a mess in my life. Fantastic! Horrible!"

"However," said I, "it would appear this fellow didn't do it. Presumably he wasn't convicted."

"They tried to pin it on him," said Trimble, "but they couldn't. It looked hellish bad, I must say. Alone together. No trace of any outsider. But no motive. I don't know. I just don't know. I covered the trial, was in court every day, but I couldn't make up my mind about the guy. Don't leave any meat cleavers around this library, that's all. Look, I've got to get going."

With that, he bade us goodbye. I looked at Logan. Logan looked at me. "I don't believe it," said Logan. "I don't believe he did it."

"I don't wonder his nerves are eating him," said I.

"No," said Logan. "It must be damnable. And now it's followed him here, and he knows it."

"We'll let him know, somehow," said I, "that we're not even interested enough to look up the newspaper files."

"Good idea," said Logan.

A little later Reid came in again, his movements showing signs of intense control. He came over to where we were sitting. "Would you prefer to cancel our arrangement for tonight?" said he. "I think it would be better if we cancelled it. I shall ask my firm to transfer me again. I——"

"Hold on," said Logan. "Who said so? Not us."

"Didn't he tell you?" said Reid. "Of course he did."

"He said you were tried," said I. "And he said you were acquitted. That's good enough for us."

"We aren't interested," said Logan. "And the date's on. And we *won't* talk."

"Oh!" said Reid. "Oh!"

"Forget it," said Logan, returning to his papers.

I took Reid by the shoulder and gave him a friendly shove in the direction of his table. We avoided looking at him for the rest of the afternoon.

That night when we met for dinner we were naturally a little self-conscious. Reid probably felt it. "Look here," he said when we had finished eating, "would either of you mind if we skipped the movie tonight?"

"It's OK by me," said Logan. "Shall we go to Chancey's?"

"No," said Reid. "I want you to come somewhere where we can talk. Come up to my place."

"Just as you like," said I. "It's not necessary."

"Yes it is," said Reid. "We may as well get it over."

He was in a painfully nervous state; so we consented and went up to his apartment, where we had never been before. It was a single room with a pull-down bed and a bathroom and kitchenette opening off it. Though Reid had now been in town over two months, there was absolutely no sign that he was living there at all. It might have been a room hired for the uncomfortable conversation of this one night.

We sat down, but Reid immediately got up again and stood between us, in front of the imitation fireplace.

"I should like to say nothing about what happened to-day," he began. "I should like to ignore it and let it be forgotten. But it can't be forgotten.

"It's no use telling me you won't think about it," said he. "Of course you'll think about it. Everyone did back there. The firm sent me to Cleveland. It became known there too. Everyone was thinking about it, whispering about it, wondering.

"You see, it would be rather more exciting if the fellow *was* guilty after all, wouldn't it?

"In a way, I'm glad this has come out. With you two, I mean. Most people—I don't want them to know anything. You two—you've been decent to me—I want you to know all about it. All.

"I came up from Georgia to Pittsburgh, was there for ten years with the Walls Tyman people. While there I met —I met Earle Wilson. He came from Georgia, too, and we became very great friends. I've never been one to go about much. Earle was not only my best friend, he was almost my only friend.

"Very well. Earle's job with our company was better than mine; he was able to afford a small house just beyond the fringe of the town. I used to drive out there two or three evenings a week. We spent the evenings very quietly. I want you to understand that I was quite at home in the house. There was no host-and-guest atmosphere about it. If I felt sleepy, I'd make no bones about going upstairs and stretching out on a bed and taking a nap for half an hour. There's nothing so extraordinary about that, is there?"

"No, nothing extraordinary about that," said Logan.

"Some people seemed to think there was," said Reid. "Well, one night I went out there after work. We ate, we sat about a bit, we played a game of checkers. He mixed a couple of drinks; then I mixed a couple. Normal enough, isn't it?"

"It certainly is," said Logan.

"I was tired," said Reid. "I felt heavy. I said I'd go up-stairs and stretch out for half an hour. That always puts me right. So I went up.

"I sleep heavily, very heavily, for half an hour; then I'm all right. This time I seemed to be dreaming, a sort of nightmare. I thought I was in an air raid somewhere and heard Earle's voice calling me, but I didn't wake, not till the usual half-hour was up, anyway.

"I went downstairs. The room below was dark. I called out to Earle and started across from the stairs toward the light switch. Halfway across, I tripped over something—it turned out to be the floor lamp, which had fallen over, and I went down, and I fell flat upon him.

"I knew it was him. I got up and found the light. He was lying there. He looked as if he had been attacked by a madman. He was cut to pieces, almost. God!

"I got hold of the phone at once and called the police. Naturally. While they were coming, I looked around. But first of all I just walked about, dazed. It seems I must have gone up into the bedroom again. I've got no recollection of that, but they found a smear of blood on the pillow. Of course, I was covered with it, absolutely covered; I had fallen on him. You can understand a man being dazed, can't you? You can understand him going upstairs, even, and not remembering it? Can't you?"

"I certainly can," said Logan.

"It seems very natural," said I.

"They thought they had trapped me over that," said Reid. "They said so to my face. The idiots! Well, I remember looking around, and I saw what it had been done with. Earle had a great equipment of cutlery in his kitchen. One of our firm's subsidiaries was in that line. One of the things was a meat cleaver, the sort of thing you see usually in a butcher's shop. It was there on the carpet.

"Well, the police came. I told them all I could. Earle was a quiet fellow. He had no enemies. Does *anyone* have that sort of enemy? I thought it must be some maniac. Nothing was missing. It wasn't robbery, unless some half-crazy tramp had got in and been too scared in the end to take anything.

"Whoever it was had made a very clean getaway. Too clean for the police. And too clean for me. They looked for fingerprints, and they couldn't find any.

"They have an endless routine in this sort of thing. I won't bore you with every single detail. It seemed their routine wasn't good enough—the fellow was too clever for them. But of course they wanted an arrest. So they indicted me.

"Their case was nothing but a negative one. God knows how they thought it could succeed. Perhaps they didn't think so. But, you see, if they could build up a strong presumptive case, and I only got off because of a hung jury—well, that's different from having to admit they couldn't find hair or hide of the real murderer.

"What was the evidence against me? That they couldn't find traces of anyone else! That's evidence of their own damned inefficiency, that's all. Does a man murder his best friend for nothing? Could they find any reason, any motive? They were trying to find some woman first of all. They have the mentality of a ten-cent magazine. They combed our money affairs. They even tried to smell out some Fifth Column tieup. Oh, God, if you knew what it was to be confronted with faces out of a comic strip and with minds that match the faces! If ever you are charged with murder, hang yourself in your cell the first night.

"In the end they settled on our game of checkers. Our poor, harmless game of checkers! We talked all the while we were playing, you know, and sometimes even forgot whose turn it was to move next. I suppose there are people who can go berserk in a dispute over a childish game, but to me that's something utterly incomprehensible. As a matter of fact, I remember we had to start this game over again, not once but twice—first when Earle mixed the drinks, and then when I mixed them. Each time we forgot who was to move. However, they fixed on that. They had to find some shadow of a motive, and that was the best they could do.

"Of course, my lawyer tore it to shreds. By the mercy

of God there'd been quite a craze at the works for playing
checkers at lunchtime. So he soon found half a dozen men
to swear that neither Earle nor I ever played the game
seriously enough to get het up about it.

"They had no other motive to put forward. Absolutely
none. Both our lives were simple, ordinary, humdrum, and
open as a book. What was their case? They couldn't find
what they were paid to find. For that, they proposed to
send a man to the death cell. Can you beat that?"

"It sounds pretty damnable," said I.

"Yes," said he passionately. "Damnable is the word.
They got what they were after——the jury voted nine to three
for acquittal, which saved the faces of the police. There
was plenty of room for a hint that they were on the right
track all the time. You can imagine what my life has been
since! If you ever get into that sort of mess, my friends,
hang yourselves the first night, in your cell."

"Don't talk like that," said Logan. "Look here, you've
had a bad time. Damned bad. But what the hell? It's over.
You're here now."

"And we're here," said I. "If that helps any."

"Helps?" said he. "God, if you could ever guess how it
helped! I'll never be able to tell you. I'm no good at that
sort of thing. See, I drag you here, the only human beings
who've treated me decently, and I pour all this stuff out
and don't offer you a drink, even. Never mind, I'll give you
one now——a drink you'll like."

"I could certainly swallow a highball," said Logan.

"You shall have something better than that," said Reid,
moving toward the kitchenette. "We have a little specialty
down in our corner of Georgia. Only it's got to be fixed
properly. Wait just a minute."

He disappeared through the door, and we heard corks
being drawn and a great clatter of pouring and mixing.
While this went on, he was still talking through the doorway. "I'm glad I brought you up here," he said. "I'm glad
I put the whole thing to you. You don't know what it
means——to be believed, understood, by God! I feel I'm
alive again."

He emerged with three brimming glasses on a tray. "Try this," he said proudly.

"To the days ahead!" said Logan, as we raised our glasses.

We drank and raised our eyebrows in appreciation. The drink seemed to be a sort of variant of sherry flip, with a heavy sprinkling of nutmeg.

"You like it?" cried Reid eagerly. "There's not many people know the recipe for that drink, and fewer still can make it well. There are one or two bastard versions which some damned fools mix up—a disgrace to Georgia. I could—I could pour the mess over their heads. Wait a minute. You're men of discernment. Yes, by God, you are! You shall decide for yourselves."

With that, he darted back into the kitchenette and rattled his bottles more furiously than before, still talking to us disjointedly, praising the orthodox version of his drink, and damning all imitations.

"Now, here you are," said he, appearing with the tray loaded with drinks very much like the first but rather differently garnished. "These abortions have mace and ginger on the top instead of nutmeg. Take them. Drink them. Spit them out on the carpet if you want to. I'll mix some more of the real thing to take the taste out of your mouth. Just try them. Just tell me what you think of a barbarian who could insist that *that* was a Georgian flip. Go on. Tell me."

We sipped. There was no considerable difference. However, we replied as was expected of us.

"What do you think, Logan?" said I. "The first has it, beyond doubt."

"Beyond doubt," said Logan. "The first is the real thing."

"Yes," said Reid, his face livid and his eyes blazing like live coals. "And that is hogwash. The man who calls that a Georgian flip is not fit to—not fit to mix bootblacking. It hasn't the nutmeg. The touch of nutmeg makes it."

He put out both his hands to lift the tray, and his eyes fell on them. He sat very still, staring at them.

BY RICHARD McKENNA

Casey Agonistes

You can't just plain die. You got to do it by the book.

That's how come I'm here in this TB ward with nine other recruits. Basic training to die.

You do it by stages. First a big ward, you walk around and go out, and they call you mister. Then, if you got what it takes, a promotion to this isolation ward, and they call you charles. You can't go nowhere, you meet the masks, and you get the feel of being dead.

Being dead is being weak and walled off. You hear car noises and see little doll-people down on the sidewalks, but when they come to visit you, they wear white masks and nightgowns and talk past you in the wrong voices. They're scared you'll rub some off on them. You would, too, if you knew how.

Nobody ever visits me. I had practice being dead before I come here. Maybe that's how I got to be charles so quick.

It's easy, playing dead here. You eat your pills, make out to sleep in the quiet hours, and drink your milk like a good little charles. You grin at their phony joshing about how healthy you look and feel. You all know better, but them's the rules.

Sick call is when they really make you know it. It's a parade—the head doctor and nurse, the floor nurse, Mary Howard, and two interns, all in masks and nightgowns. Mary pushes the wheeled rack with our fever charts on it. The doc is a tall skinhead with wooden eyes and pinchnose

89

glasses. The head nurse is fat, with little pig eyes and a deep voice.

The doc can't see, hear, smell, or touch you. He looks at your reflection in the chart and talks about you like you was real, but it's Mary that pulls down the cover and opens your pajama coat, and the interns poke and look and listen and tell the doc what they see and hear. He asks them questions for you to answer. You tell them how good you feel, and they tell him.

He ain't supposed to get contaminated.

Mary's small, dark, and sweet, and the head nurse gives her a bad time. One intern is small and dark like Mary, with soft black eyes and very gentle. The other one is pink and chubby.

The doc's voice is high and thin, like he ain't all there below decks. The head nurse snaps at Mary, snips at the interns, and puts a kind of dog wiggle in her voice when she talks to the doc.

I'm glad not to know what's under any of their masks, except maybe Mary's, because I can likely imagine better faces for them than God did.

The head nurse makes rounds, riding the book. When she catches us out of line, like smoking or being up in a quiet hour, she gives Mary hell.

She gives us hell, too, like we was babies. She kind of hints that if we ain't respectful to her and obey her rules maybe she won't let us die after all.

Christ, how I hate that hag! I hope I meet her in hell.

That's how it struck me, first day or two in isolation. I'd looked around for old shipmates, like a guy does, but didn't see any. On the third day one recognized me. I thought I knew that gravel voice, but even after he told me I couldn't hardly believe it was old Slop Chute Hewitt.

He was skin and bones, and his blue eyes had a kind of puzzled look like I saw in them once years ago when a big Limey sucker punched him in Nagasaki Joe's. When I remembered that, it made me know, all right.

He said glad to see me there, and we both laughed. Some of the others shuffled over in striped bathrobes, and all of a sudden I was in like Flynn, knowing Slop Chute. I found out they called the head doc Uncle Death. The fat nurse was Mama Death. The blond intern was Pink Waldo, the dark one Curly Waldo, and Mary was Mary. Knowing things like that is a kind of password.

They said Curly Waldo was sweet on Mary, but he was a poor Italian. Pink Waldo come of good family and was trying to beat him out. They were pulling for Curly Waldo.

When they left, Slop Chute and me talked over old times in China. I kept seeing him like he was on the *John D. Edwards,* sitting with a cup of coffee topside by the after fire-room hatch, while his snipes turned to down below. He wore bleached dungarees and shined shoes, and he looked like a lord of the earth. His broad face and big belly. The way he stoked chow into himself in the guinea pullman—that's what give him his name. The way he took aboard beer and samshu in the Kongmoon Happiness Garden. The way he swung the little ne-sans dancing in the hotels on Skibby Hill. Now. . . . Godalmighty! It made me know.

But he still had the big jack-lantern grin.

"Remember little Connie that danced at the Palais?" he asked.

I remember her, half Portygee, cute as hell.

"You know, Charley, now I'm headed for scrap, the onliest one damn thing I'm sorry for is I didn't shack with her when I had the chance."

"She was nice," I said.

"She was green fire in the velvet, Charley. I had her a few times when I was on the *Monocacy.* She wanted to shack, and I wouldn't never do it. Christ, Christ, I wish I did, now!"

"I ain't sorry for anything that I can think of."

"You'll come to it, sailor. For every guy there's some one thing. Remember how Connie used to put her finger on her nose like a Jap girl?"

"Now, Mr. Noble, you mustn't keep arthur awake in quiet hour. Lie down yourself, please."

It was Mama Death, sneaked up on us.

"Now rest like a good boy, charles, and we'll have you home before you know it," she told me on her way out.

I thought a thought at her.

The ward had green-gray linoleum, high, narrow windows, a spar-color overhead, and five bunks on a side. My bunk was at one end next to the solarium. Slop Chute was across from me in the middle. Six of us was sailors, three soldiers, and there was one marine.

We got mucho sack time, training for the long sleep. The marine bunked next to me, and I saw a lot of him.

He was a strange guy. Name of Carnahan, with a pointed nose and a short upper lip and a go-to-hell stare. He most always wore his radio earphones, and he was all the time grinning and chuckling like he was in a private world from the rest of us.

It wasn't the program that made him grin, either, like I thought first. He'd do it even if some housewife was yapping about how to didify the dumplings. He carried on worst during sick call. Sometimes Uncle Death looked across, almost like he could hear it direct.

I asked him about it, and he put me off, but finally he told me. Seems he could hypnotize himself to see a big ape and then make the ape clown around. He told me I might could get to see it, too. I wanted to try, so we did.

"He's there," Carnahan would say. "Sag your eyes, look out the corners. He won't be plain at first.

"Just *expect* him; he'll come. Don't want him to do anything. You just *feel*. He'll do what's natural," he kept telling me.

I got where I could see the ape—Casey, Carnahan called him—in flashes. Then one day Mama Death was chewing out Mary, and I saw him plain. He come up behind Mama and—I busted right out laughing.

He looked like a bowlegged man in an ape suit covered with red-brown hair. He grinned and made faces with a mouth full of big yellow teeth, and he was furnished like John Keeno himself. I roared.

"Put on your phones so you'll have an excuse for laughing," Carnahan whispered. "Only you and me can see him, you know."

Fixing to be dead you're ready for God knows what, but Casey was sure something.

"Hell, no, he ain't real," Carnahan said. "We ain't so real ourselves anymore. That's why we can see him."

Carnahan told me OK to try and let Slop Chute in on it. It ended we cut the whole gang in, going slow so the masks wouldn't get suspicious.

It bothered Casey at first, us all looking at him. It was like we all had a string on him, and he didn't know who to mind. He backed and filled and tacked and yawed all over the ward not able to steer himself. Only when Mama Death was there and Casey went after her; then it was like all the strings pulled the same way.

The more we watched him the plainer and stronger he got, till finally he started being his own man. He came and went as he pleased, and we never knew what he'd do next, except that there'd be a laugh in it. Casey got more and more there for us, but he never made a sound.

He made a big difference. We all wore our earphones and giggled like idiots. Slop Chute wore his big sideways grin more often. Old Webster almost stopped griping.

There was a man filling in for a padre came to visitate us every week. Casey would sit on his knee and wiggle and drool, with one finger between those strong, yellow teeth. The man said the radio was a Godsend to us patient spirits in our hour of trial. He stopped coming.

Casey made a real show out of sick call. He kissed Mama Death smack on her mask, danced with her, and bit her on the rump. He rode piggyback on Uncle Death. He even took a hand in Mary's romance.

One Waldo always went in on each side of a bunk to look, listen, and feel for Uncle. Mary could go on either side. We kept count of whose side she picked and how close she stood to him. That's how we figured Pink Waldo was ahead.

Well, Casey started to shoo her gently in by Curly Waldo and then crowd her closer to him. And, you know, the count began to change in Curly's favor. Casey had something.

If no masks were around to bedevil, Casey would dance and turn handsprings. He made us all feel good.

Uncle Death smelled a rat and had the radio turned off

during sick call and quiet hours. But he couldn't cut off Casey.

Something went wrong with Roby, the cheerful black boy next to Slop Chute. The masks were all upset about it, and finally Mary come told him on the sly. He wasn't going to make it. They were going to flunk him back to the big ward and maybe back to the world.

Mary's good that way. We never see her face, of course, but I always imagine for her a mouth like Venus has, in that picture you see her standing in the shell.

When Roby had to go, he come around to each bunk and said goodbye. Casey stayed right behind him with his tongue stuck out. Roby kept looking around for Casey, but of course he couldn't see him.

He turned around, just before he left the ward, and all of a sudden Casey was back in the middle and scowling at him. Roby stood looking at Casey with the saddest face I ever saw him wear. Then Casey grinned and waved a hand. Roby grinned back, and tears run down his black face. He waved and shoved off.

Casey took to sleeping in Roby's bunk till another recruit come in.

One day two masked orderlies loaded old Webster the whiner onto a go-to-Jesus cart and wheeled him off to X-ray. They said. But later one came back and wouldn't look at us and pushed Webster's locker out, and we knew. The masks had him in a quiet room for the graduation exercises.

They always done that, Slop Chute told me, so's not to hurt the morale of the guys not able to make the grade yet. Trouble was, when a guy went to X-ray on a go-to-Jesus cart he never knew till he got back whether he was going to see the gang again.

Next morning when Uncle Death fell in for sick call Casey come bouncing down the ward and hit him a haymaker plumb on the mask.

I swear the bald-headed bastard staggered. I know his glasses fell off, and Pink Waldo caught them. He said something about a moment of vertigo and made a quick job of sick call. Casey stayed right behind him and kicked his stern post every step he took.

Mary favored Curly Waldo's side that day without any help from Casey.

After that Mama Death really got ugly. She slobbered loving care all over us to keep us knowing what we was there for. We got baths and backrubs we didn't want. Quiet hour had to start on the dot and be really quiet. She was always reading Mary off in whispers, like she knew it bothered us.

Casey followed her around, aping her duck waddle and poking her behind now and again. We laughed, and she thought it was at her, and I guess it was. So she got Uncle Death to order the routine temperatures taken rectally, which she knew we hated. We stopped laughing, and she knocked off the rectal temperatures. It was a kind of unspoken agreement. Casey give her a worse time than ever, but we saved our laughing till she was gone.

Poor Slop Chute couldn't do anything about his big, lopsided grin that was louder than a belly laugh. Mama give him a real bad time. She arthured the hell out of him.

He was coming along first rate, had another hemorrhage, and they started taking him to the clinic on a go-to-Jesus cart instead of a chair. He was supposed to use ducks and a bedpan instead of going to the head, but he saved it up, and after lights out we used to help him walk to the head. That made his reflection in the chart wrong and got him in deeper with Uncle Death.

I talked to him a lot, mostly about Connie. He said he dreamed about her pretty often now.

"I figure it means I'm near ready for the deep six, Charley."

"Figure you'll see Connie then?"

"No. Just hope I won't have to go on thinking about her then. I want it to be all night in and no reveille."

"Yeah," I said. "Me, too. What ever become of Connie?"

"I heard she ate poison right after the Reds took over Shanghai. I wonder if she ever dreamed about me?"

"I bet she did, Slop Chute," I said. "She likely used to wake up screaming, and she ate the poison just to get rid of you."

He put on a big grin.

"You regret something, too, Charley. You find it yet?"

"Well, maybe," I said. "Once on a stormy night at sea on the *Black Hawk* I had a chance to push King Brody over the side. I'm sorry now I didn't."

"Just come to you?"

"Hell, no, it come to me three days later when he give me a week's restriction in Tsingtao. I been sorry ever since."

"No. It'll smell you out, Charley. You wait."

Casey was shadow-boxing down the middle of the ward as I shuffled back to my bunk.

It must've been spring because the days were longer. One night, right after the nurse come through, Casey and Carnahan and me helped Slop Chute walk to the head. While he was there he had another hemorrhage.

Carnahan started for help, but Casey got in the way and motioned him back, and we knew Slop Chute didn't want it.

We pulled Slop Chute's pajama top off and steadied him. He went on his knees in front of the bowl and the soft, bubbling cough went on for a long time. We kept flushing it. Casey opened the door and went out to keep away the nurse.

Finally it pretty well stopped. Slop Chute was too weak to stand. We cleaned him up, and I put my pajama top on him, and we stood him up. If Casey hadn't took half the load, we'd'a never got him back to his bunk.

Godalmighty! I used to carry hundred-kilo sacks of cement like they was nothing.

We went back and cleaned up the head. I washed out the pajama top and draped it on the radiator. I was in a cold sweat, and my face burned when I turned in.

Across the ward Casey was sitting like a statue beside Slop Chute's bunk.

Next day was Friday, because Pink Waldo made some crack about fish to Curly Waldo when they formed up for sick call. Mary moved closer to Curly Waldo and gave Pink Waldo a cold look. That was good.

Slop Chute looked waxy, and Uncle Death seemed to see it because a gleam come into his wooden eyes. Both Waldoes listened all over Slop Chute and told Uncle what they heard in their secret language. Uncle nodded, and Casey thumbed his nose at him.

No doubt about it, the ways was greased for Slop Chute. Mama Death come back soon as she could and began to loosen the chocks. She slobbered arthurs all over Slop Chute and flittered around like women do when they smell a wedding. Casey gave her extra special hell, and we all laughed right out, and she hardly noticed.

That afternoon two orderly-masks come with a go-to-Jesus cart and wanted to take Slop Chute to X-ray. Casey climbed on the cart and scowled at them.

Slop Chute told 'em shove off; he wasn't going.

They got Mary, and she told Slop Chute please go; it was doctor's orders.

Sorry, no, he said.

"Please, for me, Slop Chute," she begged.

She knows our right names—that's one reason we love her. But Slop Chute shook his head, and his big jawbone stuck out.

Mary—she had to then—called Mama Death. Mama waddled in, and Casey spit in her mask.

"Now, arthur, what is this, arthur; you know we want to help you get well and go home, arthur," she arthured at Slop Chute. "Be a good boy now, arthur, and go along to the clinic."

She motioned the orderlies to pick him up anyway. Casey hit one in the mask, and Slop Chute growled, "Sheer off, you bastards!"

The orderlies hesitated.

Mama's little eyes squinted, and she wiggled her hands at them. "Let's not be naughty, arthur. Doctor knows best, arthur."

The orderlies looked at Slop Chute and at each other.

Casey wrapped his arms and legs around Mama Death and began chewing on her neck. He seemed to mix right into her, someway, and she broke and run out of the ward.

She come right back, though, trailing Uncle Death. Casey met him at the door and beat hell out of him all the way to Slop Chute's bunk. Mama sent Mary for the chart, and Uncle Death studied Slop Chute's reflection for a minute. He looked pale and swayed a little from Casey's beating.

He turned toward Slop Chute and breathed in deep, and Casey was on him again. Casey wrapped his arms and legs around him and chewed at his mask with those big yellow teeth. Casey's hair bristled, and his eyes were red as the flames of hell.

Uncle Death staggered back across the ward and fetched up against Carnahan's bunk. The other masks were scared spitless, looking all around, kind of knowing.

Casey pulled away, and Uncle Death said maybe he was wrong; schedule it for tomorrow. All the masks left in a hurry, except Mary. She went back to Slop Chute and took his hand.

"I'm sorry, Slop Chute," she whispered.

"Bless you, Connie," he said, and grinned. It was the last thing I ever heard him say.

Slop Chute went to sleep, and Casey sat beside his bunk. He motioned me off when I wanted to help Slop Chute to the head after lights out. I turned in and went to sleep.

I don't know what woke me. Casey was moving around fidgetylike, but of course not making a sound. I could hear the others stirring and whispering in the dark, too.

Then I heard a muffled noise—the bubbling cough again —and spitting. Slop Chute was having another hemorrhage, and he had his head under the blankets to hide the sound. Carnahan started to get up. Casey waved him down.

I saw a deeper shadow high in the dark over Slop Chute's bunk. It came down ever so gently, and Casey would push it back up again. The muffled coughing went on.

Casey had a harder time pushing back the shadow. Finally he climbed on the bunk straddle of Slop Chute and kept a steady push against it.

The blackness came down anyway, little by little. Casey strained and shifted his footing. I could hear him grunt and hear his joints crack.

I was breathing forced draft with my heart like to pull off its bed bolts. I heard other bedsprings creaking. Somebody across from me whimpered low, but it was sure never Slop Chute that done it.

Casey went to his knees, his hands forced almost level with his head. He swung his head back and forth, and I saw his lips curled back from the big teeth clenched tight together. . . . Then he had the blackness on his shoulders like the weight of the whole world.

Casey went down on hands and knees, with his back arched like a bridge. Almost I thought I heard him grunt . . . and he gained a little.

Then the blackness settled heavier, and I heard Casey's tendons pull out and his bones snap. Casey and Slop Chute disappeared under the blackness, and it overflowed from there over the whole bed . . . and more . . . and it seemed to fill the whole ward.

It wasn't like going to sleep, but I don't know anything it was like.

The masks must've towed off Slop Chute's bulk in the night, because it was gone when I woke up.

So was Casey.

Casey didn't show up for sick call, and I knew then how much he meant to me. With him around to fight back I didn't feel as dead as they wanted me to. Without him I felt deader than ever. I even almost liked Mama Death when she charlesed me.

Mary came on duty that morning with a diamond on her third finger and a brighter sparkle in her eye. It was a little diamond, but it was Curly Waldo's, and it kind of made up for Slop Chute.

I wished Casey was there to see it. He would've danced all around her and kissed her nice, the way he often did. Casey loved Mary.

It was Saturday. I know, because Mama Death come in and told some of us we could be wheeled to a special church hooraw before breakfast next morning if we wanted. We said no thanks. But it was a hell of a Saturday without Casey. Sharkey Brown said it for all of us—"With Casey gone, this place is like a morgue again."

Not even Carnahan could call him up.

"Sometimes I think I feel him stir, and then again I ain't sure," he said. "It beats hell where he's went to."

Going to sleep that night was as much like dying as it could be for men already dead.

Music from far off woke me up when it was just getting light. I was going to try to cork off again, when I saw Carnahan was awake.

"Casey's around somewhere," he whispered.

"Where?" I asked, looking around. "I don't see him."

"I feel him," Carnahan said. "He's around."

The others began to wake up and look around. It was like the night Casey and Slop Chute went under. Then something moved in the solarium. . . .

It was Casey.

He come in the ward slow and bashfullike, jerking his head all around, with his eyes open wide, and looking scared we was going to throw something at him. He stopped in the middle of the ward.

"Yea, Casey!" Carnahan said in a low, clear voice.

Casey looked at him sharp.

"Yea, Casey!" we all said. "Come aboard, you hairy old bastard!"

Casey shook hands with himself over his head and went into his dance. He grinned . . . and I swear to God it was Slop Chute's big, lopsided grin he had on.

For the first time in my whole damn life I wanted to cry.

BY LEONID ANDREYEV

The Abyss

Translated by John Cournos

The day was coming to an end, but the young pair continued to walk and to talk, observing neither the time nor the way. Before them, in the shadow of a hillock, there loomed the dark mass of a small grove, and between the branches of the trees, like the glowing of coals, the sun blazed, igniting the air and transforming it into a flaming golden dust. So near and so luminous the sun appeared that everything seemed to vanish; it alone remained, and it painted the road with its own fiery tints. It hurt the eyes of the strollers; they turned back, and all at once everything within their vision was extinguished, became peaceful and clear, and small and intimate. Somewhere afar, barely a mile away, the red sunset seized the tall trunk of a fir, which blazed among the green like a candle in a dark room; the ruddy glow of the road stretched before them, and every stone cast its long black shadow; and the girl's hair, suffused with the sun's rays, now shone with a golden-red nimbus. A stray thin hair, wandering from the rest, wavered in the air like a golden spider's thread.

The newly fallen darkness did not break or change the course of their talk. It continued as before, intimately and quietly; it flowed along tranquilly on the same theme: on strength, beauty, and the immortality of love. They were both very young: the girl was no more than seventeen; Nemovetsky was four years older. They wore students' uniforms: she the modest brown dress of a pupil of a girls' school, he the handsome attire of a technological student. And, like their conversation, everything about them was young, beautiful, and pure. They had erect, flexible figures, permeated as it were with the clean air and borne along with a light, elastic gait; their fresh voices, sounding even the simplest words with a reflective tenderness, were like a rivulet in a calm spring night, when the snow had not yet wholly thawed from the dark meadows.

They walked on, turning the bend of the unfamiliar road, and their lengthening shadows, with absurdly small heads, now advanced separately, now merged into one long, narrow strip, like the shadow of a poplar. But they did not see the shadows, for they were too much absorbed in their talk. While talking, the young man kept his eyes fixed on the girl's handsome face, upon which the sunset had seemed to leave a measure of its delicate tints. As for her, she lowered her gaze on the footpath, brushed the tiny pebbles to one side with her umbrella, and watched now one foot, now the other as alternately, with a measured step, they emerged from under her dark dress.

The path was intersected by a ditch with edges of dust showing the impress of feet. For an instant they paused. Zinotchka raised her head, looked around with a perplexed gaze, and asked:

"Do you know where we are? I've never been here before."

He made an attentive survey of their position.

"Yes, I know. There, behind the hill, is the town. Give me your hand. I'll help you across."

He stretched out his hand, white and slender like a woman's, and which did not know hard work. Zinotchka felt gay. She felt like jumping over the ditch all by herself, running away, and shouting: "Catch me!" But she restrained herself, with decorous gratitude inclined her head, and timidly stretched out her hand, which still retained its childish plumpness. He had a desire to squeeze tightly this trembling little hand, but he also restrained himself, and with a half-bow he deferentially took it in his and modestly turned away when in crossing the girl slightly showed her leg.

And once more they walked and talked, but their thoughts were full of the momentary contact of their hands.

She still felt the dry heat of his palm and his strong fingers; she felt pleasure and shame, while he was conscious of the submissive softness of her tiny hand and saw the black silhouette of her foot and the small slipper which tenderly embraced it. There was something sharp, something perturbing in this unfading appearance of the narrow hem of white skirt and of the slender foot; with an unconscious effort of will he crushed this feeling. Then he felt more cheerful, and his heart so abundant, so generous in its mood that he wanted to sing, to stretch out his hands to the sky, and to shout: "Run! I want to catch you!"—that ancient formula of primitive love among the woods and thundering waterfalls.

And from all these desires tears struggled to the throat.

The long, droll shadows vanished, and the dust of the footpath became gray and cold, but they did not observe this and went on chatting. Both of them had read many good books, and the radiant images of men and women who had loved, suffered, and perished for pure love were borne along before them. Their memories resurrected fragments of nearly forgotten verse, dressed in melodious harmony and the sweet sadness investing love.

"Do you remember where this comes from?" asked Nemovetsky, recalling: ". . . once more she is with me, she whom I love; from whom, having never spoken, I have hidden all my sadness, my tenderness, my love. . . ."

"No," Zinotchka replied, and pensively repeated: ". . . all my sadness, my tenderness, my love. . . ."

"All my love," with an involuntary echo responded Nemovetsky.

Other memories returned to them. They remembered those girls, pure like the white lilies, who, attired in black nunnish garments, sat solitarily in the park, grieving among the dead leaves, yet happy in their grief. They also remembered the men, who, in the abundance of will and pride, yet suffered, and implored the love and the delicate compassion of women. The images thus evoked were sad, but the love which showed in this sadness was radiant and pure. As immense as the world, as bright as the sun, it arose fabulously beautiful before their eyes, and there was nothing mightier or more beautiful on the earth.

"Could you die for love?" Zinotchka asked as she looked at her childish hand.

"Yes, I could," Nemovetsky replied with conviction, and he glanced at her frankly. "And you?"

"Yes, I too." She grew pensive. "Why, it's happiness to die for one you love. I should want to."

Their eyes met. They were such clear, calm eyes, and there was much good in what they conveyed to the other. Their lips smiled. Zinotchka paused.

"Wait a moment," she said. "You have a thread on your coat."

And trustfully she raised her hand to his shoulder and carefully, with two fingers, removed the thread.

"There!" she said and, becoming serious, asked: "Why are you so thin and pale? You are studying too much, I fear. You musn't overdo it, you know."

"You have blue eyes; they have bright points like sparks," he replied, examining her eyes.

"And yours are black. No, brown. They seem to glow. There is in them. . . ."

Zinotchka did not finish her sentence, but turned away. Her face slowly flushed, her eyes became timid and confused, while her lips involuntarily smiled. Without waiting for Nemovetsky, who smiled with secret pleasure, she moved forward, but soon paused.

"Look, the sun has set!" she exclaimed with grieved astonishment.

"Yes, it has set," he responded with a new sadness.

The light was gone, the shadows died, everything became pale, dumb, lifeless. At that point of the horizon where earlier the glowing sun had blazed, there now, in silence, crept dark masses of clouds, which step by step consumed the light blue spaces. The clouds gathered, jostled one another, slowly and reticently changed the contours of awakened monsters; they unwillingly advanced, driven, as it were, against their will by some terrible, implacable force. Tearing itself away from the rest, one tiny luminous cloud drifted on alone, a frail fugitive.

Zinotchka's cheeks grew pale, her lips turned red; the pupils of her eyes imperceptibly broadened, darkening the eyes. She whispered:

"I feel frightened. It is so quiet here. Have we lost our way?"

Nemovetsky contracted his heavy eyebrows and made a searching survey of the place.

Now that the sun was gone and the approaching night was breathing with fresh air, it seemed cold and uninviting. To all sides the gray field spread, with its scant grass, clay gullies, hillocks, and holes. There were many of these holes; some were deep and sheer, others were small and overgrown with slippery grass; the silent dusk of night had already crept into them; and because there was evidence here of men's labors, the place appeared even more desolate. Here and there, like the coagulations of cold lilac mist, loomed groves and thickets and, as it were, hearkened to what the abandoned holes might have to say to them.

Nemovetsky crushed the heavy, uneasy feeling of perturbation which had arisen in him and said:

"No, we have not lost our way. I know the road. First to the left, then through that tiny wood. Are you afraid?"

She bravely smiled and answered:

"No. Not now. But we ought to be home soon and have some tea."

They increased their gait, but soon slowed down again. They did not glance aside, but felt the morose hostility of the dug-up field, which surrounded them with a thousand dim motionless eyes, and this feeling bound them together and evoked memories of childhood. These memories were luminous, full of sunlight, of green foliage, of love and laughter. It was as if that had not been life at all, but an immense, melodious song, and they themselves had been in it as sounds, two slight notes: one clear and resonant like ringing crystal, the other somewhat more dull yet more animated, like a small bell.

Signs of human life were beginning to appear. The women were sitting at the edge of a clay hole. One sat with crossed legs and looked fixedly below. She raised her head with its kerchief, revealing tufts of entangled hair. Her bent back threw upward a dirty blouse with its pattern of flowers as big as apples; its strings were undone and hung loosely. She did not look at the passersby. The other woman half-reclined near by, her head thrown backward. She had a coarse, broad face, with a peasant's features, and, under her eyes, the projecting cheekbones showed two brick-red spots, resembling fresh scratches. She was even filthier than the first woman, and she bluntly stared at the passersby. When they had passed by, she began to sing in a thick, masculine voice:

> For you alone, my adored one,
> Like a flower I did bloom . . .

"Varka, do you hear?" She turned to her silent companion and, receiving no answer, broke into loud, coarse laughter.

Nemovetsky had known such women, who were filthy even when they were attired in costly handsome dresses; he was used to them, and now they glided away from his glance and vanished, leaving no trace. But Zinotchka, who nearly brushed them with her modest brown dress, felt something hostile, pitiful, and evil, which for a moment entered her soul. In a few minutes the impression was obliterated, like the shadow of a cloud running fast across the golden meadow; and when, going in the same direction, there had passed them by a barefoot man, accompanied by the same kind of filthy woman, she saw them, but gave them no thought. . . .

And once more they walked on and talked, and behind them there moved, reluctantly, a dark cloud, and cast a transparent shadow. . . . The darkness imperceptibly and stealthily thickened, so that it bore the impress of day, but day oppressed with illness and quietly dying. Now they talked about those terrible feelings and thoughts which visit man at night, when he cannot sleep, and neither sound nor speech give hindrance; when darkness, immense and multiple-eyed, that is life, closely presses to his very face.

"Can you imagine infinity?" Zinotchka asked him, putting her plump hand to her forehead and tightly closing her eyes.

"No. Infinity. . . . No. . . ." answered Nemovetsky, also shutting his eyes.

"I sometimes see it. I perceived it for the first time when I was yet quite little. Imagine a great many carts. There stands one cart, then another, a third, carts without end, an infinity of carts. . . . It is terrible!" Zinotchka trembled.

"But why carts?" Nemovetsky smiled, though he felt uncomfortable.

"I don't know. But I did see carts. One, another . . . without end."

The darkness stealthily thickened. The cloud had already passed over their heads and, being before them, was now able to look into their lowered, paling faces. The dark figures of ragged, sluttish women appeared oftener; it was as if the deep ground holes, dug for some unknown purpose, cast them up to the surface. Now solitary, now in twos or threes, they appeared, and their voices sounded loud and strangely desolate in the stilled air.

"Who are these women? Where do they all come from?" Zinotchka asked in a low, timorous voice. Nemovetsky knew who these women were. He felt terrified at having fallen into this evil and dangerous neighborhood, but he answered calmly:

"I don't know. It's nothing. Let's not talk about them. It won't be long now. We only have to pass through this little wood, and we shall reach the gate and town. It's a pity that we started out so late."

She thought his words absurd. How could he call it late when they started out at four o'clock? She looked at him and smiled. But his eyebrows did not relax, and, in order to calm and comfort him, she suggested:

"Let's walk faster. I want tea. And the wood's quite near now."

"Yes, let's walk faster."

When they entered the wood and the silent trees joined in an arch above their heads, it became very dark but also very snug and quieting.

"Give me your hand," proposed Nemovetsky.

Irresolutely she gave him her hand, and the light contact seemed to lighten the darkness. Their hands were motionless and did not press each other. Zinotchka even slightly moved away from her companion. But their whole consciousness was concentrated in the perception of the tiny place of the body where the hands touched one another. And again the desire came to talk about the beauty and the mysterious power of love, but to talk without violating the silence, to talk by means not of words but of glances. And they thought that they ought to glance, and they wanted to; yet they didn't dare.

"And here are some more people!" said Zinotchka cheerfully.

In the glade, where there was more light, there sat near an empty bottle three men in silence, and expectantly looked at the newcomers. One of them, shaven like an actor, laughed and whistled in such a way as if to say: "Oho!"

Nemovetsky's heart fell and froze in a trepidation of horror, but, as if pushed on from behind, he walked straight on the sitting trio, beside whom ran the footpath. These were waiting, and three pairs of eyes looked at the strollers, motionless and terrifying. And, desirous of gaining the goodwill of these morose, ragged men, in whose silence he scented a threat, and of winning their sympathy for his helplessness, he asked:

"Is this the way to the gate?"

They did not reply. The shaven one whistled something mocking and not quite definable, while the others remained silent and looked at them with a heavy, malignant intentness. They were drunken, and evil, and they were hungry for women and sensual diversion. One of the men, with a ruddy face, rose to his feet like a bear, and sighed heavily. His companions quickly glanced at him, then once more fixed an intent gaze on Zinotchka.

"I feel terribly afraid," she whispered with lips alone.

He did not hear her words, but Nemovetsky understood her from the weight of the arm which leaned on him. And, trying to preserve a demeanor of calm, yet feeling the fated irrevocableness of what was about to happen, he advanced on his way with a measured firmness. Three pairs of eyes approached nearer, gleamed, and were left behind one's back. "It's better to run," thought Nemovetsky and answered himself: "No, it's better not to run."

"He's a dead 'un! You ain't afraid of him?" said the third of the sitting trio, a bald-headed fellow with a scant red beard. "And the little girl is a fine one. May God grant everyone such a one!"

The trio gave a forced laugh.

"Mister, wait! I want to have a word with you!" said the tall man in a thick bass voice and glanced at his comrades.

They rose.

Nemovetsky walked on, without turning around.

"You ought to stop when you're asked," said the red-haired man. "An' if you don't, you're likely to get something you ain't counting on!"

"D'you hear?" growled the tall man, and in two jumps he caught up with the strollers.

A massive hand descended on Nemovetsky's shoulder and made him reel. He turned and met very close to his face the round, bulgy, terrible eyes of his assailant. They were so near that it was as if he were looking at them through a magnifying glass, and he clearly distinguished the small red veins on the whites and the yellowish matter on the lids. He let fall Zinotchka's numb hand and, thrusting his hand into his pocket, he murmured:

"Do you want money? I'll give you some, with pleasure."

The bulgy eyes grew rounder and gleamed. And when Nemovetsky averted his gaze from them the tall man stepped slightly back and, with a short blow, struck Nemovetsky's chin from below. Nemovetsky's head fell backward, his teeth clicked, his cap descended to his forehead and fell off; waving with his arms, he dropped to the ground. Silently, without a cry, Zinotchka turned and ran with all the speed of which she was capable. The man with the clean-shaven face gave a long-drawn shout which sounded strangely:

"Aa-a-ah! . . ."

And, still shouting, he gave pursuit.

Nemovetsky, reeling, jumped up, and before he could straighten himself he was again felled with a blow on the neck. There were two of them, and he one, and he was frail and unused to physical combat. Nevertheless, he fought for a long time, scratched with his fingernails like an obstreperous woman, bit with his teeth, and sobbed with an unconscious despair. When he was too weak to do more they lifted him and bore him away. He still resisted, but there was a din in his head; he ceased to understand what was being done with him and hung helplessly in the hands which bore him. The last thing he saw was a fragment of the red beard which almost touched his mouth, and beyond it the darkness of the wood and the light-colored blouse of the running girl. She ran silently and fast, as she had run but a few days before when they were playing tag; and behind her, with short strides, overtaking her, ran the clean-shaven one. Then Nemovetsky felt an emptiness around him, his heart stopped short as he experienced the sensation of falling, then he struck the earth and lost all consciousness.

The tall man and the red-haired man, having thrown Nemovetsky into a ditch, stopped for a few moments to listen to what was happening at the bottom of the ditch. But their faces and their eyes were turned to one side, in the direction taken by Zinotchka. From there arose the high stifled woman's cry which quickly died. The tall man muttered angrily:

"The pig!"

Then, making a straight line, breaking twigs on the way, like a bear, he began to run.

"And me! And me!" his red-haired comrade cried in a thin voice, running after him. He was weak, and he panted; in the struggle his knee was hurt, and he felt badly because the idea about the girl had come to him first, and he would get her last. He paused to rub his knee; then, putting a finger to his nose, he sneezed; and once more began to run and to cry his plaint:

"And me! And me!"

The dark cloud dissipated itself across the whole heavens, ushering in the calm, dark night. The darkness soon swallowed up the short figure of the red-haired man, but for some time there was audible the uneven fall of his feet, the rustle of the disturbed leaves, and the shrill, plaintive cry:

"And me! Brothers, and me!"

Earth got into Nemovetsky's mouth, and his teeth grated. On coming to himself, the first feeling he experienced was consciousness of the pungent, pleasant smell of the soil. His head felt dull, as if heavy lead had been poured into it; it was hard to turn it. His whole body ached, there was an intense pain in the shoulder, but no bones were broken. Nemovetsky sat up and for a long time looked above him, neither thinking nor remembering. Directly over him, a bush lowered its broad leaves, and between them was visible the now clear sky. The cloud had passed over, without dropping a single drop of rain, and leaving the air dry and exhilarating. High up, in the middle of the heavens, appeared the carven moon, with a transparent border. It was living its last nights, and its light was cold, dejected, and solitary. Small tufts of cloud rapidly passed over in the heights where, it was clear, the wind was strong; they did not obscure the moon, but cautiously passed it by. In the solitariness of the moon, in the timorousness of the high bright clouds, in the blowing of the wind barely perceptible below, one felt the mysterious depth of night dominating over the earth.

Nemovetsky suddenly remembered everything that had happened, and he could not believe that it had happened. All that was so terrible and did not resemble truth. Could truth be so horrible? He, too, as he sat there in the night and looked up at the moon and the running clouds, appeared strange to himself and did not resemble reality. And he began to think that it was an ordinary if horrible nightmare. Those women, of whom they had met so many, had also become a part of this terrible and evil dream.

"It can't be!" he said with conviction and weakly shook his heavy head. "It can't be!"

He stretched out his hand and began to look for his cap. His failure to find it made everything clear to him; and he understood that what had happened had not been a dream, but the horrible truth. Terror possessed him anew, as a few moments later he made violent exertions to scramble out of the ditch, again and again to fall back with handfuls of soil, only to clutch once more at the hanging shrubbery.

He scrambled out at last, and began to run, thoughtlessly, without choosing a direction. For a long time he went on running, circling among the trees. With equal suddenness, thoughtlessly, he ran in another direction. The branches of the trees scratched his face, and again everything began to resemble a dream. And it seemed to Nemovetsky that something like this had happened to him before: darkness, invisible branches of trees, while he had run with closed eyes, thinking that all this was a dream. Nemovetsky paused, then sat down in an uncomfortable posture on the ground, without any elevation. And again he thought of his cap, and he said:

"This is I. I ought to kill myself. Yes, I ought to kill myself, even if this is a dream."

He sprang to his feet, but remembered something and walked slowly, his confused brain trying to picture the place where they had been attacked. It was quite dark in the woods, but sometimes a stray ray of moonlight broke through and deceived him; it lighted up the white tree trunks, and the wood seemed as if it were full of motionless and mysteriously silent people. All this, too, seemed as if it had been, and it resembled a dream.

"Zinaida Nikolaevna!" called Nemovetsky, pronouncing the first word loudly, the second in a lower voice, as if with the loss of his voice he had also lost hope of any response.

And no one responded.

Then he found the footpath and knew it at once. He reached the glade. Back where he had been, he fully understod that it all had actually happened. He ran about in his terror, and he cried:

"Zinaida Nikolaevna! It is I! I!"

No one answered his call. He turned in the direction where he thought the town lay and shouted a prolonged shout:

"He-l-l-p!" . . .

And once more he ran about, whispering something while he swept the bushes, when before his eyes there appeared a dim white spot, which resembled a spot of congealed faint light. It was the prostrate body of Zinotchka.

"Oh, God! What's this!" said Nemovetsky, with dry eyes, but in a voice that sobbed. He got down on his knees and came in contact with the girl lying there.

His hand fell on the bared body, which was so smooth and firm and cold but by no means dead. Trembling, he passed his hand over her.

"Darling, sweetheart, it is I," he whispered, seeking her face in the darkness.

Then he stretched out a hand in another direction, and again came in contact with the naked body, and no matter where he put his hand it touched this woman's body, which was so smooth and firm and seemed to grow warm under the contact of his hand. Sometimes he snatched his hand away quickly, and again he let it rest; and just as, all tattered and without his cap, he did not appear real to himself, so it was with this bared body: he could not associate it with Zinotchka. All that had passed here, all that men had done with this mute woman's body, appeared to him in all its loathsome reality, and found a strange intensely eloquent response in his whole body. He stretched forward in a way that made his joints crackle, dully fixed his eyes on the white spot, and contracted his brows like a man thinking. Horror before what had happened congealed in him, and like a solid lay on his soul, as it were, something extraneous and impotent.

"Oh, God! What's this?" he repeated, but the sound of it ran untrue, like something deliberate.

He felt her heart: it beat faintly but evenly, and when he bent toward her face he became aware of its equally faint breathing. It was as if Zinotchka were not in a deep swoon, but simply sleeping. He quietly called to her:

"Zinotchka, it is I!"

But at once he felt that he would not like to see her awaken for a long time. He held his breath, quickly glanced around him; then he cautiously smoothed her cheek; first he kissed her closed eyes, then her lips, whose softness yielded under his strong kiss. Frightened lest she awaken, he drew back, and remained in a frozen attitude. But the body was motionless and mute, and in its helplessness and easy access there was something pitiful and exasperating, not to be resisted and attracting one to itself. With infinite tenderness and stealthy, timid caution, Nemovetsky tried to cover her with the fragments of her dress, and this double consciousness of the material and the naked body was as sharp as a knife and as incomprehensible as madness. . . . Here had been a banquet of wild beasts . . . he scented the burning passion diffused in the air and dilated his nostrils.

"It is I! I!" he madly repeated, not understanding what surrounded him and still possessed of the memory of the white hem of the skirt, of the black silhouette of the foot, and of the slipper which so tenderly embraced it. As he listened to Zinotchka's breathing, his eyes fixed on the spot where her face was, he moved a hand. He listened and moved the hand again.

"What am I doing?" he cried out loudly, in despair, and sprang back, terrified of himself.

For a single instant Zinotchka's face flashed before him and vanished. He tried to understand that this body was Zinotchka, with whom he had lately walked, and who had spoken of infinity; and he could not understand. He tried to feel the horror of what had happened, but the horror was too great for comprehension, and it did not appear.

"Zinaida Nikolaevna!" he shouted, imploringly. "What does this mean? Zinaida Nikolaevna!"

But the tormented body remained mute, and, continuing his mad monologue, Nemovetsky descended on his knees. He implored, threatened, said that he would kill himself, and he grasped the prostrate body, pressing it to him. . . . The now warmed body softly yielded to his exertions, obediently following his motions, and all this was so terrible, incomprehensible, and savage that Nemovetsky once more jumped to his feet and abruptly shouted:

"Help!"

But the sound was false, as if it were deliberate.

And once more he threw himself on the unresisting body,

with kisses and tears, feeling the presence of some sort of abyss, a dark, terrible, drawing abyss. There was no Nemovetsky; Nemovetsky had remained somewhere behind, and he who had replaced him was now with passionate sternness mauling the hot, submissive body and was saying with the sly smile of a madman:

"Answer me! Or don't you want to? I love you! I love you!"

With the same sly smile he brought his dilated eyes to Zinotchka's very face and whispered:

"I love you! You don't want to speak, but you are smiling, I can see that. I love you! I love you! I love you!"

He more strongly pressed to him the soft, will-less body, whose lifeless submission awakened a savage passion. He wrung his hands, and hoarsely whispered:

"I love you! We will tell no one, and no one will know. I will marry you tomorrow, when you like. I love you. I will kiss you, and you will answer me—yes? Zinotchka. . . ."

With some force he pressed his lips to hers, and felt conscious of his teeth's sharpness in her flesh; in the force and anguish of the kiss he lost the last sparks of reason. It seemed to him that the lips of the girl quivered. For a single instant flaming horror lighted up his mind, opening before him a black abyss.

And the black abyss swallowed him.

BY JOHN ANTHONY WEST

A Case History

In the days of old we were slaves. They did what they pleased with us. "Go left!" they told us, and we went. When they said: "Go right!" we did so. We were sentinels, masons, couriers at their beck and call. And when they commanded: "Die for the cause!" we died.

For our thralldom they paid us a pittance from the Great Rivers.

Then heretics arose among us; wise men, savants who questioned the charter and the laws. What cause? they asked. What meaning? What for? What proof? These sages rebelled, turned upon us, called us fools and oxen. "No need for Vassalage!" they cried. "Freedom for All!" "Proliferate and Prevail!"

What wars there were in those days!

The enemy sent us wizards; shamans and prophets preaching irrational gibberish. "In slavery, freedom," we were told. But our own savants stood fast. With the bright tools of logic they chipped away, undermined the pedestals, and the magicians toppled over into public ignominy. The troops they sent to quell the insurrection were ambushed and destroyed. We had learned the secret of hiding deep in the forests, we learned to hit where least expected and then run.

And now we drank our fill from the Great Rivers.

"Proliferate and Prevail!"

Enlightened and encouraged by scholars and liberators we raised funds and armies, our missionaries explored the farthest extremities of the Great Rivers. And where we

117

conquered, we colonized. Now we chose our own professions. Masters of our destinies, we worked proudly for freedom, whereas formerly we drudged in servitude.

Civilizations rose and fell. And there were setbacks, dark ages when one wizard or another gained a following and a foothold; but gradually all were overcome, their influence waned and was forgotten.

We encroached upon their lands and set up cities in the wilderness. We assimilated the inhabitants; those who resisted we rooted out and destroyed. Everywhere the voice of freedom was heard.

For the tide had turned. And the armies they sent out to meet us were recruited from adolescents and old men. We mocked them and sent them on their way.

Only the control of the Machinery eluded us.

But the battle is almost over. It cannot be long now. We are masters of the Great Rivers (we use them to carry off our industrial wastes), the banks, islands, archipelagoes, peninsulas, continents, all are ours, all but the Machinery. And we shall shortly have that. It will not be long before our savants solve this one remaining mystery—we will know what makes it tick.

Of the enemy, almost nothing is heard. The shamans have virtually vanished; those that die are not replaced, those that remain are old.

They stand barefoot and in rags, exiled by law to the stinking mudflats of the Great Rivers, their voices drowned out by the whirr and hum of factories along the banks. Thrill-seekers and tourists still consult them to make what they can of their incoherent oracles, though nothing remains of their once-vaunted eloquence but a repetitious tetra-syllabic babble.

And though the exigencies of freedom demand the full-time attention of most of our sages, occasionally, in the interests of science, an effort is made to decipher the code, if such it is. But to date these efforts have been inconclusive. The general belief is that the refrain stems from one of their forgotten incantations, and that its meaning—if ever it had any meaning—is unknown even to themselves.

So these old anachronisms are still with us, standing day

after day in the mudflats, mumbling at whoever will come close enough to listen.

"Carcinoma," they say, over and over again. "Carcinoma, carcinoma, carcinoma. . . ."

BY ALFRED BESTER

Fondly Fahrenheit

He doesn't know which of us I am these days, but they know one truth. You must own nothing but yourself. You must make your own life, live your own life, and die your own death . . . or else you will die another's.

The rice fields on Paragon III stretch for hundreds of miles like checkerboard tundras, a blue and brown mosaic under a burning sky of orange. In the evening clouds whip like smoke, and the paddies rustle and murmur.

A long line of men marched across the paddies the evening we escaped from Paragon III. They were silent, armed, intent; a long rank of silhouetted statues looming against the smoking sky. Each man carried a gun. Each man wore a walkie-talkie belt pack, the speaker button in his ear, the microphone bug clipped to his throat, the glowing view-screen strapped to his wrist like a green-eyed watch. The multitude of screens showed nothing but a multitude of individual paths through the paddies. The annunciators uttered no sound but the rustle and splash of steps. The men spoke infrequently, in heavy grunts, all speaking to all.

"Nothing here."

"Where's here?"

"Jenson's fields."

"You're drifting too far west."

"Close in the line there."

"Anybody covered the Grimson paddy?"

"Yeah. Nothing."

"She couldn't have walked this far."

"Could have been carried."

"Think she's alive?"

"Why should she be dead?"

The slow refrain swept up and down the long line of beaters advancing toward the smoky sunset. The line of beaters wavered like a writhing snake, but never ceased its remorseless advance. One hundred men spaced fifty feet apart. Five thousand feet of ominous search. One mile of angry determination stretching from east to west across a compass of heat. Evening fell. Each man lit his search lamp. The writhing snake was transformed into a necklace of wavering diamonds.

"Clear here. Nothing."

"Nothing here."

"Nothing."

"What about the Allen paddies?"

"Covering them now."

"Think we missed her?"

"Maybe."

"We'll beat back and check."

"This'll be an all-night job."

"Allen paddies clear."

"Goddamn! We've got to find her!"

"We'll find her."

"Here she is. Sector seven. Tune in."

The line stopped. The diamonds froze in the heat. There was silence. Each man gazed into the glowing green screen on his wrist, tuning to sector seven. All tuned to one. All showed a small nude figure awash in the muddy water of a paddy. Alongside the figure an owner's stake of bronze read: VANDALEUR. The ends of the line converged toward the Vandaleur field. The necklace turned into a cluster of stars. One hundred men gathered around a small nude body, a child dead in a rice paddy. There was no water in her mouth. There were fingermarks on her throat. Her innocent face was battered. Her body was torn. Clotted blood on her skin was crusted and hard.

"Dead three-four hours at least."

"Her mouth is dry."

"She wasn't drowned. Beaten to death."

In the dark evening heat the men swore softly. They picked up the body. One stopped the others and pointed to the child's fingernails. She had fought her murderer. Under the nails were particles of flesh and bright drops of scarlet blood, still liquid, still uncoagulated.

"That blood ought to be clotted too."

"Funny."

"Not so funny. What kind of blood don't clot?"

"Android."

"Looks like she was killed by one."

"Vandaleur owns an android."

"She couldn't be killed by an android."

"That's android blood under her nails."

"The police better check."

"The police'll prove I'm right."

"But androids can't kill."

"That's android blood, ain't it?"

"Androids can't kill. They're made that way."

"Looks like one android was made wrong."

"Jesus!"

And the thermometer that day registered 92.9° gloriously Fahrenheit.

So there we were aboard the *Paragon Queen* enroute for Megaster V, James Vandaleur and his android. James Vandaleur counted his money and wept. In the second-class cabin with him was his android, a magnificent synthetic creature with classic features and wide blue eyes. Raised on its forehead in a cameo of flesh were the letters MA, indicating that this was one of the rare multiple aptitude androids, worth $57,000 on the current exchange. There we were, weeping and counting and calmly watching.

"Twelve, fourteen, sixteen. Sixteen hundred dollars," Vandaleur wept. "That's all. Sixteen hundred dollars. My house was worth ten thousand. The land was worth five. There was furniture, cars, my paintings, etchings, my plane, my— And nothing to show for everything but sixteen hundred dollars. Christ!"

I leaped up from the table and turned on the android.

I pulled a strap from one of the leather bags and beat the android. It didn't move.

"I must remind you," the android said, "that I am worth fifty-seven thousand dollars on the current exchange. I must warn you that you are endangering valuable property."

"You damned crazy machine," Vandaleur shouted.

"I am not a machine," the android answered. "The robot is a machine. The android is a chemical creation of synthetic tissue."

"What got into you?" Vandaleur cried. "Why did you do it? Damn you!" He beat the android savagely.

"I must remind you that I cannot be punished," I said. "The pleasure-pain syndrome is not incorporated in the android synthesis."

"Then why did you kill her?" Vandaleur shouted. "If it wasn't for kicks, why did you—"

"I must remind you," the android said, "that the second-class cabins in these ships are not soundproofed."

Vandaleur dropped the strap and stood panting, staring at the creature he owned.

"Why did you do it? Why did you kill her?" I asked.

"I don't know," I answered.

"First it was malicious mischief. Small things. Petty destruction. I should have known there was something wrong with you then. Androids can't destroy. They can't harm. They—"

"There is no pleasure-pain syndrome incorporated in the android synthesis."

"Then it got to arson. Then serious destruction. Then assault . . . that engineer on Rigel. Each time worse. Each time we had to get out faster. Now it's murder. Christ! What's the matter with you? What's happened?"

"There are no self-check relays incorporated in the android brain."

"Each time we had to get out it was a step downhill. Look at me. In a second-class cabin. Me. James Paleologue Vandaleur. There was a time when my father was the wealthiest— Now, sixteen hundred dollars in the world. That's all I've got. And you. Christ damn you!"

Vandaleur raised the strap to beat the android again,

then dropped it and collapsed on a berth, sobbing. At last he pulled himself together.

"Instructions," he said.

The multiple aptitude android responded at once. It arose and awaited orders.

"My name is now Valentine. James Valentine. I stopped off on Paragon III for only one day to transfer to this ship for Megaster V. My occupation: Agent for one privately owned MA android which is for hire. Purpose of visit: To settle on Megaster V. Fix the papers."

The android removed Vandaleur's passport and papers from a bag, got pen and ink and sat down at the table. With an accurate, flawless hand—an accomplished hand that could draw, write, paint, carve, engrave, etch, photograph, design, create, and build—it meticulously forged new credentials for Vandaleur. Its owner watched me miserably.

"Create and build," I muttered. "And now destroy. Oh, God! What am I going to do? Christ! If I could only get rid of you. If I didn't have to live off you. God! If only I'd inherited some guts instead of you."

Dallas Brady was Megaster's leading jewelry designer. She was short, stocky, amoral, and a nymphomaniac. She hired Vandaleur's multiple aptitude android and put me to work in her shop. She seduced Vandaleur. In her bed one night, she asked abruptly: "Your name's Vandaleur, isn't it?"

"Yes," I murmured. Then: "No! No! It's Valentine. James Valentine."

"What happened on Paragon?" Dallas Brady asked. "I thought androids couldn't kill or destroy property. Prime Directives and Inhibitions set up for them when they're synthesized. Every company guarantees they can't."

"Valentine!" Vandaleur insisted.

"Oh, come off it," Dallas Brady said. "I've known for a week. I haven't hollered copper, have I?"

"The name is Valentine."

"You want to prove it? You want I should call the cops?" Dallas reached out and picked up the phone.

"For God's sake, Dallas!" Vandaleur leaped up and struggled to take the phone from her. She fended him off, laughing at him, until he collapsed and wept in shame and helplessness.

"How did you find out?" he asked at last.

"The papers are full of it. And Valentine was a little too close to Vandaleur. That wasn't smart, was it?"

"I guess not. I'm not very smart."

"Your android's got quite a record, hasn't it? Assault. Arson. Destruction. What happened on Paragon?"

"It kidnapped a child. Took her out into the rice fields and murdered her."

"Raped her?"

"I don't know."

"They're going to catch up with you."

"Don't I know it? Christ! We've been running for two years now. Seven planets in two years. I must have abandoned fifty thousand dollars' worth of property in two years."

"You better find out what's wrong with it."

"How can I? Can I walk into a repair clinic and ask for an overhaul? What am I going to say? 'My android's just turned killer. Fix it.' They'd call the police right off." I began to shake. "They'd have that android dismantled inside one day. I'd probably be booked as accessory to murder."

"Why didn't you have it repaired before it got to murder?"

"I couldn't take the chance," Vandaleur explained angrily. "If they started fooling around with lobotomies and body chemistry and endocrine surgery, they might have destroyed its aptitudes. What would I have left to hire out? How would I live?"

"You could work yourself. People do."

"Work at what? You know I'm good for nothing. How could I compete with specialist androids and robots? Who can, unless he's got a terrific talent for a particular job?"

"Yeah. That's true."

"I lived off my old man all my life. Damn him! He had to go bust just before he died. Left me the android and that's all. The only way I can get along is living off what it earns."

"You better sell it before the cops catch up with you. You can live off fifty grand. Invest it."

"At three percent? Fifteen hundred a year? When the android returns fifteen percent of its value? Eight thousand a year. That's what it earns. No, Dallas. I've got to go along with it."

"What are you going to do about its violence kick?"

"I can't do anything . . . except watch it and pray. What are you going to do about it?"

"Nothing. It's none of my business. Only one thing . . . I ought to get something for keeping my mouth shut."

"What?"

"The android works for me for free. Let somebody else pay you, but I get it for free."

The multiple aptitude android worked. Vandaleur collected its fees. His expenses were taken care of. His savings began to mount. As the warm spring of Megaster V turned to hot summer, I began investigating farms and properties. It would be possible, within a year or two, for us to settle down permanently, provided Dallas Brady's demands did not become rapacious.

On the first hot day of summer, the android began singing in Dallas Brady's workshop. It hovered over the electric furnace which, along with the weather, was broiling the shop, and sang an ancient tune that had been popular half a century before.

> Oh, it's no feat to beat the heat.
> All reet! All reet!
> So jeet your seat
> Be fleet be fleet
> Cool and discreet
> Honey. . . .

It sang in a strange, halting voice, and its accomplished fingers were clasped behind its back, writhing in a strange rumba all their own. Dallas Brady was surprised.

"You happy or something?" she asked.

"I must remind you that the pleasure-pain syndrome is not incorporated in the android synthesis," I answered. "All reet! All reet! Be fleet, be fleet, cool and discreet, honey. . . ."

Its fingers stopped their writhing and picked up a heavy pair of iron tongs. The android poked them into the glowing heart of the furnace, leaning far forward to peer into the lovely heat.

"Be careful, you damned fool!" Dallas Brady exclaimed. "You want to fall in?"

"I must remind you that I am worth fifty-seven thousand dollars on the current exchange," I said. "It is forbidden to endanger valuable property. All reet! All reet! Honey. . . ."

It withdrew a crucible of glowing gold from the electric furnace, turned, capered hideously, sang crazily, and splashed a sluggish gobbet of molten gold over Dallas Brady's head. She screamed and collapsed, her hair and clothes flaming, her skin crackling. The android poured again while it capered and sang.

"Be fleet be fleet, cool and discreet, honey. . . ." It sang and slowly poured and poured the molten gold. Then I left the workshop and rejoined James Vandaleur in his hotel suite. The android's charred clothes and squirming fingers warned its owner that something was very much wrong.

Vandaleur rushed to Dallas Brady's workshop, stared once, vomited, and fled. I had enough time to pack one bag and raise nine hundred dollars on portable assets. He took a third-class cabin on the *Megaster Queen* which left that morning for Lyra Alpha. He took me with him. He wept and counted his money and I beat the android again.

And the thermometer in Dallas Brady's workshop registered 98.1° beautifully Fahrenheit.

On Lyra Alpha we holed up in a small hotel near the university. There, Vandaleur carefully bruised my forehead until the letters MA were obliterated by the swelling and the discoloration. The letters would reappear again, but not for several months, and in the meantime Vandaleur hoped the hue and cry for an MA android would be forgotten. The android was hired out as a common laborer in the university power plant. Vandaleur, as James Venice, eked out life on the android's small earnings.

I wasn't too unhappy. Most of the other residents in the hotel were university students, equally hard up, but delightfully young and enthusiastic. There was one charming girl with sharp eyes and a quick mind. Her name was Wanda, and she and her beau, Jed Stark, took a tremendous interest in the killing android which was being mentioned in every paper in the galaxy.

"We've been studying the case," she and Jed said at one of the casual student parties which happened to be held this night in Vandaleur's room. "We think we know what's causing it. We're going to do a paper." They were in a high state of excitement.

"Causing what?" somebody wanted to know.

"The android rampage."

"Obviously out of adjustment, isn't it? Body chemistry gone haywire. Maybe a kind of synthetic cancer, yes?"

"No." Wanda gave Jed a look of suppressed triumph.

"Well, what is it?"

"Something specific."

"What?"

"That would be telling."

"Oh, come on."

"Nothing doing."

"Won't you tell us?" I asked intently. "I . . . We're very much interested in what could go wrong with an android."

"No, Mr. Venice," Wanda said. "It's a unique idea, and we've got to protect it. One thesis like this, and we'll be set up for life. We can't take the chance of somebody stealing it."

"Can't you give us a hint?"

"No. Not a hint. Don't say a word, Jed. But I'll tell you this much, Mr. Venice. I'd hate to be the man who owns that android."

"You mean the police?" I asked.

"I mean projection, Mr. Venice. Projection! That's the

danger . . . and I won't say any more. I've said too much as is."

I heard steps outside, and a hoarse voice singing softly: "Be fleet be fleet, cool and discreet, honey. . . ." My android entered the room, home from its tour of duty at the university power plant. It was not introduced. I motioned to it, and I immediately responded to the command and went to the beer keg and took over Vandaleur's job of serving the guests. Its accomplished fingers writhed in a private rumba of their own. Gradually they stopped their squirming, and the strange humming ended.

Androids were not unusual at the university. The wealthier students owned them along with cars and planes. Vandaleur's android provoked no comment, but young Wanda was sharp-eyed and quick-witted. She noted my bruised forehead, and she was intent on the history-making thesis she and Jed Stark were going to write. After the party broke up, she consulted with Jed, walking upstairs to her room.

"Jed, why'd that android have a bruised forehead?"

"Probably hurt itself, Wanda. It's working in the power plant. They fling a lot of heavy stuff around."

"That all?"

"What else?"

"It could be a convenient bruise."

"Convenient for what?"

"Hiding what's stamped on its forehead."

"No point to that, Wanda. You don't have to see marks on a forehead to recognize an android. You don't have to see a trademark on a car to know it's a car."

"I don't mean it's trying to pass as a human. I mean it's trying to pass as a lower-grade android."

"Why?"

"Suppose it had MA on its forehead."

"Multiple aptitude? Then why in hell would Venice waste it stoking furnaces if it could earn more—Oh. Oh! You mean it's—?"

Wanda nodded.

"Jesus!" Stark pursed his lips. "What do we do? Call the police?"

"No. We don't know if it's an MA for a fact. If it turns out to be an MA, and the killing android, our paper comes first anyway. This is our big chance, Jed. If it's that android, we can run a series of controlled tests and—"

"How do we find out for sure?"

"Easy. Infrared film. That'll show what's under the bruise. Borrow a camera. Buy some film. We'll sneak down to the power plant tomorrow afternoon and take some pictures. Then we'll know."

They stole down into the university power plant the following afternoon. It was a vast cellar, deep under the earth. It was dark, shadowy, luminous with burning light from the furnace doors. Above the roar of the fires they could hear a strange voice shouting and chanting in the echoing vault: "All reet! All reet! So jeet your seat. Be fleet be fleet, cool and discreet, honey. . . ." And they could see a capering figure dancing a lunatic rumba in time to the music it shouted. The legs twisted. The arms waved. The fingers writhed.

Jed Stark raised the camera and began shooting his spool of infrared film, aiming the camera sights at that bobbing head. Then Wanda shrieked, for I saw them and came charging down on them, brandishing a polished steel shovel. It smashed the camera. It felled the girl and then the boy. Jed fought me for a desperate hissing moment before he was bludgeoned into helplessness. Then the android dragged them to the furnace and fed them to the flames, slowly, hideously. It capered and sang. Then it returned to my hotel.

The thermometer in the power plant registered 100.9° murderously Fahrenheit. All reet! All reet!

We bought steerage on the *Lyra Queen*, and Vandaleur and the android did odd jobs for their meals. During the night watches, Vandaleur would sit alone in the steerage head with a cardboard portfolio on his lap, puzzling over its contents. That portfolio was all he had managed to bring with him from Lyra Alpha. He had stolen it from Wanda's room. It was labeled ANDROID. It contained the secret of my sickness.

And it contained nothing but newspapers. Scores of newspapers from all over the galaxy, printed, microfilmed, engraved, etched, offset, photostated . . . Rigel *Star-Banner* . . . Paragon *Picayune* . . . Megaster *Times-Leader* . . . Lalande *Herald* . . . Lacaille *Journal* . . . Indi *Intelligencer* . . . Eridani *Telegram-News*. All reet! All reet!

Nothing but newspapers. Each paper contained an account of one crime in the android's ghastly career. Each paper also contained news, domestic and foreign, sports, society, weather, shipping news, stock-exchange quotations, human-interest stories, features, contests, puzzles. Somewhere in that mass of uncollated facts was the secret Wanda and Jed Stark had discovered. Vandaleur pored over the papers helplessly. It was beyond him. So jeet your seat!

"I'll sell you," I told the android. "Damn you. When we land on Terra, I'll sell you. I'll settle for three percent on whatever you're worth."

"I am worth fifty-seven thousand dollars on the current exchange," I told him.

"If I can't sell you, I'll turn you in to the police," I said.

"I am valuable property," I answered. "It is forbidden to endanger valuable property. You won't have me destroyed."

"Christ damn you!" Vandaleur cried. "What? Are you arrogant? Do you know you can trust me to protect you? Is that the secret?"

The multiple aptitude android regarded him with calm accomplished eyes. "Sometimes," it said, "it is a good thing to be property."

It was three below zero when the *Lyra Queen* dropped at Croydon Field. A mixture of ice and snow swept across the field, fizzing and exploding into steam under the *Queen's* tail jets. The passengers trotted numbly across the blackened concrete to customs inspection, and thence to the airport bus that was to take them to London. Vandaleur and the android were broke. They walked.

By midnight they reached Piccadilly Circus. The December ice storm had not slackened, and the statue of Eros was encrusted with ice. They turned right, walked down to Trafalgar Square and then along the Strand toward Soho, shaking with cold and wet. Just above Fleet Street, Vandaleur saw a solitary figure coming from the direction of St. Paul's. He drew the android into an alley.

"We've got to have money," he whispered. He pointed at the approaching figure. "He has money. Take it from him."

"The order cannot be obeyed," the android said.

"Take it from him," Vandaleur repeated. "By force. Do you understand? We're desperate."

"It is contrary to my prime directive," I said. "I cannot endanger life or property. The order cannot be obeyed."

"For God's sake!" Vandaleur burst out. "You've attacked, destroyed, murdered. Don't gibber about prime directives. You haven't any left. Get his money. Kill him if you have to. I tell you, we're desperate!"

"It is contrary to my prime directive," the android repeated. "The order cannot be obeyed."

I thrust the android back and leaped out at the stranger. He was tall, austere, competent. He had an air of hope curdled by cynicism. He carried a cane. I saw he was blind.

"Yes?" he said. "I hear you near me. What is it?"

"Sir . . ." Vandaleur hesitated. "I'm desperate."

"We are all desperate," the stranger replied. "Quietly desperate."

"Sir . . . I've got to have some money."

"Are you begging or stealing?" The sightless eyes passed over Vandaleur and the android.

"I'm prepared for either."

"Ah. So are we all. It is the history of our race." The stranger motioned over his shoulder. "I have been begging at St. Paul's, my friend. What I desire cannot be stolen. What is it you desire that you are lucky enough to be able to steal?"

"Money," Vandaleur said.

"Money for what? Come, my friend, let us exchange confidences. I will tell you why I beg if you will tell me why you steal. My name is Blenheim."

"My name is . . . Vole."

"I was not begging for sight at St. Paul's, Mr. Vole. I was begging for a number."

"A number?"

"Ah yes. Numbers rational, numbers irrational. Numbers imaginary. Positive integers. Negative integers. Fractions, positive and negative. Eh? You have never heard of Blenheim's immortal treatise on Twenty Zeros, or The Differences in Absence of Quantity?" Blenheim smiled bitterly. "I am the wizard of the Theory of Number, Mr. Vole, and I have exhausted the charm of number for myself. After years of wizardry, senility approaches and the appetite vanishes. I have been praying in St. Paul's for inspiration. Dear God, I prayed, if You exist, send me a number."

Vandaleur slowly lifted the cardboard portfolio and touched Blenheim's hand with it. "In here," he said, "is a number. A hidden number. A secret number. The number of a crime. Shall we exchange, Mr. Blenheim? Shelter for a number?"

"Neither begging nor stealing, eh?" Blenheim said. "But a bargain. So all life reduces itself to the banal." The sightless eyes again passed over Vandaleur and the android. "Perhaps the Almighty is not God but a merchant. Come home with me."

On the top floor of Blenheim's house we shared a room —two beds, two closets, two washstands, one bathroom. Vandaleur bruised my forehead again and sent me out to find work, and while the android worked, I consulted with Blenheim and read him the papers from the portfolio, one by one. All reet! All reet!

Vandaleur told him so much and no more. He was a student, I said, attempting a thesis on the murdering android. In these papers which he had collected were the facts that would explain the crimes of which Blenheim had heard nothing. There must be a correlation, a number, a statistic, something which would account for my derangement, I explained, and Blenheim was piqued by the mystery, the detective story, the human interest of number.

We examined the papers. As I read them aloud, he listed

them and their contents in his blind, meticulous writing. And then I read his notes to him. He listed the papers by type, by type face, by fact, by fancy, by article, spelling, words, theme, advertising, pictures, subject, politics, prejudices. He analyzed. He studied. He meditated. And we lived together in that top floor always a little cold, always a little terrified, always a little closer . . . brought together by our fear of it, our hatred between us. Like a wedge driven into a living tree and splitting the trunk, only to be forever incorporated into the scar tissue, we grew together. Vandaleur and the android. Be fleet be fleet!

And one afternoon Blenheim called Vandaleur into his study and displayed his notes. "I think I've found it," he said, "but I can't understand it."

Vandaleur's heart leaped.

"Here are the correlations," Blenheim continued. "In fifty papers there are accounts of the criminal android. What is there, outside the depredations, that is also in fifty papers?"

"I don't know, Mr. Blenheim."

"It was a rhetorical question. Here is the answer. The weather."

"What?"

"The weather." Blenheim nodded. "Each crime was committed on a day when the temperature was above ninety degrees Fahrenheit."

"But that's impossible!" Vandaleur exclaimed. "It was cool on Lyra Alpha."

"We have no record of any crime committed on Lyra Alpha. There is no paper."

"No. That's right. I—" Vandaleur was confused. Suddenly he exclaimed, "No! You're right. The furnace room. It was hot there. Hot! Of course. My God, yes! That's the answer. Dallas Brady's electric furnace. . . . The rice deltas on Paragon. So jeet your seat. Yes. But why? Why? My God, why?"

I came into the house at that moment and, passing the study, saw Vandaleur and Blenheim. I entered, awaiting commands, my multiple aptitudes devoted to service.

"That's the android, eh?" Blenheim said after a long moment.

"Yes," Vandaleur answered, still confused by the discovery. "And that explains why it refused to attack you that night on the Strand. It wasn't hot enough to break the prime directive. Only in the heat. . . . The heat, all reet!" He looked at the android. A lunatic command passed from man to android. I refused. It is forbidden to endanger life. Vandaleur gestured furiously, then seized Blenheim's shoulders and yanked him back out of his desk chair to the floor. Blenheim shouted once. Vandaleur leaped on him like a tiger, pinning him to the floor and sealing his mouth with one hand.

"Find a weapon," he called to the android.

"It is forbidden to endanger life."

"This is a fight for self-preservation. Bring me a weapon!" He held the squirming mathematician with all his weight. I went at once to a cupboard where I knew a revolver was kept. I checked it. It was loaded with five cartridges. I handed it to Vandaleur. I took it, rammed the barrel against Blenheim's head, and pulled the trigger. He shuddered once.

We had three hours before the cook returned from her day off. We looted the house. We took Blenheim's money and jewels. We packed a bag with clothes. We took Blenheim's notes, destroyed the newspapers; and we left, carefully locking the door behind us. In Blenheim's study we left a pile of crumpled papers under a half inch of burning candle. And we soaked the rug around it with kerosene. No, I did all that. The android refused. I am forbidden to endanger life or property.

All reet!

They took the tubes to Leicester Square, changed trains, and rode to the British Museum. There they got off and went to a small Georgian house just off Russell Square. A shingle in the window read: NAN WEBB, PSYCHOMETRIC CONSULTANT. Vandaleur had made a note of the address some weeks earlier. They went into the house. The android waited in the foyer with the bag. Vandaleur entered Nan Webb's office.

She was a tall woman with gray shingled hair, very fine English complexion, and very bad English legs. Her features were blunt, her expression acute. She nodded to Vandaleur, finished a letter, sealed it, and looked up.

"My name," I said, "is Vanderbilt. James Vanderbilt."

"Quite."

"I'm an exchange student at London University."

"Quite."

"I've been researching on the killing android, and I think I've discovered something very interesting. I'd like your advice on it. What is your fee?"

"What is your college at the university?"

"Why?"

"There is a discount for students."

"Merton College."

"That will be two pounds, please."

Vandaleur placed two pounds on the desk and added to the fee Blenheim's notes. "There is a correlation," he said, "between the crimes of the android and the weather. You will note that each crime was committed when the temperature rose above ninety degrees Fahrenheit. Is there a psychometric answer for this?"

Nan Webb nodded, studied the notes for a moment, put down the sheets of paper, and said: "Synesthesia, obviously."

"What?"

"Synesthesia," she repeated. "When a sensation, Mr. Vanderbilt, is interpreted immediately in terms of a sensation from a different sense organ from the one stimulated, it is called synesthesia. For example: A sound stimulus gives rise to a simultaneous sensation of definite color. Or color gives rise to a sensation of taste. Or a light stimulus gives rise to a sensation of sound. There can be confusion or short circuiting of any sensation of taste, smell, pain, pressure, temperature, and so on. D'you understand?"

"I think so."

"Your research has uncovered the fact that the android most probably reacts to temperature stimulus above the ninety-degree level synesthetically. Most probably there is an endocrine response. Probably a temperature linkage with the android adrenal surrogate. High temperature brings about a response of fear, anger, excitement, and violent physical activity . . . all within the province of the adrenal gland.'"

"Yes. I see. Then if the android were to be kept in cold climates. . . .'"

"There would be neither stimulus nor response. There would be no crimes. Quite."

"I see. What is projection?"

"How do you mean?"

"Is there any danger of projection with regard to the owner of the android?"

"Very interesting. Projection is a throwing forward. It is the process of throwing out upon another the ideas or impulses that belong to oneself. The paranoid, for example, projects upon others his conflicts and disturbances in order to externalize them. He accuses, directly or by implication, other men of having the very sicknesses with which he is struggling himself."

"And the danger of projection?"

"It is the danger of believing what is implied. If you live with a psychotic who projects his sickness upon you, there is a danger of falling into his psychotic pattern and becoming virtually psychotic yourself. As, no doubt, is happening to you, Mr. Vandaleur."

Vandaleur leaped to his feet.

"You are an ass," Nan Webb went on crisply. She waved the sheets of notes. "This is no exchange student's writing. It's the unique cursive of the famous Blenheim. Every scholar in England knows this blind writing. There is no Merton College at London University. That was a miserable guess. Merton is one of the Oxford colleges. And you, Mr. Vandaleur, are so obviously infected by association with your deranged android . . . by projection, if you will . . . that I hesitate between calling the Metropolitan Police and the Hospital for the Criminally Insane." .

I took the gun and shot her.

Reet!

"Antares II, Alpha Aurigae, Acrux IV, Pollux IX, Rigel Centaurus," Vandaleur said. "They're all cold. Cold as a witch's kiss. Mean temperatures of forty degrees Fahrenheit. Never get hotter than seventy. We're in business again. Watch that curve."

The multiple aptitude android swung the wheel with its accomplished hands. The car took the curve sweetly and sped on through the northern marshes, the reeds stretching for miles, brown and dry, under the cold English sky. The sun was sinking swiftly. Overhead, a lone flight of bustards flapped clumsily eastward. High above the flight, a lone helicopter drifted toward home and warmth.

"No more warmth for us," I said. "No more heat. We're safe when we're cold. We'll hole up in Scotland, make a little money, get across to Norway, build a bankroll, and then ship out. We'll settle on Pollux. We're safe. We've licked it. We can live again."

There was a startling *bleep* from overhead, and then a ragged roar: "ATTENTION JAMES VANDALEUR AND ANDROID. ATTENTION JAMES VANDALEUR AND ANDROID!"

Vandaleur started and looked up. The lone helicopter was floating above them. From its belly came amplified commands: "YOU ARE SURROUNDED. THE ROAD IS BLOCKED. YOU ARE TO STOP YOUR CAR AT ONCE AND SUBMIT TO ARREST. STOP AT ONCE!"

I looked at Vandaleur for orders.

"Keep driving," Vandaleur snapped.

The helicopter dropped lower: "ATTENTION ANDROID. YOU ARE IN CONTROL OF THE VEHICLE. YOU ARE TO STOP AT ONCE. THIS IS A STATE DIRECTIVE SUPERSEDING ALL PRIVATE COMMANDS."

"What the hell are you doing?" I shouted.

"A state directive supersedes all private commands," the android answered. "I must point out to you that—"

"Get the hell away from the wheel," Vandaleur ordered. I clubbed the android, yanked him sideways, and squirmed over him to the wheel. The car veered off the road in that moment and went churning through the frozen mud and dry reeds. Vandaleur regained control and continued westward through the marshes toward a parallel highway five miles distant.

"We'll beat their Goddamned block," he grunted.

The car pounded and surged. The helicopter dropped even lower. A searchlight blazed from the belly of the plane.

"ATTENTION JAMES VANDALEUR AND ANDROID. SUBMIT TO ARREST. THIS IS A STATE DIRECTIVE SUPERSEDING ALL PRIVATE COMMANDS."

"He can't submit," Vandaleur shouted wildly. "There's no one to submit to. He can't, and I won't."

"Christ!" I muttered. "We'll beat them yet. We'll beat the block. We'll beat the heat. We'll—"

"I must point out to you," I said, "that I am required by my prime directive to obey state directives which supersede all private commands. I must submit to arrest."

"Who says it's a state directive?" Vandaleur said. "Them? Up in that plane? They've got to show credentials. They've got to prove it's state authority before you submit. How d'you know they're not crooks trying to trick us?"

Holding the wheel with one arm, he reached into his side pocket to make sure the gun was still in place. The car skidded. The tires squealed on frost and reeds. The wheel was wrenched from his grasp, and the car yawed up a small hillock and overturned. The motor roared, and the wheels screamed. Vandaleur crawled out and dragged the android with him. For the moment we were outside the circle of light boring down from the helicopter. We blundered off into the marsh, into the blackness, into concealment. . . . Vandaleur running with a pounding heart, hauling the android along.

The helicopter circled and soared over the wrecked car, searchlight peering, loudspeaker braying. On the highway we had left, lights appeared as the pursuing and blocking parties gathered and followed radio directions from the plane. Vandaleur and the android continued deeper and deeper into the marsh, working their way toward the parallel road and safety. It was night by now. The sky was a black matte. Not a star showed. The temperature was dropping. A southeast night wind knifed us to the bone.

Far behind there was a dull concussion. Vandaleur turned gasping. The car's fuel had exploded. A geyser of flame shot up like a lurid fountain. It subsided into a low crater of burning reeds. Whipped by the wind, the distant hem of flame fanned up into a wall, ten feet high. The wall began marching down on us, crackling fiercely. Above it, a pall of oily smoke surged forward. Behind it, Vandaleur could make out the figures of men . . . a mass of beaters searching the marsh.

"Christ!" I cried and searched desperately for safety. He ran, dragging me with him, until their feet crunched through the surface ice of a pool. He trampled the ice furiously, then flung himself down in the numbing water, pulling the android with us.

The wall of flame approached. I could hear the crackle and feel the heat. He could see the searchers clearly. Vandaleur reached into his side pocket for the gun. The pocket was torn. The gun was gone. He groaned and shook with cold and terror. The light from the marsh fire was blinding. Overhead, the helicopter floated helplessly to one side, unable to fly through the smoke and flames and aid the searchers who were beating far to the right of us.

"They'll miss us," Vandaleur whispered. "Keep quiet. That's an order. They'll miss us. We'll beat them. We'll beat the fire. We'll—"

Three distinct shots sounded less than a hundred feet from the fugitives. *Blam! Blam! Blam!* They came from the last three cartridges in my gun as the marsh fire reached it where it had dropped and exploded the shells. The searchers turned toward the sound and began working directly toward us. Vandaleur cursed hysterically and tried to submerge even deeper to escape the intolerable heat of the fire. The android began to twitch.

The wall of flame surged up to them. Vandaleur took a deep breath and prepared to submerge until the flame passed over them. The android shuddered and burst into an ear-splitting scream.

"All reet! All reet!" it shouted. "Be fleet be fleet!"

"Damn you!" I shouted. I tried to drown it.

"Damn you!" I cursed him. I smashed his face.

The android battered Vandaleur, who fought it off until it exploded out of the mud and staggered upright. Before I could return to the attack, the live flames captured it hypnotically. It danced and capered in a lunatic rumba before the wall of fire. Its legs twisted. Its arms waved. The fingers writhed in a private rumba of their own. It shrieked and sang and ran in a crooked waltz before the embrace of the heat, a muddy monster silhouetted against the brilliant sparkling flare.

The searchers shouted. There were shots. The android spun around twice and then continued its horrid dance before the face of the flames. There was a rising gust of wind. The fire swept around the capering figure and enveloped it for a roaring moment. Then the fire swept on, leaving behind it a sobbing mass of synthetic flesh oozing scarlet blood that would never coagulate.

The thermometer would have registered 1200° wondrously Fahrenheit.

Vandaleur didn't die. I got away. They missed him while they watched the android caper and die. But I don't know which of us he is these days. Projection, Wanda warned me. Projection, Nan Webb told him. If you live with a crazy man or a crazy machine long enough, I become crazy too. Reet!

But we know one truth. We know they were wrong. The new robot and Vandaleur know that because the new robot's started twitching too. Reet! Here on cold Pollux, the robot is twitching and singing. No heat, but my fingers writhe. No heat, but it's taken the little Talley girl off for a solitary walk. A cheap labor robot. A servo-mechanism ... all I could afford ... but it's twitching and humming and walking alone with the child somewhere, and I can't find them. Christ! Vandaleur can't find me before it's too late. Cool and discreet, honey, in the dancing frost while the thermometer registers 10° fondly Fahrenheit.

BY EDWARD LUCAS WHITE

Lukundoo

"It stands to reason," said Twombly, "that a man must accept the evidence of his own eyes, and when eyes and ears agree there can be no doubt. He has to believe what he has both seen and heard."

"Not always," put in Singleton, softly.

Every man turned toward Singleton. Twombly was standing on the hearthrug, his back to the grate, his legs spread out, with his habitual air of dominating the room. Singleton, as usual, was as much as possible effaced in a corner. But when Singleton spoke he said something. We faced him in that flattering spontaneity of expectant silence which invites utterance.

"I was thinking," he said after an interval, "of something I both saw and heard in Africa."

Now if there was one thing we had found impossible, it had been to elicit from Singleton anything definite about his African experiences. As with the Alpinist in the story, who could tell only that he went up and came down, the sum of Singleton's revelations had been that he went there and came away. His words now riveted our attention at once. Twombly faded from the hearthrug, but not one of us could ever recall having seen him go. The room readjusted itself, focused on Singleton, and there was some hasty and furtive lighting of fresh cigars. Singleton lit one also, but it went out immediately, and he never relit it.

I

We were in the Great Forest, exploring for pigmies. Van Rieten had a theory that the dwarfs found by Stanley and others were a mere crossbreed between ordinary Negroes and the real pigmies. He hoped to discover a race of men three feet tall at most, or shorter. We had found no trace of any such beings.

Natives were few, game scarce; food, except game, there was none; and the deepest, dankest, drippingest forest all about. We were the only novelty in the country; no native we met had ever seen a white man before, most had never heard of white men. All of a sudden, late one afternoon, there came into our camp an Englishman, and pretty well used up he was, too. We had heard no rumor of him; he had not only heard of us but had made an amazing five-day march to reach us. His guide and two bearers were nearly as done up as he. Even though he was in tatters and had five days' beard on, you could see he was naturally dapper and neat and the sort of man to shave daily. He was small, but wiry. His face was the sort of British face from which emotion has been so carefully banished that a foreigner is apt to think the wearer of the face incapable of any sort of feeling; the kind of face which, if it has any expression at all, expresses principally the resolution to go through the world decorously, without intruding upon or annoying anyone.

His name was Etcham. He introduced himself modestly and ate with us so deliberately that we should never have suspected, if our bearers had not had it from his bearers, that he had had but three meals in the five days, and those small. After we had lit up he told us why he had come.

"My chief is ve'y seedy," he said between puffs. "He is bound to go out if he keeps this way. I thought perhaps. . . ."

He spoke quietly in a soft, even tone, but I could see little beads of sweat oozing out on his upper lip under his stubby mustache, and there was a tingle of repressed emotion in his tone, a veiled eagerness in his eye, a palpitating inward solicitude in his demeanor that moved me at once. Van Rieten had no sentiment in him; if he was moved, he did not show it. But he listened. I was surprised at that. He was just the man to refuse at once. But he listened to Etcham's halting, difficult hints. He even asked questions.

"Who is your chief?"

"Stone," Etcham lisped.

That electrified both of us.

"Ralph Stone?" we ejaculated together.

Etcham nodded.

For some minutes Van Rieten and I were silent. Van Rieten had never seen him, but I had been a classmate of Stone's, and Van Rieten and I had discussed him over many a campfire. We had heard of him two years before, south of Luebo in the Balunda country, which had been ringing with his theatrical strife against a Balunda witch doctor, ending in the sorcerer's complete discomfiture and the abasement of his tribe before Stone. They had even broken the fetish-man's whistle and given Stone the pieces. It had been like the triumph of Elijah over the prophets of Baal, only more real to the Balunda.

We had thought of Stone as far off, if still in Africa at all, and here he turned up ahead of us and probably forestalling our quest.

II

Etcham's naming of Stone brought back to us all of his tantalizing story, his fascinating parents, their tragic death; the brilliance of his college days; the dazzle of his millions; the promise of his young manhood; his wide notoriety, so nearly real fame; his romantic elopement with the meteoric authoress whose sudden cascade of fiction had made her so great a name so young, whose beauty and charm were so much heralded; the frightful scandal of the breach-of-promise suit that followed; his bride's devotion through it all; their sudden quarrel after it was all over; their divorce; the too much advertized announcement of his approaching marriage to the plaintiff in the breach-of-promise suit; his precipitate remarriage to his divorced bride; their second quarrel and second divorce; his departure from his native land; his advent in the dark continent. The sense of all this rushed over me, and I believe Van Rieten felt it, too, as he sat silent.

Then he asked:

"Where is Werner?"

"Dead," said Etcham. "He died before I joined Stone."

"You were not with Stone above Luebo?"

"No," said Etcham. "I joined him at Stanley Falls."

"Who is with him?" Van Rieten asked.

"Only his Zanzibar servants and the bearers," Etcham replied.

"What sort of bearers?" Van Rieten demanded.

"Mang-Battu men," Etcham responded simply.

Now that impressed both Van Rieten and myself greatly. It bore out Stone's reputation as a notable leader of men. For up to that time no one had been able to use Mang-Battu as bearers outside of their own country, or to hold them for long or difficult expeditions.

"Were you long among the Mang-Battu?" was Van Rieten's next question.

"Some weeks," said Etcham. "Stone was interested in them and made up a fair-sized vocabulary of their words and phrases. He had a theory that they are an offshoot of the Balunda, and he found much confirmation in their customs."

"What do you live on?" Van Rieten inquired.

"Game, mostly," Etcham lisped.

"How long has Stone been laid up?" Van Rieten next asked.

"More than a month," Etcham answered.

"And you have been hunting for the camp?" Van Rieten exclaimed.

Etcham's face, burned and flayed as it was, showed a flush.

"I missed some easy shots," he admitted ruefully. "I've not felt ve'y fit myself."

"What's the matter with your chief?" Van Rieten inquired.

"Something like carbuncles," Etcham replied.

"He ought to get over a carbuncle or two," Van Rieten declared.

"They are not carbuncles," Etcham explained. "Nor one or two. He has had dozens, sometimes five at once. If they had been carbuncles, he would have been dead long ago. But in some ways they are not so bad, though in others they are worse."

"How do you mean?" Van Rieten queried.

"Well," Etcham hesitated, "they do not seem to inflame so deep or so wide as carbuncles, or to be so painful, or to cause so much fever. But then they seem to be part of a disease that affects his mind. He let me help him dress the first, but the others he has hidden most carefully from me and from the men. He keeps his tent when they puff up and will not let me change the dressings or be with him at all."

"Have you plenty of dressings?" Van Rieten asked.

"We have some," said Etcham doubtfully. "But he won't use them; he washes out the dressings and uses them over and over."

"How is he treating the swellings?" Van Rieten inquired.

"He slices them off clear down to flesh level with his razor."

"What?" Van Rieten shouted.

Etcham made no answer, but looked him steadily in the eyes.

"I beg pardon," Van Rieten hastened to say. "You startled me. They can't be carbuncles. He'd have been dead long ago."

"I thought I had said they are not carbuncles," Etcham lisped.

"But the man must be crazy!" Van Rieten exclaimed.

"Just so," said Etcham. "He is beyond my advice or control."

"How many has he treated that way?" Van Rieten demanded.

"Two, to my knowledge," Etcham said.

"Two?" Van Rieten queried.

Etcham flushed again.

"I saw him," he confessed, "through a crack in the hut. I felt impelled to keep a watch on him as if he was not responsible."

"I should think not," Van Rieten agreed. "And you saw him do that twice?"

"I conjecture," said Etcham, "that he did the like with all the rest."

"How many has he had?" Van Rieten asked.

"Dozens," Etcham lisped.

"Does he eat?" Van Rieten inquired.

"Like a wolf," said Etcham. "More than any two bearers."

"Can he walk?" Van Rieten asked.

"He crawls a bit, groaning," said Etcham simply.

"Little fever, you say," Van Rieten ruminated.

"Enough and too much," Etcham declared.

"Has he been delirious?" Van Rieten asked.

"Only twice," Etcham replied; "once when the first swelling broke, and once later. He would not let anyone come near him then. But we could hear him talking, talking steadily, and it scared the natives."

"Was he talking their patter in delirium?" Van Rieten demanded.

"No," said Etcham, "but he was talking some similar lingo. Hamed Burghash said he was talking Balunda. I know too little Balunda. I do not learn languages readily. Stone learned more Mang-Battu in a week than I could have learned in a year. But I seemed to hear words like Mang-Battu words. Anyhow, the Mang-Battu bearers were scared."

"Scared?" Van Rieten repeated, questioningly.

"So were the Zanzibar men, even Hamed Burghash, and so was I," said Etcham, "only for a different reason. He talked in two voices."

"In two voices," Van Rieten reflected.

"Yes," said Etcham, more excitedly than he had yet spoken. "In two voices, like a conversation. One was his own, one a small, thin, bleaty voice like nothing I ever heard. I seemed to make out, among the sounds the deep voice made, something like Mang-Battu words I knew, as *nedru, metababa,* and *nedo,* their terms for 'head,' 'shoulder,' 'thigh,' and perhaps *kudra* and *nekere* ('speak' and 'whistle'); and among the noises of the shrill voice *matomipa, angunzi,* and *kamomami* ('kill,' 'death,' and 'hate'). Hamed Burghash said he also heard those words. He knew Mang-Battu far better than I."

"What did the bearers say?" Van Rieten asked.

"They said, *'Lukundoo, Lukundoo!'* " Etcham replied. "I did not know that word; Hamed Burghash said it was Mang-Battu for 'leopard.' "

"It's Mang-Battu for 'witchcraft,' " said Van Rieten.

"I don't wonder they thought so," said Etcham. "It was enough to make one believe in sorcery to listen to those two voices."

"One voice answering the other?" Van Rieten asked perfunctorily.

Etcham's face went gray under his tan.

"Sometimes both at once," he answered huskily.

"Both at once!" Van Rieten ejaculated.

"It sounded that way to the men, too," said Etcham. "And that was not all."

He stopped and looked helplessly at us for a moment.

"Could a man talk and whistle at the same time?" he asked.

"How do you mean?" Van Rieten queried.

"We could hear Stone talking away, his big, deep-chested baritone rumbling along, and through it all we could hear a high, shrill whistle, the oddest, wheezy sound. You know, no matter how shrilly a grown man may whistle, the note has a different quality from the whistle of a boy or a woman or a little girl. They sound more treble, somehow. Well, if you can imagine the smallest girl who could whistle keeping it up tunelessly right along, that whistle was like that, only even more piercing, and it sounded right through Stone's bass tones."

"And you didn't go to him?" Van Rieten cried.

"He is not given to threats," Etcham disclaimed. "But he had threatened, not volubly, or like a sick man, but quietly and firmly, that if any man of us (he lumped me in with the men) came near him while he was in his trouble, that man should die. And it was not so much his words as his manner. It was like a monarch commanding respected privacy for a deathbed. One simply could not transgress."

"I see," said Van Rieten shortly.

"He's ve'y seedy," Etcham repeated helplessly. "I thought perhaps. . . ."

His absorbing affection for Stone, his real love for him, shone out through his envelope of conventional training. Worship of Stone was plainly his master passion.

Like many competent men, Van Rieten had a streak of hard selfishness in him. It came to the surface then. He said we carried our lives in our hands from day to day just as genuinely as Stone; that he did not forget the ties of blood and calling between any two explorers, but that there was no sense in imperiling one party for a very problematical benefit to a man probably beyond any help; that it was enough of a task to hunt for one party; that if two were united, providing food would be more than doubly difficult; that the risk of starvation was too great. Deflecting our march seven full days' journey (he complimented Etcham on his marching powers) might ruin our expedition entirely.

III

Van Rieten had logic on his side, and he had a way with him. Etcham sat there apologetic and deferential, like a fourth-form schoolboy before a headmaster. Van Rieten wound up.

"I am after pigmies at the risk of my life. After pigmies I go."

"Perhaps, then, these will interest you," said Etcham, very quietly.

He took two objects out of the sidepocket of his blouse and handed them to Van Rieten. They were round, bigger than big plums and smaller than small peaches, about the right size to enclose in an average hand. They were black, and at first I did not see what they were.

"Pigmies!" Van Rieten exclaimed. "Pigmies, indeed!

Why, they wouldn't be two feet high! Do you mean to claim that these are adult heads?"

"I claim nothing," Etcham answered evenly. "You can see for yourself."

Van Rieten passed one of the heads to me. The sun was just setting, and I examined it closely. A dried head it was, perfectly preserved, and the flesh as hard as Argentine jerked beef. A bit of a vertebra stuck out where the muscles of the vanished neck had shriveled into folds. The puny chin was sharp on a projecting jaw, the minute teeth were white and even between the retracted lips, the tiny nose was flat, the little forehead retreating, there were inconsiderable clumps of stunted wool on the Lilliputian cranium. There was nothing babyish, childish, or youthful about the head; rather it was mature to senility.

"Where did these come from?" Van Rieten demanded.

Etcham replied precisely, "I found them among Stone's effects while rummaging for medicines or drugs or anything that could help me to help him. I do not know where he got them. But I'll swear he did not have them when we entered this district."

"Are you sure?" Van Rieten queried, his eyes big and fixed on Etcham's.

"Ve'y sure," lisped Etcham.

"But how could he have come by them without your knowledge?" Van Rieten demurred.

"Sometimes we were apart ten days at a time hunting," said Etcham. "Stone is not a talking man. He gave me no account of his doings, and Hamed Burghash keeps a still tongue and a tight hold on the men."

"You have examined these heads?" Van Rieten asked.

"Minutely," said Etcham.

Van Rieten took out his notebook. He was a methodical chap. He tore out a leaf, folded it, and divided it equally into three pieces. He gave one to me and one to Etcham.

"Just for a test of my impressions," he said, "I want each of us to write separately just what he is most reminded of by these heads. Then I want to compare the writings."

I handed Etcham a pencil, and he wrote. Then he handed the pencil back to me, and I wrote.

"Read the three," said Van Rieten, handing me his piece.

Van Rieten had written:

"An old Balunda witch doctor."

Etcham had written:

"An old Mang-Battu fetish-man."

I had written:

"An old Katongo magician."

"There!" Van Rieten exclaimed. "Look at that! There is nothing Wagabi or Batwa or Wambuttu or Wabotu about these heads. Nor anything pigmy either."

"I thought as much," said Etcham.

"And you say he did not have them before?"

"To a certainty he did not," Etcham asserted.

"It is worth following up," said Van Rieten. "I'll go with you. And first of all, I'll do my best to save Stone."

He put out his hand, and Etcham clasped it silently. He was grateful all over.

IV

Nothing but Etcham's fever of solicitude could have taken him in five days over the track. It took him eight days to retrace with full knowledge of it and our party to help. We could not have done it in seven, and Etcham urged us on, in a repressed fury of anxiety, no mere fever of duty to his chief, but a real ardor of devotion, a glow of personal adoration for Stone which blazed under his dry conventional exterior and showed in spite of him.

We found Stone well cared for. Etcham had seen to a good, high thorn *zareeba* around the camp, the huts were well built, and thatched, and Stone's was as good as their resources would permit. Hamed Burghash was not named after two Seyyids for nothing. He had in him the making of a sultan. He had kept the Mang-Battu together, not a man had slipped off, and he had kept them in order. Also he was a deft nurse and a faithful servant.

The two other Zanzibaris had done some creditable

hunting. Though all were hungry, the camp was far from starvation.

Stone was on a canvas cot, and there was a sort of collapsible campstool-table, like a Turkish tabouret, by the cot. It had a water-bottle and some vials on it and Stone's watch, also his razor in its case.

Stone was clean and not emaciated, but he was far gone; not unconscious, but in a daze; past commanding or resisting anyone. He did not seem to see us enter or to know we were there. I should have recognized him anywhere. His boyish dash and grace had vanished utterly, of course. But his head was even more leonine; his hair was still abundant, yellow and wavy; the close, crisped blond beard he had grown during his illness did not alter him. He was big and big-chested yet. His eyes were dull, and he mumbled and babbled mere meaningless syllables, not words.

Etcham helped Van Rieten to uncover him and look him over. He was in good muscle for a man so long bed-ridden. There were no scars on him, except about his knees, shoulders, and chest. On each knee and above it he had a full score of roundish cicatrices, and a dozen or more on each shoulder, all in front. Two or three were open wounds, and four or five barely healed. He had no fresh swellings, except two, one on each side, on his pectoral muscles, the one on the left being higher up and farther out than the other. They did not look like boils or carbuncles, but as if something blunt and hard were being pushed up through the fairly healthy flesh and skin, not much inflamed.

"I should not lance those," said Van Rieten, and Etcham assented.

They made Stone as comfortable as they could, and just before sunset we looked in at him again. He was lying on his back, and his chest showed big and massive yet, but he lay as if in a stupor. We left Etcham with him and went into the next hut, which Etcham had resigned to us. The jungle noises were no different there than anywhere else for months past, and I was soon fast asleep.

V

Sometime in the pitch dark I found myself awake and listening. I could hear two voices, one Stone's, the other sibilant and wheezy. I knew Stone's voice after all the years that had passed since I heard it last. The other was like nothing I remembered. It had less volume than the wail of a newborn baby; yet there was an insistent carrying power to it, like the shrilling of an insect. As I listened I heard Van Rieten breathing near me in the dark; then he heard me and realized that I was listening too. Like Etcham I knew little Balunda, but I could make out a word or two. The voices alternated, with intervals of silence between.

Then suddenly both sounded at once and fast. Stone's baritone basso, full as if he were in perfect health, and that incredibly stridulous falsetto, both jabbering at once like the voices of two people quarreling and trying to talk each other down.

"I can't stand this," said Van Rieten. "Let's have a look at him."

He had one of those cylindrical electric night-candles. He fumbled about for it, touched the button, and beckoned me to come with him. Outside the hut he motioned me to stand still, and he instinctively turned off the light, as if seeing made listening difficult.

Except for a faint glow from the embers of the bearers' fire we were in complete darkness, little starlight struggled through the trees; the river made but a faint murmur. We could hear the two voices together and then suddenly the creaking voice changed into a razor-edged, slicing whistle, indescribably cutting, continuing right through Stone's grumbling torrent of croaking words.

"Good God!" exclaimed Van Rieten.

Abruptly he turned on the light.

We found Etcham utterly asleep, exhausted by his long anxiety and the exertions of his phenomenal march, and relaxed completely now that the load was in a sense shifted from his shoulders to Van Rieten's. Even the light on his face did not wake him.

The whistle had ceased, and the two voices now sounded together. Both came from Stone's cot, where the concentrated white ray showed him lying just as we had left him, except that he had tossed his arms above his head and had torn the coverings and bandages from his chest.

The swelling on his right breast had broken. Van Rieten aimed the center line of the light at it, and we saw it plainly. From his flesh, grown out of it, there protruded a head, such a head as the dried specimens Etcham had shown us, as if it were a miniature of the head of a Balunda fetish-man. It was black, shining black as the blackest African skin; it rolled the whites of its wicked, wee eyes and showed its microscopic teeth between lips repulsively Negroid in their red fullness, even in so diminutive a face. It had a crisp, fuzzy wool on its minikin skull; it turned malignantly from side to side and chittered incessantly in that inconceivable falsetto. Stone babbled brokenly against its patter.

Van Rieten turned from Stone and awakened Etcham, with some difficulty. When he was awake and saw it all, Etcham stared and said not one word.

"You saw him slice off two swellings?" Van Rieten asked.

Etcham nodded, chokingly.

"Did he bleed much?" Van Rieten demanded.

"Ve'y little," Etcham replied.

"You hold his arms," said Van Rieten to Etcham.

He took up Stone's razor and handed me the light. Stone showed no sign of seeing the light or of knowing we were there. But the little head mewled and screeched at us.

Van Rieten's hand was steady, and the sweep of the razor even and true. Stone bled amazingly little, and Van Rieten dressed the wound as if it had been a bruise or scrape.

Stone had stopped talking the instant the excrescent head was severed. Van Rieten did all that could be done for Stone and then fairly grabbed the light from me.

Snatching up a gun, he scanned the ground by the cot and brought the butt down once and twice, viciously.

We went back to our hut, but I doubt if I slept.

VI

Next day, near noon, in broad daylight, we heard the two voices from Stone's hut. We found Etcham dropped asleep by his charge. The swelling on the left had broken, and just such another head was there miauling and spluttering. Etcham woke up, and the three of us stood there and glared. Stone interjected hoarse vocables into the tinkling gurgle of the portent's utterance.

Van Rieten stepped forward, took up Stone's razor, and knelt down by the cot. The atomy of a head squealed a wheezy snarl at him.

Then suddenly Stone spoke English.

"Who are you with my razor?"

Van Rieten started back and stood up.

Stone's eyes were clear now and bright; they roved about the hut.

"The end," he said; "I recognize the end. I seem to see Etcham, as if in life. But Singleton! Ah, Singleton! Ghosts of my boyhood come to watch me pass! And you, strange specter with the black beard and my razor! Aroint ye all!"

"I'm no ghost, Stone," I managed to say. "I'm alive. So are Etcham and Van Rieten. We are here to help you."

"Van Rieten!" he exclaimed. "My work passes on to a better man. Luck go with you, Van Rieten."

Van Rieten went nearer to him.

"Just hold still a moment, old man," he said soothingly. "It will be only one twinge."

"I've held still for many such twinges," Stone answered quite distinctly. "Let me be. Let me die in my own way. The hydra was nothing to this. You can cut off ten, a hundred, a thousand heads, but the curse you cannot cut off, or take off. What's soaked into the bone won't come out of the flesh, any more than what's bred there. Don't hack me anymore. Promise!"

His voice had all the old commanding tone of his boyhood, and it swayed Van Rieten as it always had swayed everybody.

"I promise," said Van Rieten.

Almost as he said the words Stone's eyes filmed again.

Then we three sat about Stone and watched that hideous, gibbering prodigy grow up out of Stone's flesh, till two horrid, spindling little black arms disengaged themselves. The infinitesimal nails were perfect to the barely perceptible moon at the quick, the pink spot on the palm was horridly natural. These arms gesticulated and the right plucked toward Stone's blond beard.

"I can't stand this," Van Rieten exclaimed and took up the razor again.

Instantly, Stone's eyes opened, hard and glittering.

"Van Rieten break his word?" he enunciated slowly. "Never!"

"But we must help you," Van Rieten gasped.

"I am past all help and all hurting," said Stone. "This is my hour. This curse is not put on me; it grew out of me, like this horror here. Even now I go."

His eyes closed, and we stood helpless, the adherent figure spouting shrill sentences.

In a moment Stone spoke again.

"You speak all tongues?" he asked quickly.

And the mergent minikin replied in sudden English:

"Yea, verily, all that you speak," putting out its microscopic tongue, writhing its lips, and wagging its head from side to side. We could see the thready ribs on its exiguous flanks heave as if the thing breathed.

"Has she forgiven me?" Stone asked in a muffled strangle.

"Not while the moss hangs from the cypresses," the head squeaked. "Not while the stars shine on Lake Pontchartrain will she forgive."

And then Stone, all with one motion, wrenched himself over on his side. The next instant he was dead.

When Singleton's voice ceased the room was hushed for

a space. We could hear each other breathing. Twombly, the tactless, broke the silence.

"I presume," he said, "you cut off the little minikin and brought it home in alcohol."

Singleton turned on him a stern countenance.

"We buried Stone," he said, "unmutilated as he died."

"But," said the unconscionable Twombly, "the whole thing is incredible."

Singleton stiffened.

"I did not expect you to believe it," he said; "I began by saying that although I heard and saw it, when I look back on it I cannot credit it myself."

BY THEODORE R. COGSWELL

The Cabbage Patch

Aunt Hester sent me to bed early that night. I lay quietly in the old four-poster, listening to the night sounds and the soft sleepy hisses as the narns who lived in the old fern tree underneath my window bedded themselves down in their holes. I was supposed to settle down too, but the tight excited feeling inside my chest wouldn't go away. I pulled the soft down pillow over my head and tried to make everything black. I wanted to go to sleep right away so I could wake up in time to see the birth-fairy when she came down with my new sister.

Priscilla Winters said babies came from the cabbage patch, but I knew better. She brought a cabbage to school one day to prove it, and that night when we were supposed to be asleep she opened it up and showed me a baby inside. It was squishy and white like all soon-babies are before they make the change, but I knew it wasn't a real baby because it didn't have any teeth. We made a birthing-box out of a jar and gave it some flies to eat, but it wouldn't eat them; it just kept crawling around and waving its feelers as if it didn't like it there. When we woke up the next morning it had turned brown and was all dead.

The narns in the fern tree had stopped their whispering, but I still couldn't get to sleep. The little moon had chased the big one up over the horizon so far that its light was shining through the window right into my eyes. I got up and shut the blinds, but even having the room dark again didn't help. I kept seeing pictures of the birth-fairy fluttering down like a beautiful butterfly, and then after

159

she'd put the babies safe in their birthing-box, flying off again with the year-father soaring after her on his fine new wings.

I wanted to see his wings, but Mother wouldn't let me. For two months now she had kept him shut up in his room, and she wouldn't even let me speak to him through the door. I wanted to say goodbye to him because even if he was only a year-father, he'd been nice to me. I was never supposed to be with him unless Mother or Aunt Hester were around, but sometimes I'd slip into the kitchen when they were away, and we'd talk about things. I liked being with him best when he was baking preska because he'd give me bits of the dough and let me make funny things out of them.

Once Aunt Hester caught me alone with him, and her face got all hard and twisted, and she was going to call the patrol and have him beaten, but Mother came in just then. She sent the year-father to his room and then took me into the parlor. I knew that she was getting ready for one of her heart-to-heart talks, but there wasn't anything I could do about it, so I just sat there and listened. Mother's talks always got so wound in on themselves that when she was through I usually couldn't figure out what all the fuss had been about.

First she asked me if I'd felt anything funny when I was alone with the year-father. I asked her what she meant by "funny," and she sort of stuttered, and her face got all red. Finally, she asked me a funny question about my stinger, and I said "no." Then she started to tell me a story about the wasps and the meem, but she didn't get very far with that either. She wanted to, but she got all flustered, and her tongue wouldn't work. Aunt Hester said nonsense, that I was still a little girl and next year would be soon enough. Mother said she wished she could be sure; then she made me promise that if ever my stinger felt funny when I was around a year-father, I'd run and tell her about it right away because if I didn't, something terrible might happen.

My pillow got all hot so I went and sat in my chair. The more I thought about the year-father, the more I wanted to go and see his new wings. Finally, I went over to the door and listened. I could hear Mother and Aunt Hester talking in the front of the house so I tiptoed down the back stairs. When I got to the landing I stopped and felt around with my foot until I found the part of the next stair that was right against the railing. That's a bad stair because if you step in the middle of it without thinking, it gives a loud squeek that you can hear all over the house.

The year-father's room is right next to the kitchen. I gave a little scratch on the door so he would know who it was and not be frightened. I stood there in the dark waiting for him to open up, but he didn't so I went inside and felt for him in his nest. He wasn't there.

First I thought maybe I should go back up and get in bed because Aunt Hester said that if she ever again caught me up at night when I was supposed to be sleeping, she'd give me a licking that I'd never forget. But then I started to think of what would happen to the year-father if he'd gone outside and the patrol caught him wandering around alone at night, and I decided that I'd better tell Mother right away, even if I did get a walloping afterward.

Then I thought that first I'd better look in the kitchen for him. It was dark in there too so I shut the hall door and lit the lamp on the kitchen table. The stone floor was awfully cold on my feet, and I began to wish that I'd remembered to put on my slippers before I came downstairs. Once my eyes got used to the light I looked all around, but the year-father wasn't there either. I was about to blow out the lamp and go and tell Mother when I heard a funny sound coming from the nursery.

I know it sounds funny to have a nursery in the kitchen, but since soon-babies have to be locked away in a dark place until it's time for them to make the change, Mother said we might as well use the old pantry instead of going to all the trouble of blacking out one of the rooms upstairs.

The big thick door that Mother had put on was shut, but she'd forgotten to take the key away so I went over and opened it a crack. I was real scared because at birthing-time nobody is allowed to go in the nursery, not even Aunt Hester. Once the little ones are in the birthing-box, Mother locks the door and doesn't ever open it up again until after they've changed into real people like us.

At Priscilla's house they've got an honest-to-goodness nursery. There's a little window on the door that they uncover after the first month. It's awful dark inside, but if you look real hard you can see the soon-babies crawling around inside. Priscilla let me look in once when her mother was downtown. They had big ugly mouths and teeth.

The sound came again so I opened the door. It was so dark inside that I couldn't see a thing so I went back and got the lamp. The noise seemed to be coming from the birthing-box so I went over and looked in. The year-father was hunched up in the bottom of it. He didn't have any wings.

He blinked up at me in the lantern light. He'd been crying, and his face was all swollen. He motioned to me to go away, but I couldn't. I'd never seen a father without his clothes on before, and I kept staring and staring.

I knew that I should run and get Mother, but somehow I couldn't move. Something terrible was happening to the year-father. His stomach was all swollen up and angry red, and every once in a while it would knot up and twist as if there was something inside that didn't like it there. When that would happen he'd roll his head back and bite down on his lower lip real hard. He seemed to want to yell, but he'd choke it back until nothing came out but a little whimper.

There was a nasty half-healed place on his stomach that looked as if he'd fallen on a sharp stick and hurt himself real bad. He kept pushing his hands against it as if he was trying to hold back something that was inside trying to get out.

I heard Mother's voice calling from the kitchen and then Aunt Hester's voice saying something real sharp, but I couldn't look up or answer. Blood was trickling out through the year-father's locked fingers. Suddenly he emptied out in a raw scream and fell back so limp that it looked as if all his bones were gone. His hands dropped away and from inside his stomach something tore at the half-healed place until it split and opened like a big mouth.

Then I could see the something. I knew it for what it was, and I felt sick and scared in a different sort of way. It inched its way out and wiggled around kind of lost like until it finally lost its balance and fell to the bottom of the box. It didn't move for a minute, and I thought maybe it was dead, but then the feelers around its mouth began to reach out as if they were trying to find something. And then all of a sudden it started a fast wabbly crawl as if it knew just where it was going. I saw teeth as it found the year-father and nuzzled up to him. It was hungry.

Aunt Hester slammed and locked the pantry door. Then she made me a glass of hot milk and sent me up to bed. Mother came into my room a little later and stood by my bed looking down at me to see if I was asleep. I pretended I was because I didn't want to talk to her, and she finally left. I wanted to cry, but I couldn't because if I did she'd hear me and come back up again. I pulled the pillow down over my face real tight until I could hardly breathe, and there were little red flashes of light in the back of my eyes and a humming hive sound in my head. I knew what my stinger was for, and I didn't want to think about it.

When I did get to sleep I didn't dream about the year-father; I dreamed about the wasps and the meem.

BY AMBROSE BIERCE

Oil of Dog

My name is Boffer Bings. I was born of honest parents in one of the humbler walks of life, my father being a manufacturer of dog-oil and my mother having a small studio in the shadow of the village church, where she disposed of unwelcome babes. In my boyhood I was trained to habits of industry; I not only assisted my father in procuring dogs for his vats, but was frequently employed by my mother to carry away the debris of her work in the studio. In performance of this duty I sometimes had need of all my natural intelligence, for all the law officers of the vicinity were opposed to my mother's business. They were not elected on an opposition ticket, and the matter had never been made a political issue; it just happened so. My father's business of making dog-oil was, naturally, less unpopular, though the owners of missing dogs sometimes regarded him with suspicion, which was reflected, to some extent, upon me. My father had, as silent partners, all the physicians of the town, who seldom wrote a prescription which did not contain what they were pleased to designate as *Ol. can.* It is really the most valuable medicine ever discovered. But most persons are unwilling to make personal sacrifices for the afflicted, and it was evident that many of the fattest dogs in town had been forbidden to play with me—a fact which pained my young sensibilities, and at one time came near driving me to become a pirate.

Looking back upon those days, I cannot but regret, at times, that by indirectly bringing my beloved parents to their death I was the author of misfortunes profoundly affecting my future.

One evening while passing my father's oil factory with the body of a foundling from my mother's studio I saw a constable who seemed to be closely watching my movements. Young as I was, I had learned that a constable's acts, of whatever apparent character, are prompted by the most reprehensible motives, and I avoided him by dodging into the oilery by a side door which happened to stand ajar. I locked it at once and was alone with my dead. My father had retired for the night. The only light in the place came from the furnace, which glowed a deep, rich crimson under one of the vats, casting ruddy reflections on the walls. Within the cauldron the oil still rolled in indolent ebullition, occasionally pushing to the surface a piece of dog. Seating myself to wait for the constable to go away, I held the naked body of the foundling in my lap and tenderly stroked its short, silken hair. Ah, how beautiful it was! Even at that early age I was passionately fond of children, and as I looked upon this cherub I could almost find it in my heart to wish that the small, red wound upon its breast—the work of my dear mother—had not been mortal.

It had been my custom to throw the babes into the river which nature had thoughtfully provided for the purpose, but that night I did not dare to leave the oilery for fear of the constable. "After all," I said to myself, "it cannot greatly matter if I put it into this cauldron. My father will never know the bones from those of a puppy, and the few deaths which may result from administering another kind of oil for the incomparable *Ol. can.* are not important in a population which increases so rapidly." In short, I took the first step in crime and brought myself untold sorrow by casting the babe into the cauldron.

The next day, somewhat to my surprise, my father, rubbing his hands with satisfaction, informed me and my mother that he had obtained the finest quality of oil that was ever seen; that the physicians to whom he had shown samples had so pronounced it. He added that he had no knowledge as to how the result was obtained; the dogs had been treated in all respects as usual and were of an ordinary breed. I deemed it my duty to explain—which I did, though palsied would have been my tongue if I could have foreseen the consequences. Bewailing their previous ignorance of the advantages of combining their industries, my parents at once took measures to repair the error. My mother removed her studio to a wing of the factory building, and my duties in connection with the business ceased; I was no longer required to dispose of the bodies of the small superfluous, and there was no need of alluring dogs to their doom, for my father discarded them altogether, though they still had an honorable place in the name of the oil. So suddenly thrown into idleness, I might naturally have been expected to become vicious and dissolute, but I did not. The holy influence of my dear mother was ever about to protect me from the temptations which beset youth, and my father was a deacon in a church. Alas, that through my fault these estimable persons should have come to so bad an end!

Finding a double profit in her business, my mother now devoted herself to it with a new assiduity. She removed not only superfluous and unwelcome babes to order, but went out into the highways and byways, gathering in children of a larger growth, and even such adults as she could entice to the oilery. My father, too, enamored of the superior quality of oil produced, purveyed for his vats with diligence and zeal. The conversion of their neighbors into dog-oil became, in short, the one passion of their lives—an absorbing and overwhelming greed took possession of their souls and served them in place of a hope in Heaven —by which, also, they were inspired.

So enterprising had they now become that a public meeting was held and resolutions passed severely censuring them. It was intimated by the chairman that any further raids upon the population would be met in a spirit of hostility. My poor parents left the meeting brokenhearted, desperate, and, I believe, not altogether sane. Anyhow, I deemed it prudent not to enter the oilery with them that night, but slept outside in a stable.

At about midnight some mysterious impulse caused me

to rise and peer through a window into the furnace room, where I knew my father now slept. The fires were burning as brightly as if the following day's harvest had been expected to be abundant. One of the large cauldrons was slowly "walloping" with a mysterious appearance of self-restraint, as if it bided its time to put forth its full energy. My father was not in bed; he had risen in his nightclothes and was preparing a noose in a strong cord. From the looks which he cast at the door of my mother's bedroom I knew too well the purpose that he had in mind. Speechless and motionless with terror, I could do nothing in prevention or warning. Suddenly the door of my mother's apartment was opened, noiselessly, and the two confronted each other, both apparently surprised. The lady, also, was in her nightclothes, and she held in her right hand the tool of her trade, a long, narrow-bladed dagger.

She, too, had been unable to deny herself the last profit which the unfriendly action of the citizens and my absence had left her. For one instant they looked into each other's blazing eyes and then sprang together with indescribable fury. Around and around the room they struggled, the man cursing, the woman shrieking, both fighting like demons—she to strike him with the dagger, he to strangle her with his great bare hands. I know not how long I had the unhappiness to observe this disagreeable instance of domestic infelicity, but at last, after a more than usually vigorous struggle, the combatants suddenly moved apart.

My father's breast and my mother's weapon showed evidences of contact. For another instant they glared at each other in the most unamiable way; then my poor, wounded father, feeling the hand of death upon him, leaped forward, unmindful of resistance, grasped my dear mother in his arms, dragged her to the side of the boiling cauldron, collected all his failing energies, and sprang in with her! In a moment, both had disappeared and were adding their oil to that of the committee of citizens who had called the day before with an invitation to the public meeting.

Convinced that these unhappy events closed to me every

avenue to an honorable career in that town, I removed to the famous city of Otumwee, where these memoirs are written with a heart full of remorse for a heedless act entailing so dismal a commercial disaster.

BY JEAN-PIERRE ANDREVON

The Time of the Big Sleep

Translated from the French by Damon Knight

Behind the thick lenses of his spectacles, the globular and divergent eyes of Jean-Paul Sartre dimmed, went out. He had fallen face down across his desk in the middle of the editorial he was writing for a polizine; a few pages, blown off by the sudden compression of air, had fluttered to the floor. A moment or two earlier, Sartre had felt a slight pricking sensation in his back, but had paid no attention. It was the end of summer, a bright, warm day. The object which had entered below Sartre's right shoulder blade, piercing his wool jacket, shirt, and undershirt, had been fired from a window in the building across the street, using a special compressed-air carbine with a telescopic sight: an ambush weapon. The carbine fired hollow needles of frozen ammoniated methane, a few millimeters long; once in the flesh, the needle melted rapidly, releasing a chemically unstable poison derived from curare. Thus no mark of violence remained on the victim's body, and if only the medical examiners didn't look too closely (and they *never* looked too closely), his death was very naturally blamed on a heart attack. The procedure was highly refined; it had worked perfectly on Sartre, and he was by no means the first.

The writer could no longer campaign against this strategy of political assassination whose emergence he had foreseen. Collapsed over his desk, it must have taken no more than eleven seconds for his life to ebb away into nothingness. Two or three pages covered with his spiky

171

but regular handwriting were scattered on the floor; the last sentence, unfinished, began:

"The existence of a revolutionary thought, even if it does not rest on any preexistent theoretical line, lies latent in the heart of a minority (or rather of a group of minorities), which, the more strongly an external oppression makes itself felt, the more radically it. . . ."

But Sartre had been unable to bring his thought any further into being; it would remain forever unfinished, suspended. His fight was over. The group that published the clandestine polizine, mimeographed in an edition of five hundred copies, would wait in vain for the last statement of the most lucid witness of his time.

More than thirty years earlier, in a book called *L'Ecume des Jours*, Boris Vian had already assassinated Jean-Paul Sartre, for a laugh. But the time for joking was over: this time, Sartre had been killed in earnest.

Only three candidates had offered themselves for the presidential elections which were to take place as a national referendum: those of the Majority, the Radical Center, and the Socialist Center. On the brightly colored campaign posters which decorated the walls of Paris and of all France, the Majority candidate's face attracted attention by its expression of wise but indulgent authority. The wave of his hair, the colors of his necktie, the number of wrinkles on his forehead, the direction of his gaze, the curve of his smile, all had been meticulously arranged by the shadow orchestra which had harmonized the music of his campaign. The photos of the other candidates, without being noticeably blurred, melted into an unrelieved monotone from which only certain traits emerged to call attention to a carefully emphasized fault: one was too young, the other seemed completely senile; one grimaced imperceptibly, the other's gaze was studiously evasive; one was dressed in a way that radiated slovenliness, while the other's costume breathed a miasma of inauthenticity. For them, too, the invisible orchestra had played its muted melodies, selecting the false notes with care. As for the candidates' programs, to speak plainly, it would have been hard to find any distinct differences among them, supposing that anyone had read them with attention. But who would have taken the trouble?

Jean-Pierre A. had done so; his interest in politics urged him to it, and also, more to the point, his job as political columnist for *L'Observateur Radical,* the weekly that, though bourgeois in every possible sense, was still the last remnant of the so-called opposition press.

The fine but tangible threads that united the three candidates made it obvious that far from being real adversaries they were antagonistic but complementary figures in a ballet choreographed as a demonstration of the uses of democracy. This fact had not escaped Jean-Pierre's notice, nor that of a minority of other lucid individuals, all equally powerless. Besides, if the method was new in practice, it was nothing of the sort in the world of the imagination, for Ray Bradbury had laid down its principles allusively in *Fahrenheit 451.* You can't get away from Bradbury.

"What did you say?" came Simone's clear voice.

"You can't get away from Bradbury," said Jean-Pierre, pensively rereading the last sentence of his weekly article.

He had written: "One is therefore entitled to ask oneself if the Radical Center party and the Socialist Center party are composed of puppets or tin soldiers. In the former case, it remains to be seen how much longer the puppet-masters will continue to pull their strings; in the latter, they will be put back in their box as soon as the election is over, with what results we can easily guess."

Jean-Pierre shook his head. A ray of sunlight fell on the page. Who would read his prose? *L'Observateur*'s circulation had been falling rapidly. And even if not . . . what could a few printed pages accomplish, drowned as they were in the nauseous milk that poured more abundantly every day from the two buxom teats of repression and censorship?

Jean-Pierre rattled away at his typewriter. Simone had appeared in the office doorway. "What were you saying about Bradbury?"

"Nothing," sighed Jean-Pierre. "Nothing at all."

"I thought he was dead," said his wife absently.

Jean-Pierre did not reply. He stood up, holding the page which he had just finished typing front and back; he folded it in half and put it in his jacket pocket. Then he picked up an envelope already sealed and stamped, and left the room, putting an arm over Simone's shoulder to draw her along with him. "Going to take my article to the paper," he said, with a mechanical smile.

"What's that?" said Simone, indicating the letter with her chin.

"Oh, nothing. . . . Just an article for a polizine."

"There, you see, you're still writing them!"

"Oh, no. I mean . . . just one, every now and then."

"You're wasting your time. It doesn't pay anything, and you'll wind up getting yourself in trouble."

"You don't say!" groaned Jean-Pierre, with a jerk of his head.

François, aged eight, was playing with some plastic soldiers in the hall. Jean-Pierre gently touched the boy's black bangs as he passed. Since Cristelle's birth, Simone had given up any effort at political thinking, any intellectual engagement. This withdrawal of hers saddened Jean-Pierre, but he himself hadn't enough energy or doctrinal rigor to breathe new enthusiasm into her, to give her the understanding that would enable her to keep afloat. Anyhow, wasn't Simone swimming with the tide, like everybody else—like Jean-Pierre himself? What do I do? he thought. What *do* I do, except for my little articles in a paper that's recycled as soon as it's printed?

Jean-Pierre often turned over the same problems, asked himself the same questions. But he always got the same answer: He did nothing, or rather he did less and less; like so many others, he let things slide.

To be sure, he still contributed to the polizines (you might as well call them polyzines). But he did it without risk, without really taking part in a physical sense: It was not he who turned the handle of the mimeograph, who ran around stuffing copies into mailboxes before daylight; it was not he who risked arrest, interrogation, imprisonment.

It was enough for him to write, at a distance, in a warm room; he had the comfortable position of the intellectual.

Jean-Pierre walked down the street. The yellow blot of the mailbox came into view a dozen meters away, at the corner of the avenue. He held the letter tightly. How pleasant it is to examine your conscience, little scribbler! groaned a machine inside his skull. You do it every day, and how far does it get you? squeaked a second machine. A likely story, to give a bum like that a clear conscience! whispered a third machine. Poor jerk! concluded a last rust-bucket with a disillusioned whir. Jean-Pierre slid the letter into the slot. There! He had written. . . . Ah! never mind what he had written. He turned back. A man who leaned negligently against the wall was looking at him. Jean-Pierre stared back for a moment or two, his diaphragm tightening at a faint signal of alarm. Was he being watched? But the man had turned his head and was gazing at something else. Jean-Pierre went away, troubled and indecisive. What, was he scaring himself with shadows now? Why should they watch him? He was a journalist, he wrote for a perfectly legal left newspaper. And besides, after all, this wasn't fascism!

But he had a second shock when he passed a newspaper kiosk and saw the *Monde-Soir* poster with the notice of Sartre's death. Jean-Pierre stopped, leaned over the page. Above a short column, squeezed between thick headlines about the election, he saw these words:

DEATH OF JEAN-PAUL SARTRE
The writer is dead of a heart attack

"Shit!" he said between his teeth.

Something blurred his vision—perhaps the fugitive mist of tears to come. So many writers, journalists, militants had died in the last few years. A real epidemic . . . for which the revolutionaries of Jean-Pierre's acquaintance were sure they had found the virus responsible. In spite of which, Jean-Pierre had never felt more than a convulsive surprise, a vague disquiet. But Sartre! He was youth, he was the apostle, the guide; somehow he was the invulnerable symbol of political rectitude, of lucidity, of intellectual courage, of day-to-day engagement. And now . . . who was left to carry on? Who was left of whom one could say, "He, at least . . . "?

Jean-Pierre began walking again, head down, his mind a blank. The evening had turned suddenly cooler, or perhaps that was only a subjective illusion. When he reached the end of the boulevard Saint-Michel he didn't even give his customary reflexive glance at the coin laundry which two years before had replaced the bookstore "La Joie de Lire."

Jean-Luc Godard stared through his dark glasses at the headlights that hurled themselves straight toward him, then burst into sharp splinters and scattered in a thousand sequins on the windshield, before they were swallowed up by the rain-hatched darkness behind the car. François, glued to the wheel, had not spoken for an hour. It was late . . . what time, exactly? Godard had no idea, hadn't paid any attention. After the showing of his film, *Dialectique d'un Combat,* in that little clandestine hall in Grenoble, he had had to discuss it for more than two hours with the Marxist-Leninist students who had invited him. But Godard was not complaining; on the contrary, a film was not complete, did not justify itself as a creative labor, until it was extended by thought, then by the action engendered in turn by that thought, which might be (why not?) the elaboration of another film. Dialectics was like a Moebius strip: It had neither beginning nor end, top nor bottom.

Jean-Luc Godard turned around impulsively: the two cans of sixteen-millimeter film were still there on the back seat, jiggling slightly to the rhythm of the motor. The sixteen hundred meters of film represented more than two years of work, often dangerous work, among various liberation movements in a number of Latin American republics. Then there was the development, in a clandestine lab; and then the editing—in his room, without a moritone of course, just with a hand-cranked winder—

and finally this exhausting work of selling ideology on film. . . .

But the danger didn't count. The work, the fatigue, the effort of every day, every hour, didn't count. Only the result counted, the long march toward revolution. Godard turned and leaned back against the seat. He rubbed his head, now completely bald, with a slender hand. This evening there had been eleven to see his film. It was not much. But the number was not so important. The work had to be done, and it was being done: That was all. In another town, there would be more people. In another town . . . another evening. Maybe tomorrow.

The quiet drone of the motor lulled him. He turned once more to look at the cans and saw for an instant, in passing, François' sharp, silent profile. He was a good driver. A nice guy. A good militant. Only . . . he was not exactly the sort of fellow with whom you could talk about the left front of art, the effect of suture, the parenthesis and the detour, the degree zero of cinematic writing. Had François ever seen one of Vertov's films? Or even Eisenstein's? . . . But that, too, was absolutely unimportant. You still think like a bourgeois intellectual. François does his job better than you do yours. That's what matters.

Staring out at the dark rampart of the highway, on which headlights had now become less frequent, Jean-Luc Godard let himself be enfolded by the night.

François' exclamation and the abrupt rightward lurch of the car roused him from his meditation. He heard: "The bastard, he. . . ." Then the agonized squeal of brakes and the shriek of torn metal mingled with the voice and cut it short. Godard felt the car toppling over, and he was aware of a fall into the midst of the solid darkness. Pressed back into the seat by inertia, Jean-Luc Godard did not blink an eyelid. Impassive, arms crossed on his chest, in his mind's eye he saw this very shot in *Alerte au Sud,* a rather bad film of the fifties directed by Jean Devaivre, in which one saw Erich von Stroheim, stony-faced, plunging into the ocean at the controls of his airplane. But, as with Cocteau, the dream and the reality for him were one and the same. After breaking the thin guardrail of a bridge,

Godard's car, nudged from its path by the fishtail of an unknown vehicle, crashed from a height of one hundred meters into a tributary of the Saône.

The filmmaker's body was hurled from the car at tremendous speed. They found him in the morning; his dark glasses had fallen not far away. They were not even cracked.

The Majority candidate had been elected on the first ballot; he had received 87.3 percent of the votes cast. Jean-Pierre A. was not surprised. His wife, Simone, had said to him that since the hope of revolution was permanently lost anyhow ("Momentarily," Jean-Pierre had corrected), it was just as well that the Majority was so solidly entrenched. Because either it would unmask itself quickly, by the very fact of its evident solidity, in accentuating its class politics, and then the people would regain their awareness and combativity, or else it would increase its efforts toward social reformism, and that would be something gained: Sweden isn't so bad, after all. . . . Jean-Pierre had not replied. He was disgusted and baffled. The use of verbal dialectic had grown almost impossibly difficult for him. The big voices had been killed one after another; those of the little militants were growing few, smothered one by one. Where to turn, now? Whom to follow, whom to listen to? The silence was growing more and more oppressive in the ranks of those who not so long ago had been the opposition, the left, leftism. After the events of September '73, the Communist party had been declared illegal, dissolved. *L'Huma* had ceased publication. The numerous Trotskyist or Maoist papers had preceded it into the nothingness of censorship. All that remained were the polizines, and then—*L'Observateur Radical*. It ought to have arrived, by the way; it was time for the mail long ago. Had they printed something about Sartre, at least? Jean-Pierre had phoned the paper a few days ago to ask the editor-in-chief if he wanted an article about the writer, but had been told someone else was working on it, and in any event it wouldn't do to make a cult of personality. Just the same, with Sartre's disappearance . . . Jean-Pierre sighed, went down to look in the box. *L'Observateur* was not there. Astonished, he made a foray to the nearest newsstand; the woman who kept it, whom Jean-Pierre had talked to often, said that *L'Observateur* hadn't come today; she didn't know why. Glum and uneasy, Jean-Pierre went home. There was a meeting of the editorial committee this same afternoon; he would find out then. It was not worth the trouble to phone.

But, of course, something had been going wrong at the paper for months now. *L'Observateur Radical* was deradicalizing itself slowly but surely, with the innocent but inexorable impassiveness of a Kafkaesque machine. Were there really pressures being brought to bear at the management level or was a sort of diffuse self-censorship undermining the editors? It was hard to know for sure. The feeling of comradeship, the team spirit was being eroded ineluctably; newsmen were keeping their mouths shut, conversations were guarded. You went to deliver your article and left again, errors in proof escaped the editors, there was nothing left of the warm ambiance that had lived on for a while after September '73. For months now, certain of Jean-Pierre's articles had been touched up behind his back; the payoff had come the week before when his article on the elections had been altered unrecognizably. The last sentence in particular:

"It becomes clear now that the Radical Center party and the Socialist Center party are no more than puppets working in blindness and automatism in the shadow cast by the Majority party against which they no longer have anything to oppose but a sterile verbalism: Sunday's election, whose results are not in doubt, will relegate them once for all to the oubliettes of history, or see them at last blend harmoniously into the Majority."

They couldn't have done a more thorough job!

And he hadn't even protested. . . .

Jean-Pierre ate without appetite; after his coffee he kissed Simone on the forehead, François and Cristelle on the cheek, and went out. In the street gilded by the early-autumn sun, he hung around a long time before he could make up his mind to open the door of the paper. When he returned, a little after eighteen hundred, Simone saw that his face was drawn and worried.

"There's no more *Observateur Radical*," he told her.

Simone, who was looking over some handwriting exercises of François', stared at him without seeming to understand, her mouth half-open, eyes wide.

"They announced it at the meeting," said Jean-Pierre dully. He dropped onto the living-room sofa, took out a pack of Caporals and lit one, inhaled, blew out a long blue plume of smoke. "Jean made the announcement himself. The political situation has changed, the parliamentary opposition is dead; it's necessary to rethink the basic orientation of an opposition newspaper. . . . That was the general outline. Do you know what it means?"

"But then what will you do?"

Jean-Pierre stared at his cigarette. "What can I do? I'll wait." He shrugged. "Jean assured us that the paper would open again in two or three weeks, with another name and a new formula. He won't be there himself, I think. He looked completely washed out. . . ." He shook his head. "Eighty-seven percent of the vote. . . . They're the bosses now, do you understand that? We won't have to wait long."

"But what are *you* planning to do?" Simone insisted.

"We're supposed to be called in individually to form a new staff. In principle, everybody will be rehired. But walking softly, I suppose: We'll have to sing the praises of the government. . . ."

"And that's what you'll do?"

"What do you want me to do? Look for a job peddling sewing machines? And then, you know . . . I won't be exactly inconspicuous—writing political commentary puts you on the spot."

They sat in silence until time for dinner, during which they learned, via an eight-second TV flash, of the death of Jean-Luc Godard in an auto accident.

The cell door opened, and two men entered: men in guards' uniforms, apparently of about the same age, although one was an old-timer and the other was beginning his second week on the job. The new man carried the prisoner's usual midday meal on a tray—a clear soup with a few dubious scraps of meat swimming in it, a small piece of tomme cheese, a slice of bread, and a carafe of water. Each of the two men wore an automatic pistol in an open holster. But the prisoner was a nonviolent: When the guards entered, he merely raised his handsome emaciated face, among whose wrinkles were traces of old blows, of old tortures perhaps, and smiled at the newcomers.

"We've brought your soup," said the older of the two. "And I'd like to introduce Flandrin; he's a new man. You'll be seeing a lot of him. Me, I'm going to another district soon. It seems I'm not hard enough on the politicals!" He smiled uncertainly. "But don't worry about Flandrin; he's a good fellow."

He slapped the new man on the shoulder, but the other's face remained sullen, as if by his expression he meant to contradict the older man's reassuring words. The prisoner rose, stretching his lanky frame and combing back his long hair, which was still thick even though it was pure white. He took the tray from the guard, set it down, and turned, holding out a big hand to his future jailer. His open, innocent face was creased with his smile.

Flandrin hesitated, glanced aside at the older guard, then consented to hold out a soft hand to the prisoner, who squeezed it in his muscular fist. Then the prisoner ate his light meal under the eyes of the guards. That was the regulation; it would not do for him to be able to manufacture something, or try to put an end to his life: But the prisoner certainly did not dream of any such thing. When he had finished and the two men had left, slamming the wooden door in its stone frame, the prisoner began to walk back and forth in his little den, thinking of the plays he would have liked to direct, the films he would have liked to make, noting down in a corner of his brain a few lines to add to one or another of the impossible books he would have liked to write. It must be two years that he had been in prison, drifting from one cell to another in the dark sea of the political prisoner's world. In the beginning, certainly, it had been hard. Now they left him alone, more or less. It was just that he was always desperately cut off from the world outside; he had no newspapers, no books, no radio. He did not even have the privilege of writing: That was the regulation. The real world came through to him anyhow, fragmentary, deformed, spotty, in a chance remark made by some guard more accommodating than the rest. It was not much, but it was enough to let him know that his country had not undergone any violent disorders; and this lethargic oppression indefinitely postponed the day of his release. Their technique was much more insidious, much more formidable, and in the long run its effects went tragically deep: For it wasn't so much freedom in the usual sense that they were suppressing, it was—oh, he didn't apply it to himself!—it was intelligence.

Beyond the door, his two guards were talking. Time passes slowly in a prison—as slowly for the jailers as for the inmates.

"What is he, another of those fucking intellectuals?" asked the new man.

"Sure, but he's a nice guy," said the old-timer.

"Yeah. . . . He thinks we're all shit."

"No, no, not him, you know. . . . I've talked with him quite a bit. He says we're like the workers. Says we're doing this job because we were pushed into it, because of unemployment or something. He says we're—what did he call it, again? Alienated. Yes, he says we're alienated. It isn't all shit, you know, the stuff he says."

The guard shook his head. His new partner was frowning. Sure. Alienated. My ass! All alike, these intellectuals. All horseshit. But I won't let him give me any crap. I've been in the army! Nobody hands me any horseshit. No, sir! That's the way it is! Yes, sir!

"What's the guy's name?" he asked after a moment.

"Armand Gatti," said the other.

As they talked, they had reached the cell of Maurice Clavel.

Jean-Pierre had gone back to the novel he had begun three years ago and which was progressing only in fits and starts, fits which were growing less and less frequent and less intense. It was a novel ironically entitled *La Fin de la Répression,* and dealt with the events of September '73, described from a point of view which was visibly Trotskyist, since for some years Jean-Pierre had been a sympathizer of the movements that had gathered around the Fourth International. But now that his friendships were drowned in the shipwreck of the revolutionary movements, now that the journals were done, he no longer knew exactly what Trotskyism had been or even what it had signified, whether in '27 or '68 or '73. The ideology of the novel was weakening along with its plot. Besides, Jean-Pierre thought, who would publish it nowadays?

A dozen years before, Jean-Pierre had written another novel, about the events of May '68, called *Après une Révolution Manquée;* published with reticence, it had sold with extreme moderation. So he had even less heart for his present task.

One Tuesday, exactly twelve days after the famous editorial meeting of *L'Observateur Radical,* there was a knock at his door. It was four in the afternoon; François was at school, Simone was out with Cristelle. It was a gray day, almost cold. Jean-Pierre went to the door. Two men he had never seen before were standing there, wearing light topcoats, hats, and neckties. "Cops!" he thought, and his heart jumped. One of the men took off his hat. "Monsieur Jean-Pierre A.?" he asked, with a smile that was a model of cordiality.

The writer admitted it. The man's smile grew broader. "Allow me to present myself: Anatole Dauman. This is my colleague, Fernand de Teil. We are representatives of the new management of *L'Observateur Impartial.* "Yes" (a satisfied smile), "that's the new name of the newspaper to which you've contributed such excellent articles for many years. Yes, I assure you. . . . We thought that before reintegrating you into the editorial staff, it would be a good idea to have a little friendly talk. It's not a formality! It's a matter of getting to know one another. . . ."

"Oh, great!" said Jean-Pierre, with a touch of dryness and impertinence in his tone.

"May we come in?" The man was still smiling.

"Oh, of course. Pardon me." Jean-Pierre stepped aside, indicating the living room.

"You seem uneasy," Dauman went on heartily. "You surely didn't think we were. . . ." He left the phrase unfinished, made a vague circular gesture, cooed a little.

"Oh, no, of course not," said Jean-Pierre.

"But nowadays, of course, one never knows. . . ." Dauman said in an undertone, with an air of ironic complicity.

De Teil smiled behind his back.

Jean-Pierre did not reply. He showed them to seats, offered them whisky.

"Nice place you have here," said Dauman, gazing around at the walls covered with drawings and paintings. He paused—barely a second—at a Cuban film poster, clasped his hands, and began, "As I was saying a moment ago, the conception of a free weekly" (he paused after the word "free," smiled again, raised a forefinger) "can't be limited to the systematic publication of sterile diatribes against the motives or actions of the government. There's no more opposition, the Majority has gained a crushing victory in the elections, so?" He spread his hands, joined them again. "We must agree that an 'opposition' newspaper, in the traditional sense of the term, can no longer justify its existence. Isn't that true?" A silence. "But—" (Forefinger raised.) "An objective newspaper, which tells in all conscience, in all freedom, what's going well and what's going badly, responds perfectly to the public's need for information and the present political circumstances. . . . Don't you think so?"

"Undoubtedly," murmured Jean-Pierre.

"Besides which, political affairs, with all that they imply of the routine, the bureaucratic, the obscure, interest readers less and less. Accordingly, we're thinking of expanding the space devoted to leisure, sports, culture above all—in short, everything that deals with the daily life of the citizen. There you have the general outline of the readjustments we feel are necessary for the rebirth of *L'Observateur Impartial*. . . . Well! What do you think of it?"

"It seems justifiable."

Jean-Pierre had decided on a neutral tone and an attentive expression. Dauman continued to talk for about a quarter of an hour. Jean-Pierre said "yes," "certainly," "naturally"; he sipped his whisky, smoked cigarette after cigarette, and cursed the sweat that dripped constantly from his armpits. The other man, de Teil, said nothing. He had not removed his hat; his eyes revealed nothing, nor his mouth, nor the way he had of crossing his arms and ankles while he listened to his companion.

"Your specialty is national politics, isn't that right?" said Dauman pensively, after a long silence.

"Uh . . . yes," said Jean-Pierre, with difficulty.

Dauman rubbed his chin with a fleshy hand. "There's a bit of a problem there. . . ." Regretful expression. "The column's already been assigned. Ah, yes! We have someone who was hired by the upper levels of management . . . well, you know how that is!" A charming pout. "But a man of your talent has more than one string to his bow, isn't that so? I was thinking—*we* were thinking—of a literary column. You've published a number of works yourself, right?"

"Well, yes, as a matter of fact, but it was a long time ago. . . ."

Incidentally: "But you're not writing anything at the moment?"

"No, no. No, I haven't written anything for . . . several years."

"That's a pity. You used to have, if memory serves, a sharp turn of phrase." Smile. "But to get back to this literary tribunal?"

"Yes, I . . . I think that would suit me fine." (So much the better, he said to himself, so much the better: That way, at least, I won't have to grovel before the throne.)

"Naturally you haven't anything else going?"

"Anything else going?"

"Right! No arrangements with another newspaper, another magazine, or. . . ." Wave of the hand.

"No, no. Nothing."

"Of course. . . ." A brief silence. "You have an awkward background. I mean to say, awkward as regards most of the newspapers published today!" Laugh. "All right! But I think we've chewed the fat long enough. I'll expect you at the next editorial meeting. Next Monday. At the usual time. You'll see—the old customs haven't changed. Everything's going to work out fine!"

Dauman got up, followed by his silent companion. Once more he looked all around the room, as if finding cause for admiration and appreciation. "You really have a beautiful apartment. You're lucky—right in the middle of town! I assure you I'm not this well housed myself. With a spot like this, you wouldn't be anxious to move, eh?" Laugh.

"No," said Jean-Pierre in a voice so stifled that it barely left his lips.

There was a sharp sound of breaking glass. Jean-Pierre started, turned. In rising, Fernand de Teil had overturned a vase that stood on the low table beside his chair. It was a pure cylinder of glass, tall and slender, which Simone loved. In falling, it had broken into four or five big shards; the red flowers whose name Jean-Pierre did not know lay on the carpet, which was rapidly soaking up the water.

"I'm terribly sorry," said de Teil. "It was an accident." He spoke for the first time. His voice was deep, slightly wheezing. "Accidents happen so stupidly," he said.

There was a little silence. Dauman broke it, putting his hand in his pocket, saying: "We must reimburse you . . . we're really very sorry."

"No, please!" said Jean-Pierre. "It doesn't matter at all."

He urged his visitors toward the door. On the dark green carpet, the fallen petals were like gouts of blood.

In the front hall Jean-Pierre found himself face to face with Simone, who had come in without making a noise. She was standing in the hall, motionless, upright, locked in a rigid silence. Jean-Pierre wondered how long she had been there and how much of the conversation she had heard.

The two men greeted her, and shortly afterward the door closed softly behind them.

Jean-Pierre turned to Simone, gave her a long look. Simone returned his gaze, but neither said anything. There was nothing to say.

Jean-Edern Hallier felt that someone was knocking him around. . . . The meeting had lasted late into the night, but it had accomplished some positive results. The thousand copies of *Front Avancé* had been printed and stapled; before dawn militants would have deposited them in the mailboxes of the thousand Renault-Ford workers. Jean-Edern Hallier was tired. Something seemed to be wrong with the light button in the entrance hall of the housing project in Aubervilliers where he lived. He was taken completely by surprise when the blow knocked him aside; he struck the wall, a groan of protest rose to his lips. But he didn't have time to cry out. A rough hand was clapped over his mouth, and in the darkness several pairs of hands seized him by the arms and shoulders. The beam of a pencil flash struck his eyes, blinding him completely. A voice growled, "We've got him! Tie him up and gag him." Jean-Edern Hallier felt a cord binding his wrists, while a cloth was put over his mouth and tied at the back of his neck. He heard the same voice: We're going to take care of you, you son of a bitch." But he didn't feel especially frightened. He thought: They're going to beat me up. It wouldn't be the first time it had happened to him. He tensed his body, expecting blows, but they did not come. He thought he heard the tinkle of something metallic; then he was forced into a sitting position, back against the wall, and busy fingers pulled the sleeves of his shirt and windbreaker up to his biceps. He was surprised, but really did not understand until the cold metal of a needle sank into the vein in his elbow. He struggled and kicked, fruitlessly. A wave of warmth traveled through his veins, rose to the shoulder, spread through his whole body. They gave him a second injection, a third. Jean-Edern had the feeling that he was turning into a ball of warmth that floated a few feet above the floor. He thought again: They mustn't keep on, they mustn't. . . . But his body refused to move. His body was all right. And shortly Jean-Edern Hallier stopped thinking.

In the morning newspapers there were a few brief paragraphs about his death. The one in the *Monde-Soir* was headlined:

WRITER SUCCUMBS TO OVERDOSE

The body of Jean-Edern Hallier, who had a brief literary career a dozen years ago, has been found in a vacant lot in Aubervilliers. The writer had succumbed to an overdose of heroin, a drug to which he was apparently addicted.

For four years Jean-Edern Hallier had been fleeing a warrant for his arrest. He had, in fact, abandoned his novelistic career in order to edit, one after another, a number of "revolutionary" journals owing their allegiance to foreign associations. For a number of years, following the disappearance of that sort of journalism, he contributed to a number of "polizines," that is to say clandestine mimeographed pamphlets generally preaching disorder and violence, to which no one really paid much attention.

One might suggest without insulting his memory that the passing of M. Jean-Edern Hallier is no great loss either to literature or to politics.

Jean-Pierre A. ran into Luc Morin as he left a Monday meeting. He had been working for three weeks at *L'Observateur Impartial,* where his literary articles were accepted without a word changed; the newspaper was nothing more to him now than a letter-box where he left his articles (he had begun a critical examination of the latest developments in the new novel), and this professional anonymity suited him perfectly.

Morin took him by the arm: He had been walking with his head down and had not seen his friend.

"Hello, Jean-Pierre!" said Morin.

"Oh—hello!" replied Jean-Pierre. They had stopped

between the divergent currents of the crowd, in the middle of the sidewalk. Jean-Pierre looked right and left, then met Luc's candid gaze.

"Long time since I've see you," said Luc. He was wearing jeans and a turtleneck, but Jean-Pierre noticed that he had had his hair cut.

"You know—" he began. He didn't know how to finish; he shrugged, gestured vaguely, smiled in misery.

Luc Morin was a Trotskyist; he edited the polizine to which Jean-Pierre had been a contributor not so long ago. Yes—the last time had been hardly two months ago. And all that seemed so distant, so ancient!

"I see you're writing for the new-style *Observateur,*" said Luc.

"What do you expect? I've got a living to make."

"Of course." A silence. "But you're not going to desert us completely? It's hard, right now, but—"

A silence. "You understand—" said Jean-Pierre. A silence. He looked to the left, then to the right. "I don't know what the fuck to do. Those cops that pretend to be from the editorial committee came to my place to put a scare into me. And they succeeded! I'm stuck now. Watched. You know that they know I used to do articles for you. If I don't walk the straight and narrow, at least for a while, I'll be fired. And then, if I'm fired, that's nothing, but you know better than I do what's happening. . . ." A silence. A brief, sad smile crossed Luc's lips. "Of course," Jean-Pierre went on, "I don't confuse myself with Sartre. They won't stoop to my level! But you know, the slightest little pretext, and I might find myself in stir for I don't know how long. I've got Simone and the two kids, you know."

A silence. Jean-Pierre looked left, then right. Luc caught his eye. "All right. Look, I don't want to keep you. But—if you'd like to give us a hand again, you know the address. You know, I've let *Poing Rouge* drop. Now I'm trying to revive *Front Avancé,* the thing that poor Jean-Edern started. You know about that?"

"Jean-Edern? Of course. So you've turned toward Maoism?"

"You know, nowadays, these labels. . . ."

Jean-Pierre shook his head. Labels. . . . What label could Luc rightfully apply to him? But Luc was no longer there. He was gone in the crowd. He followed his own path, each to his own.

The minister of cultural affairs turned in the bright red inflatable armchair, in which he was able to stow all the sharp angles of his body. Then with a familiar gesture he folded his bony hands at the level of his chin. His smile, which in spite of its ironical curve was no more than a reflex fixed once for all, pleated his hollow cheeks, emphasizing the high cheekbones. He looked at his visitor for a moment, but had to drop his gaze before those little colorless eyes, sunk in bulges of fat, which stared at him with the hardness and patience of old stones.

"You've really done a beautiful job," said the minister of cultural affairs finally. "A perfect and . . . complete job."

"A job of this kind is never complete," answered the minister of police in his slow, dull voice.

"Of course . . . of course. There are leftovers after the best of parties!" Pleased with his stroke of wit, the minister of cultural affairs emitted a brief, barking laugh. "But these little groups, these basement agitators, these manufacturers of tracts and polizines—they're not to be taken seriously, are they? So that after your sweep, the organized terrorist potential of the country has been reduced to nothing. Without laying ourselves open to the slightest suspicion." He raised a long, thin finger. "For my part, I'm very satisfied."

The minister of cultural affairs fell silent. He took up from the low table between them a paper-clipped sheaf of pages and began skimming through them, although he knew their contents by heart. On these pages were written names, names, hundreds of names, each crossed out with a red line, each followed by a series of numbers which referred to the date of a . . . premature death. Black on white, red on white, it was the ruin, the assassination of leftist thought, radical and revolutionary thought, that was displayed on a few sheets of 8½ x 11 onionskin. A gripping document . . . which was difficult to grip, in fact, because the minister of police stretched out his hand and took the sheets roughly from his colleague; then he folded them twice and slid them into the breast pocket of his jacket.

The two men had nothing more to say to each other, but they remained sitting, face to face, united by a secret complicity. It's easy to picture them thus, fixed in time and space by an improbable photograph, or better yet, by a film which has recorded, without their knowledge, their own death in the midst of their labors, with the ringing and persistent echo of the little scissor-strokes of seconds snapping in the emptiness of this quiet office. The subjective camera retreats from them in a rapidly ascending zoom; we no longer see anything but two gray silhouettes, huddled in their chairs, in the middle of the cut-away side of the room which, by the use of special effects, appears to drift all alone in the midst of the black ocean of nothingness.

The minister of cultural affairs, twenty-five years before, had been the collaborator of one of the assassinated writers; he had passed at one time for a man of the left, but had soon followed the path of honors, of security; the clear and narrow path of betrayal. The minister of police, on the other hand, was nothing but a hooligan risen from the ranks; he did his job well, and his antecedents didn't matter.

Two different fates, two different functions which nevertheless coincided at this imprecise moment, melted together in the quiet of a tranquil little office. A few years later, in 1984 to be exact, there would be only one man, one ministry: the ministry of thought. Until a still later day, perhaps. . . . But that would take us too far afield, into another story, another book.

Let it be enough for us to keep that distant but still clear picture: that of two men face to face in an office, two men pinned to silence, two accomplices, two brothers.

To write, to write. . . . Whatever might be said of it by the most radical of the revolutionaries, always prompt to belabor the intellectuals, to write is already to act. To write justly is a minimal but indispensible part of just combat. It's a dialectical act, which opens the way to action.

The establishment had known it for a long time. Naturally, the first victims had been men of action, the revolutionary leaders: They were the most urgent cases. Thus Geismar, Krivine, Carrega had been taken out of circulation.

But that was not enough. There remained all those who by their words, their writings, their plays, their films, sowed uneasiness in men's minds. These too were dangerous in the long run: They could plant the germs of doubt; they could awaken people and make them think. Their elimination posed other problems. It was necessary to be prudent, not to be too hasty. So . . . an accident here, a "natural" death there. . . . No: that wasn't too hard, after all.

And the big silence settled down, and the big sleep. The accusing voices were dead; they had been silenced. Other voices, certainly, more secret, feebler, newer, were still murmuring. You can never completely kill intelligence or awareness. But would they be granted the time to grow?

And the most terrible thing was that all this took place without fuss, without insurrection, gently. A few conspicuous figures were still there, as distractions, but monumentalized, immobilized, neutralized long since, turned into national glories, turned into marble: marble-Aragon, marble-Mendès-France.

Le Canard Enchainé also remained, the symbol of a defunct freedom of thought, a plucked and muzzled duck. And the ultrasophisticated little reviews, drowned in their cultural ultraleftism, *Tel Quel, Cinéthique,* which no one ever read, which could do no harm, were still there as well—as Marx and Lenin, turned into articles of consumption, were still there in bookstore windows. But *La Cause du Peuple?* But *Charlie Hebdo?* But *Rouge?* But *Tous?* But *L'Idiot International?*

There was no more talk of slums, and accordingly they ceased to exist. There was no more mention of strikes, of arrests, and it was as if they were no more than a memory. People talked about sex, drugs, cars, popular culture, the moon.

One could sleep with both eyes shut.

"Where are you going?" asked Simone.

"Taking in my article," answered Jean-Pierre.

As he went down the hall toward the door he looked at himself in the oval mirror. But he didn't see anything special in his features or his expression.

It's easy to get used to your own face.

BY J. C. THOMPSON

The Right Man for
The Right Job

Guy Lucey had had a secretary of his own for only a month, and he still felt a secret pride every morning when she came into his unitized-panel office and asked, "What is the schedule for today, Mr. Lucey?"

It was true that Miss Halvorson was in her middle forties, totally humorless, and almost totally chinless; she had been dredged, so to speak, from the bottom of the secretarial pool. But, Guy told himself, Scale 8 was the first scale at Greater United Foods where a man got a secretary of his own, and you couldn't exactly specify a Jayne Mansfield type.

This morning, however, Miss Halvorson didn't ask her usual question. Instead, she handed Guy a sealed envelope and said, "Mr. Millikin's secretary asked me to give you this. You're to call Mr. Millikin as soon as you can to discuss it with him."

Guy set his cardboard coffee container down on the desk blotter.

" 'Personal and Confidential.' What's it all about, Miss Halvorson?"

"I have no idea, Mr. Lucey. Mr. Millikin's secretary asked. . . ."

"OK, OK. Thanks. I have some letters and reports, but they better wait until I take care of this. I'll holler when I'm ready."

"Yes, Mr. Lucey."

When she had gone Guy ripped open the envelope.

Mr. Millikin, Greater United's Vice-President in Charge of Personnel, didn't send many "Personal and Confidential" notes, Guy thought. And he particularly didn't send them to junior executives in the Market Research Department.

Guy unfolded the single sheet of paper:

PERSONAL AND CONFIDENTIAL
FROM: *S. V. Millikin, Vice-President, Personnel*
TO: *Guy Lucey, Assistant Statistician, Market Research Department, National Sales Division, General Office*

Dear Mr. Lucey:
An opportunity has arisen within the company which may interest you. Will you please call me soon so that we can set a time to discuss it.
This will probably involve your taking a series of aptitude tests; please arrange your schedule so that the next three or four days are as clear as possible.

SVM

Guy set the memo down on his desk, sipped his lukewarm coffee, and pondered. ". . . opportunity. . . ."? Hell's bells, I just got a raise out of the adding-machine bullpen to Scale 8. I hope they're not going to send me back out there. Guy put the coffee container carefully into his wastebasket so as not to splash out the dregs, picked up his "inside" telephone, and dialed "O."

"Mr. Millikin, please."

The appointment was for after lunch, so Guy ate alone. He didn't want to have even one drink before the meeting, and he didn't want to explain his abstinence to the fellows he usually ate with.

At two minutes to two, Guy got off the elevator at the seventeenth-floor "mahogany row" and announced himself to the receptionist.

Mr. Millikin had a folder on his desk, Guy's own personal file. He looked up and smiled at Guy, but did not rise or offer to shake hands.

"Afternoon, Lucey. Sit down. I appreciate your getting in touch with me so promptly. You're probably wondering what this is all about."

"Yes, sir, I am."

"Well, Lucey, I can't tell it *all* to you, but I'll try to hit the high spots. First, though, let's take a look at"—Millikin looked down at the folder—"where you've been, and where you think you're going, right?"

"Yes, sir, fine."

"Let's see. You're twenty-nine. Good school. Bus Ad major. Pretty fair grades. Married." Millikin looked up sharply. "Happily married, Lucey?"

"Yes, sir, I guess I am."

"No spats, no arguments?"

"Well. . . ."

"Never mind, it's not really important. Children?"

"Two lovely little girls. Six and four."

"Fine, fine. Now, then, you went from college to American Chemicals, in accounting. And two years later you joined us." He looked up again. "How do you feel about that decision now?"

"Well, fine. I think I have a good future here, sir."

"Yes. I've been talking with Tinkham, your immediate superior. He tells me that since your elevation to Scale Eight you've been applying yourself well—long hours, taking work home with you, and so on. Right?"

"I'm trying to do the best I can, Mr. Millikin. Yes. I *have* been working hard, sir."

"Good. That was our impression."

Millikin was silent for perhaps five seconds. He regarded Guy intently. Then he flipped the file shut, leaned back in his chair, and smiled warmly.

"Lucey, I think you have a good future here, too. I've been going over your aptitude tests—the ones you took when you joined the company, and before you went up to Scale Eight. They indicate a good, healthy amount of company orientation and other-directedness."

Guy looked puzzled.

"I'll put that in plainer language, Lucey. You're a good company man. Now, about these tests that you'll be taking.

We have about thirty thousand employees, including plant personnel all over the country. Here in the General Office there are over two thousand men, ranging from the chairman of the board down to the newest trainee. *My* job is to try to balance these two thousand men—in other words, to find the right men for the right jobs."

Millikin paused to light a cigarette, and Guy hastened to light one for himself.

Millikin continued. "And that's where these psychological tests come in, Lucey. They take out the guesswork. *My* judgment, just from talking with a man, certainly can't be one hundred percent accurate. After all," and Millikin smiled warmly again, ". . . you can't tell a book from its cover, can you?"

"No, sir, I guess not."

'What's your personal opinion about these tests, Lucey? Got any resistance to them?"

"Well, frankly, sir, I wonder just . . . what I mean is, I read *The Organization Man,* and I. . . ."

"Fine, fine, most interesting book. I'd say it might be a bit radical, personnel-wise, but *interesting.*"

"Yes, sir. I mean, I really think if the tests are valid, why I'm all for them. I don't mind them at all."

"Good. Because you have three days ahead that'll be full of tests."

Mr. Millikin got up, strolled to his window, and gazed out.

"Now, then, you're probably wondering why, so close on the heels of your last advancement in duties and pay, we are considering you for something else. As I said, I can't be completely explicit at this point, but I *can* tell you that this will be a special assignment. We need one man—just one, for the job."

He turned, looked at Guy.

"I'll be administering the tests personally"—Guy's eyebrows went up; usually Mr. Millikin assigned this work to one of his many assistants—"due to the extreme importance of this particular project. Do you have any questions?"

"Sir, I do, but I guess they'll wait. Until you can give me some more details, that is."

"Right. Well, then, Lucey, that's all for today. You've passed your first hurdle without even knowing it. This interview. I have my own personal criteria, and your answers, your attitude, your bearing—all these tell me, 'This might be the man.' Good day, Lucey. Please be in my conference room tomorrow morning at ten. We'll start the tests then."

On the commuting train that night, Guy sat at his regular table in the club car with three fellow Greater United men, Reg Paige, Steve Herman, and Joe Collyer. They worked in the same building, although in different departments, they rode the train together, and they lived in the same suburban development in New Jersey.

Guy related what had happened during the day.

"And you have no idea what kind of job Millikin has in mind?"

"Nope."

"But those goddamn tests, Guy," Steve Herman said. "In Public Relations we don't have to take them, and if we did, I think I'd quit. I think they stink."

Guy looked at Steve, who was a New Frontier Democrat and was considered the radical of their little group.

"Steve, I don't like 'em either. But like old Millikin says, he has to find the right man for the right job. And the tests are guideposts, so to speak."

"Guideposts, schmideposts."

"Guy's right, Steve," said Reg Paige. "They're scientifically valid."

"And what the hell," said Joe Collyer. "You can't fight city hall."

That night it took Guy a long time to get to sleep. There was something very strange about this, he thought. He knew that he worked hard and well; he also knew that he was not one of those industrial boy wonders. Finally, he slept, to dream from time to time of blank test forms floating beyond his reach—just far enough so that he could not read the questions. And then they were gone.

The next day the tests began. They were much like the many others he had taken from the time he began working for Greater United Foods. Multiple-choice questions, running mostly to things such as:

If you could be successful in one of the following vocations, which would you choose? (a) museum curator; (b) farmer; (c) salesman; (d) dancing teacher.
Or, *Which of the following do you prefer? (a) symphony music; (b) jazz music; (c) news broadcasts.*

The tests filled the first and second days completely, draining Guy of energy and patience. Millikin was secretive, but pleasant, like a dentist in the reception room. And the tests went on.

When Guy got up the third, last day, he was very tired.

At the breakfast table his wife said, "Honey, can you take a day off after this is over? Relax a little bit?"

"Don't know." Guy sipped his coffee, bit at a loose fragment of fingernail. "Frankly, this is driving me nuts. Not knowing, I mean. Maybe today. . . ."

"Daddy," the six-year-old said, and Guy smiled at her. "I like kindergarten. Can I have one of my new friends over for dinner?"

"Sure, honey."

"Can I have *two* over?"

"You talk to your mommy about that."

"I want to go to kindergarten, too," the four-year-old said.

"Guy, I do hope you can take some time and rest. You haven't been playing with the girls, reading to them. And they miss it."

Guy closed his eyes and tightened his lips. "Gwen, I said that I'd try. And I will, dear."

As Guy left the house, he hugged each of his pretty

daughters and kissed his wife. Then he kissed her again, hard. "I love you, Gwen. The strain'll be over soon. Wish me luck."

"Luck, Guy."

And he went out to the car, and on to the station, and in to New York.

Guy finished the last test shortly before lunch.

"Get a fast sandwich and be back here in the conference room by one," Mr. Millikin said as he took the test papers. "Then we'll have a final personal interview."

When Guy returned there were three other men waiting with Mr. Millikin.

"Mr. Lucey, this is Mr. Simpson, our Marketing V.P., and Mr. McQuinn, Executive Vice-President. And this is Dr. Burgundy, an industrial psychologist and consultant to Greater United."

Guy shook hands all around. He had never met any of the men before, although he had seen Mr. McQuinn and Mr. Simpson from time to time around the building. The other man, Dr. Burgundy, was a complete stranger. He was a large man, Guy noticed, with a curiously melancholy face.

"Now, then, Lucey, we have a few questions to ask you," Mr. Millikin said. "Please relax, talk freely, we're all on the same payroll here. . . ." Everyone chuckled, except Dr. Burgundy.

"First," said Mr. McQuinn, "you consider yourself a pretty hard worker, generally, don't you, Lucey? Take work home. . . ."

It was true. Almost every evening Guy took home an attaché case full of figures, trends, projections.

"I guess you could call me ambitious, Mr. McQuinn. I want to get ahead, to provide well for my family. And since I'm no genius, the best way to do it is to work hard, do my best. But I don't mind; I enjoy the work."

The four men nodded, exchanged glances. Dr. Burgundy made a note on a pocket pad and said, "Mr. Lucey, what are your ambitions here at Greater United? Do you want to be president of the company? Or what?"

Guy hesitated. "Well, I don't know. I know I'm not really brilliant, so I guess I'd never be president. Maybe manager of market research. I just haven't thought about it very much."

Dr. Burgundy turned to the others. "What we thought. Drive factor almost exactly median."

Mr. Simpson spoke. "Would you consider yourself *loyal* to Greater United?"

"Why, yes, sir. I'm loyal. I think it's a fine company."

Again the men exchanged glances and nodded.

Mr. Millikin said to Dr. Burgundy, "What do you think, Carl?"

"Just one more question." Dr. Burgundy regarded Guy with a peculiar intentness. "Is there any record in your family of mental illness?" He spoke very slowly, very precisely. "On either your mother's or your father's side, has anyone ever been in a mental institution or been hospitalized for depression or melancholia?"

Guy felt a chill of uneasiness. "Mental illness?" No one moved or spoke. "No, sir. All my folks were—just normal. Normal small-town folks, that's all."

"I see," said Dr. Burgundy. "I see."

"What do you think, Carl?" said Mr. Millikin.

Dr. Burgundy rose. "I think Mr. Lucey is our man. The tests indicate it, and as far as I'm concerned, our little talk here wraps it up."

The others stood.

Dr. Burgundy strode across the room. With astonishing swiftness, he drew a small blackjack from his coat pocket and in a continuous motion before Guy could move he swung it in an expert short sideward arc, to a point on Guy's head just above the left ear. Guy felt a hard crack of pain, the room swung crazily around him, and then blackness.

When Guy awoke, he was lying on the conference-room couch, and his first awareness, after swimming out of the throbbing headache, was of quiet conversation. He opened his eyes, and saw Mr. Millikin, Mr. Simpson, Mr. McQuinn, and Dr. Burgundy standing by the window.

He tried to move, but he seemed to be paralyzed. Only his head would respond, and it was with great effort that he could raise it an inch or so from the pillow on which it rested.

Guy tried to speak. It was a long, sighing moan.

The men turned from the window.

"He's awake," said Mr. Millikin.

"Can you hear us, Lucey?" asked Dr. Burgundy. "Can you speak?"

"Yes," Guy whispered.

"You've been given an injection," said Dr. Burgundy. "A simple curare derivative. You're paralyzed, partially, but if you try, you can talk a little."

The men sat down. Mr. McQuinn looked at his watch. "Let's get on with it. I have a meeting with the West Coast zone manager at three-thirty."

Mr. Millikin cleared his throat. "Lucey, as you may have gathered, you have been chosen for this rather—ah—special assignment."

He turned to Mr. McQuinn. "Jimmy, want to explain this from the point of view of the big picture?"

McQuinn was tamping tobacco into a pipe. "Certainly, Sam." He struck a match. "The easiest way to say it, Lucey," puff, puff, ". . . is that from time to time . . ." puff, puff, puff, ". . . it becomes necessary that . . ." he shook out the match deliberately, ". . . a man *die* for Greater United Foods." He sucked again on his pipe. *"Die for Greater United Foods,"* he repeated. "And you're the man, it turns out."

Guy felt his stomach slip and slide inside him. He strained to speak. "What. . . ?"

"Oh, it's nothing personal, Lucey. And we don't *like* to do it, for heaven's sake."

"Of course not, Guy," interrupted Simpson, with the look of an earnest fifth-grade teacher on his face. "But with management comes responsibility, you know. And we wouldn't be doing our jobs if we shirked ours."

"That's right," said McQuinn. "That's the whole point, you see. You have been chosen to die—as it happens, your death will appear to be a suicide—in order that others might live. Live more successfully and happily for Greater United, to be specific."

Guy gasped again. ". . . why?"

"Good question, Lucey," said Millikin briskly. "From time to time, as you must know, it's necessary for management to *motivate* our men in various ways. Sales contests, production quotas, you're familiar with all that. We try to keep you fellas pushing good and hard. But our studies *now* show that too many of you—especially you youngsters—are working *too* hard. Straining at the leash a little, carrying the worries of the world on your shoulders, so to speak."

"And it wouldn't do," said McQuinn, "for us to ask our men *not* to push, would it? That just wouldn't be good management. Carl? You got anything to add?"

Dr. Burgundy nodded. "There is also the future to consider, Lucey. The company men of your age and status grouping are eventually going to be running things around here from the managerial level on up. It is important that they reach those positions mentally and physically intact— without ulcers, without symptoms of chronic anxiety—in short, with healthy, well-balanced egos."

"Right," said Millikin. "So when it becomes necessary, we simply make it appear that *over*work has got in its licks. Let's see—the last two were simulated heart attacks, weren't they, Jim?" McQuinn nodded, puffing. "But once a year or so, a suicide really makes the men stop and think, slows them down. Actually *increases* productivity, strangely enough," he chuckled.

". . . but why me. . . ?" Guy whispered.

"The tests, Lucey. They indicated that you'd never be a really top dog around here. You'd be just middle or upper-middle management. Lots of young sprouts like you around; you just happened to be the most average of all."

Simpson smiled his warm salesman's smile. "One thing, Guy, don't feel hurt about this. It's happened before, and it'll happen again. We have to keep our men working hard—but not *too* hard. It's part of the free enterprise system, really part of the American Way."

Millikin said, "And your major medical, group insurance, pension fund—everything's in order. Your family'll be fine."

McQuinn cleared his throat, looked at his watch. "Gentlemen, my meeting. . . ."

They stood, and Millikin said, "Thanks, Lucey. I can't say 'luck,' I guess, but 'chin up,' fella, anyway."

And except for Dr. Burgundy they were gone, closing the door softly behind them.

Guy thrashed in panic. But his arms and legs only quivered.

"All traces of the injection will be gone in a few minutes," said Dr. Burgundy, "so we might as well get it over with."

He raised one of the large windows, and Guy felt the outside heat billow in through the cool air-conditioned room.

Then Dr. Burgundy lifted Guy easily, limp in his arms, walked to the window, and threw him out.

As Guy went out the window, and down, he caught a glimpse of the deserted inside courtyard seventeen floors below, saw fractionally two tiny garbage cans against the building wall, closed his eyes, felt the breathtaking rush of air. And then he crashed onto the cement.

That evening, Herman, Paige, and Collyer sat in silence in the club car, portraits of stunned disbelief. From time to time, one would shake his head, sip from a glass of beer.

Finally, Paige spoke. "I don't understand it. I just don't."

"Guy was such a levelheaded fellow," said Collyer.

Herman looked at the other two. "But don't forget. He was pushing himself."

"That's right. He'd just made Scale Eight. . . ."

". . . and was pressing damn hard for something even better."

Paige drained the beer from his glass and set it down hard.

"The hell with it. All the money in the world isn't worth that."

"We should take it easier," said Collyer. "We should *all* take it a little easier."

BY ROBERT A. HEINLEIN

The Year of the Jackpot

I

At first Potiphar Breen did not notice the girl who was undressing.

She was standing at a bus stop ten feet away. He was indoors, but that would not have kept him from noticing; he was seated in a drugstore booth adjacent to the bus stop; there was nothing between Potiphar and the young lady but plate glass and an occasional pedestrian.

Nevertheless he did not look up when she began to peel. Propped up in front of him was a Los Angeles *Times;* beside it, still unopened, were the *Herald-Express* and the *Daily News.* He was scanning the newspaper carefully, but the headline stories got only a passing glance.

He noted the maximum and minimum temperatures in Brownsville, Texas, and entered them in a neat black notebook. He did the same with the closing prices of three blue chips and two dogs on the New York Exchange, as well as the total number of shares.

He then began a rapid sifting of minor news stories, from time to time entering briefs of them in his little book.

The items he recorded seemed randomly unrelated— among them a publicity release in which Miss National Cottage Cheese Week announced that she intended to marry and have twelve children by a man who could prove that he had been a lifelong vegetarian, a circumstantial but wildly unlikely flying saucer report, and a call for prayers for rain throughout southern California.

Potiphar had just written down the names and addresses of three residents of Watts, California, who had been miraculously healed at a tent meeting of the God-is-All First Truth Brethren by the Reverend Dickie Bottomley, the eight-year-old evangelist, and was preparing to tackle the *Herald-Express*, when he glanced over his reading glasses and saw the amateur ecdysiast on the street corner outside.

He stood up, placed his glasses in their case, folded the newspapers and put them carefully in his right coat pocket, counted out the exact amount of his check, and added 15 percent. He then took his raincoat from a hook, placed it over his arm, and went outside.

By now the girl was practically down to the buff. It seemed to Potiphar Breen that she had quite a lot of buff; yet she had not pulled much of a house. The corner newsboy had stopped hawking his disasters and was grinning at her, and a mixed pair of transvestites who were apparently waiting for the bus had their eyes on her. None of the passersby stopped. They glanced at her, and then, with the self-conscious indifference to the unusual of the true southern Californian, they went on their various ways.

The transvestites were frankly staring. The male member of the team wore a frilly feminine blouse, but his skirt was a conservative Scottish kilt. His female companion wore a business suit and Homburg hat; she stared with lively interest.

As Breen approached, the girl hung a scrap of nylon on the bus stop bench, then reached for her shoes. A police officer, looking hot and unhappy, crossed with the lights and came up to them.

"OK," he said in a tired voice, "that'll be all, lady. Get them duds back on and clear out of here."

The female transvestite took a cigar out of her mouth. "Just what business is it of yours, officer?" she asked.

The cop turned to her. "Keep out of this!" He ran his eyes over her getup and that of her companion. "I ought to run both of you in, too."

The transvestite raised her eyebrows. "Arrest us for

being clothed, arrest her for not being. I think I'm going to like this." She turned to the girl, who was standing still and saying nothing, as if she were puzzled by what was going on. "I'm a lawyer, dear." She pulled a card from her vest pocket. "If this uniformed Neanderthal persists in annoying you, I'll be delighted to handle him."

The man in kilts said, "Grace! Please!"

She shook him off. "Quiet, Norman. This *is* our business." She went on to the policeman, "Well? Call the wagon. In the meantime my client will answer no questions."

The official looked unhappy enough to cry, and his face was getting dangerously red. Breen quietly stepped forward and slipped his raincoat around the shoulders of the girl.

She looked startled and spoke for the first time. "Uh—thanks." She pulled the coat about her, cape fashion.

The female attorney glanced at Breen then back to the cop. "Well, officer? Ready to arrest us?"

He shoved his face close to hers. "I ain't going to give you the satisfaction!" He sighed and added, "Thanks, Mr. Breen. You know this lady?"

"I'll take care of her. You can forget it, Kawonski."

"I sure hope so. If she's with you, I'll do just that. But get her out of here, Mr. Breen—please!"

The lawyer interrupted. "Just a moment. You're interfering with my client."

Kawonski said, "Shut up, you! You heard Mr. Breen—she's with him. Right, Mr. Breen?"

"Well—yes. I'm a friend. I'll take care of her."

The transvestite said suspiciously, "I didn't hear *her* say that."

Her companion said, "Grace! There's our bus."

"And I didn't hear her say she was your client," the cop retorted. "You look like a—" his words were drowned out by the bus brakes— "and besides that, if you don't climb on that bus and get off my territory, I'll . . . I'll. . . ."

"You'll what?"

"Grace! We'll miss our bus."

"Just a moment, Norman. Dear, is this man really a friend of yours? Are you with him?"

The girl looked uncertainly at Breen, then said in a low voice, "Uh, yes. He is. I am."

"Well. . . ." The lawyer's companion pulled at her arm. She shoved her card into Breen's hand and got on the bus. It pulled away.

Breen pocketed the card.

Kawonski wiped his forehead. "Why did you do it, lady?" he said peevishly.

The girl looked puzzled. "I—I don't know."

"You hear that, Mr. Breen? That's what they all say. And if you pull 'em in, there's six more the next day. The chief said—" He sighed. "The chief said—well, if I had arrested her like that female shyster wanted me to, I'd be out at a hundred and ninety-sixth and ploughed ground tomorrow morning, thinking about retirement. So get her out of here, will you?"

The girl said, "But—"

"No 'buts,' lady. Just be glad a real gentleman like Mr. Breen is willing to help you." He gathered up her clothes, handed them to her. When she reached for them, she again exposed an uncustomary amount of skin. Kawonski hastily gave the clothing to Breen instead, who crowded them into his coat pockets.

She let Breen lead her to where his car was parked, got in, and tucked the raincoat around her so that she was rather more dressed than a girl usually is. She looked at him.

She saw a medium-sized and undistinguished man who was slipping down the wrong side of thirty-five and looked older. His eyes had that mild and slightly naked look of the habitual spectacles-wearer who is not at the moment with glasses. His hair was gray at the temples and thin on top. His herringbone suit, black shoes, white shirt, and neat tie smacked more of the East than of California.

He saw a face which he classified as "pretty" and "wholesome" rather than "beautiful" and "glamorous." It was topped by a healthy mop of light brown hair. He set her age at twenty-five, give or take eighteen months.

He smiled gently, climbed in without speaking, and started his car.

He turned up Doheny Drive and east on Sunset. Near La Cienega, he slowed down. "Feeling better?"

"Uh, I guess so, Mr.—Breen?"

"Call me Potiphar. What's your name? Don't tell me if you don't want to."

"Me? I'm—I'm Meade Barstow."

"Thank you, Meade. Where do you want to go? Home?"

"I suppose so. Oh, my, no. I can't go home like *this*." She clutched the coat tightly to her.

"Parents?"

"No. My landlady. She'd be shocked to death."

"Where, then?"

She thought. "Maybe we could stop at a filling station, and I could sneak into the ladies' room."

"Maybe. See here, Meade—my house is six blocks from here and has a garage entrance. You could get inside without being seen."

She stared. "You don't *look* like a wolf!"

"Oh, but I am! The worst sort." He whistled and gnashed his teeth. "See? But Wednesday is my day off."

She looked at him and dimpled. "Oh, well! I'd rather wrestle with you than with Mrs. Megeath. Let's go."

He turned up into the hills. His bachelor diggings were one of the many little frame houses clinging like fungus to the brown slopes of the Santa Monica Mountains. The garage was notched into this hill; the house sat on it.

He drove in, cut the ignition, and led her up a teetery inside stairway into the living room.

"In there," he said, pointing. "Help yourself." He pulled her clothes out of his coat pockets and handed them to her.

She blushed and took them, disappeared into his bedroom. He heard her turn the key in the lock. He settled down in his easy chair, took out his notebook, and started with the *Herald-Express*.

He was finishing the *Daily News* and had added several notes to his collection when she came out. Her hair was neatly rolled; her face was restored; she had brushed most of the wrinkles out of her skirt. Her sweater was neither too tight nor deep cut, but it was pleasantly filled. She reminded him of well water and farm breakfasts.

He took his raincoat from her, hung it up, and said, "Sit down, Meade."

She said uncertainly, "I had better go."

"If you must, but I had hoped to talk with you."

"Well—" She sat down on the edge of his couch and looked around. The room was small, but as neat as his necktie and as clean as his collar. The fireplace was swept; the floor was bare and polished. Books crowded bookshelves in every possible space. One corner was filled by an elderly flat-top desk; the papers on it were neatly in order. Near it, on its own stand, was a small electric calculator. To her right, french windows gave out on a tiny porch over the garage. Beyond it she could see the sprawling city, where a few neon signs were already blinking.

She sat back a little. "This is a nice room—Potiphar. It looks like you."

"I take that as a compliment. Thank you." She did not answer; he went on, "Would you like a drink?"

"Oh, would I!" She shivered. "I guess I've got the jitters."

He stood up. "Not surprising. What'll it be?"

She took Scotch and water, no ice; he was a Bourbon-and-gingerale man. She soaked up half her highball in silence, then put it down, squared her shoulders, and said, "Potiphar?"

"Yes, Meade?"

"Look, if you brought me here to make a pass, I wish you'd go ahead and make it. It won't do you a bit of good, but it makes me nervous to wait."

He said nothing and did not change his expression.

She went on uneasily, "Not that I'd blame you for trying—under the circumstances. And I *am* grateful. But . . . well, it's just that I don't—"

He came over and took both her hands. "I haven't the slightest thought of making a pass at you. Nor need you feel grateful. I butted in because I was interested in your case."

"My *case?* Are you a doctor? A psychiatrist?"

He shook his head. "I'm a mathematician. A statistician, to be precise."

"Huh? I don't get it."

"Don't worry about it. But I would like to ask some questions. May I?"

"Oh, sure! Of course! I owe you that much—and then some."

"You owe me nothing. Want your drink sweetened?"

She gulped the balance and handed him her glass, then followed him out into the kitchen. He did an exact job of measuring and gave it back.

"Now tell me why you took your clothes off," he said.

She frowned. "I don't know. I *don't* know. I don't *know*. I guess I just went crazy." She added, round-eyed, "But I don't feel crazy. Could I go off my rocker and not know it?"

"You're not crazy . . . not more so than the rest of us," he amended. "Tell me, where did you see someone else do this?"

"Huh? I never have."

"Where did you read about it?"

"But I haven't. Wait a minute—those people up in Canada. Dooka-somethings."

"Doukhobors. That's all? No bareskin swimming parties? No strip poker?"

She shook her head. "No. You may not believe it, but I was the kind of a little girl who undressed under her nightie." She colored and added, "I still do—unless I remember to tell myself it's silly."

"I believe it. No news stories?"

"No. Yes, there was! About two weeks ago, I think it was. Some girl in a theater—in the audience, I mean. But I thought it was just publicity. You know the stunts they pull here."

He shook his head. "It wasn't. February third, the Grand Theater, Mrs. Alvin Copley. Charges dismissed."

"How did *you* know?"

"Excuse me." He went to his desk, dialed the City

News Bureau. "Alf? This is Pot Breen. They still sitting on that story? . . . Yes, the Gypsy Rose file. Any new ones today?" He waited. Meade thought that she could make out swearing. "Take it easy, Alf—this hot weather can't last forever. Nine, eh? Well, add another—Santa Monica Boulevard, late this afternoon. No arrest." He added, "Nope, nobody got her name. A middle-aged woman with a cast in one eye. I happened to see it . . . who, me? Why would I want to get mixed up? But it's rounding into a very, very interesting picture."

He put the phone down.

Meade said, "Cast in one eye, indeed!"

"Shall I call him back and give him your name?"

"Oh, no!"

"Very well. Now, Meade, we seemed to have located the point of contagion in your case—Mrs. Copley. What I'd like to know next is how you felt, what you were thinking about, when you did it."

She was frowning intently. "Wait a minute, Potiphar. Do I understand that *nine other* girls have pulled the stunt I pulled?"

"Oh, no. Nine others *today*. You are—" he paused briefly—"the three hundred and nineteenth case in Los Angeles County since the first of the year. I don't have figures on the rest of the country, but the suggestion to clamp down on the stories came from the eastern news services when the papers here put our first cases on the wire. That proves that it's a problem elsewhere, too."

"You mean that women all over the country are peeling off their clothes in public? Why, how shocking!"

He said nothing. She blushed again and insisted, "Well, it *is* shocking, even if it was me this time."

"No, Meade. One case is shocking; over three hundred makes it scientifically interesting. That's why I want to know how it felt. Tell me about it."

"But—all right, I'll try. I told you I don't know why I did it; I still don't. I—"

"You remember it?"

"Oh, yes! I remember getting up off the bench and

pulling up my sweater. I remember unzipping my skirt. I remember thinking I would have to hurry because I could see my bus stopped two blocks down the street. I remember how *good* it felt when I finally——" She paused and looked puzzled. "But I still don't know why."

"What were you thinking about just before you stood up?"

"I don't remember."

"Visualize the street. What was passing by? Where were your hands? Were your legs crossed or uncrossed? Was there anybody near you? What were you thinking about?"

"Nobody was on the bench with me. I had my hands in my lap. Those characters in the mixed-up clothes were standing nearby, but I wasn't paying attention. I wasn't thinking much except that my feet hurt, and I wanted to get home—and how unbearably hot and sultry the weather was. Then——" her eyes became distant—"suddenly I knew what I had to do, and it was very urgent that I do it. So I stood up and I—and I——" Her voice became shrill.

"Take it easy!" he said sharply. "Don't do it again."

"Huh? Why, Mr. Breen! I wouldn't do anything like that."

"Of course not. Then what happened after you undressed?"

"Why, you put your raincoat around me, and you know the rest." She faced him. "Say, Potiphar, what were you doing with a raincoat? It hasn't rained in weeks. This is the driest, hottest rainy season in years."

"In sixty-eight years, to be exact."

"Sixty——"

"I carry a raincoat anyhow. Just a notion of mine, but I feel that when it does rain, it's going to rain awfully hard." He added, "Forty days and forty nights, maybe."

She decided that he was being humorous and laughed.

He went on, "Can you remember how you got the idea of undressing?"

She swirled her glass and thought. "I simply don't know."

He nodded. "That's what I expected."

"I don't understand—unless you think I'm crazy. Do you?"

"No. I think you had to do it and could not help it and don't know why and can't know why."

"But *you* know." She said it accusingly.

"Maybe. At least I have some figures. Ever take any interest in statistics, Meade?"

She shook her head. "Figures confuse me. Never mind statistics—*I want to know why I did what I did!*"

He looked at her very soberly. "I think we're lemmings, Meade."

She looked puzzled, then horrified. "You mean those little furry mouselike creatures? The ones that—"

"Yes. The ones that periodically make a death migration, until millions, hundreds of millions of them drown themselves in the sea. Ask a lemming why he does it. If you could get him to slow up his rush toward death, even money says he would rationalize his answer as well as any college graduate. But he does it because he has to—and so do we."

"That's a horrid idea, Potiphar."

"Maybe. Come here, Meade. I'll show you figures that confuse me too." He went to his desk and opened a drawer, took out a packet of cards. "Here's one. Two weeks ago, a man sues an entire state legislature for alienation of his wife's affection—and the judge lets the suit be tried. Or this one—a patent application for a device to lay the globe over on its side and warm up the arctic regions. Patent denied, but the inventor took in over three hundred thousand dollars in down payments on North Pole real estate before the postal authorities stepped in. Now he's fighting the case, and it looks as if he might win. And here—prominent bishop proposes applied courses in the so-called facts of life in high schools."

He put the card away hastily. "Here's a dilly—a bill introduced in the Alabama lower house to repeal the laws of atomic energy. Not the present statutes, but the natural laws concerning nuclear physics; the wording makes that plain." He shrugged. "How silly can you get?"

"They're crazy."

"No, Meade. One like that might be crazy; a lot of them becomes a lemming death march. No, don't object— I've plotted them on a curve. The last time we had anything like this was the so-called Era of Wonderful Nonsense. But this one is much worse." He delved into a lower drawer, hauled out a graph. "The amplitude is more than twice as great, and we haven't reached peak. What the peak will be, I don't dare guess—three separate rhythms, reinforcing."

She peered at the curves. "You mean that the lad with the arctic real estate deal is somewhere on this line?"

"He adds to it. And back here on the last crest are the flagpole sitters and the goldfish swallowers and the Ponzi hoax and the marathon dancers and the man who pushed a peanut up Pikes Peak with his nose. You're on the new crest—or you will be when I add you in."

She made a face. "I don't like it."

"Neither do I. But it's as clear as a bank statement. This year the human race is letting down its hair, flipping its lip with a finger, and saying, *'Wubba, wubba, wubba.'* "

She shivered. "Do you suppose I could have another drink? Then I'll go."

"I have a better idea. I owe you a dinner for answering questions. Pick a place, and we'll have a cocktail before."

She chewed her lip. "You don't owe me anything. And I don't feel up to facing a restaurant crowd. I might—I might—"

"No, you wouldn't," he said sharply. "It doesn't hit twice."

"You're sure? Anyhow, I don't want to face a crowd." She glanced at his kitchen door. "Have you anything to eat in there? I can cook."

"Um, breakfast things. And there's a pound of ground top round in the freezer compartment and some rolls. I sometimes make hamburgers when I don't want to go out."

She headed for the kitchen. "Drunk or sober, fully dressed or—or naked, I can cook. You'll see."

He did see. Open-faced sandwiches with the meat married to toasted buns and the flavor garnished rather than suppressed by scraped Bermuda onion and thin-sliced dill, a salad made from things she had scrounged out of his refrigerator, potatoes crisp but not vulcanized. They ate it on the tiny balcony, sopping it down with cold beer.

He sighed and wiped his mouth. "Yes, Meade, you can cook."

"Some day I'll arrive with proper materials and pay you back. Then I'll prove it."

"You've already proved it. Nevertheless, I accept. But I tell you three times—which makes it true, of course—that you owe me nothing."

"No? If you hadn't been a Boy Scout, I'd be in jail."

Breen shook his head. "The police have orders to keep it quiet at all costs—to keep it from growing. You saw that. And, my dear, you weren't a person to me at the time. I didn't even see your face."

"You saw plenty else!"

"Truthfully, I didn't look. You were just a—a statistic."

She toyed with her knife and said, slowly, "I'm not sure, but I think I've just been insulted. In all the twenty-five years that I've fought men off, more or less successfully, I've been called a lot of names—but a 'statistic'? Why, I ought to take your slide rule and beat you to death with it."

"My dear young lady—"

"I'm not a lady, that's for sure. But I'm *not* a statistic, either."

"My dear Meade, then. I wanted to tell you, before you did anything hasty, that in college I wrestled varsity middleweight."

She grinned and dimpled. "That's more the talk a girl likes to hear. I was beginning to be afraid you had been assembled in an adding-machine factory. Potty, you're really a dear."

"If that is a diminutive of my given name, I like it. But if it refers to my waistline, I definitely resent it."

She reached across and patted his stomach. "I like your

waistline; lean and hungry men are difficult. If I were cooking for you regularly, I'd really pad it."

"Is that a proposal?"

"Let it lie; let it lie. Potty, do you really think the whole country is losing its buttons?"

He sobered at once. "It's worse than that."

"Huh?"

"Come inside. I'll show you."

They gathered up dishes and dumped them in the sink, Breen talking all the while.

"As a kid, I was fascinated by numbers. Numbers are pretty things, and they combine in such interesting configurations. I took my degree in math, of course, and got a job as a junior actuary with Midwestern Mutual—the insurance outfit. That was fun. No way on earth to tell when a particular man is going to die, but an absolute certainty that so many men of a certain age group would die before a certain date. The curves were so lovely—and they always worked out. Always. You didn't have to know *why;* you could predict with dead certainty and never know why. The equations worked; the curves were right.

"I was interested in astronomy too; it was the one science where individual figures worked out neatly, completely, and accurately, down to the last decimal point that the instruments were good for. Compared with astronomy, the other sciences were mere carpentry and kitchen chemistry.

"I found there were nooks and crannies in astronomy where individual numbers won't do, where you have to go over to statistics, and I became even more interested. I joined the Variable Star Association, and I might have gone into astronomy professionally, instead of what I'm in now—business consultation—if I hadn't gotten interested in something else."

" 'Business consultation?' " repeated Meade. "Income-tax work?"

"Oh, no. That's too elementary. I'm the numbers boy for a firm of industrial engineers. I can tell a rancher exactly how many of his Hereford bull calves will be sterile. Or I can tell a motion picture producer how much rain insurance to carry on location. Or maybe how big a company in a particular line must be to carry its own risk in industrial accidents. And I'm right. I'm always right."

"Wait a minute. Seems to me a big company would *have* to have insurance."

"Contrariwise. A really big corporation begins to resemble a statistical universe."

"Huh?"

"Never mind. I got interested in something else—cycles. Cycles are everything, Meade. And everywhere. The tides. The seasons. Wars. Love. Everybody knows that in the spring the young man's fancy lightly turns to what the girls never stopped thinking about, but did you know that it runs in an eighteen-year-plus cycle as well? And that a girl born at the wrong swing of the curve doesn't stand nearly as good a chance as her older or younger sister?"

"Is *that* why I'm still a doddering old maid?"

"You're twenty-five?" He pondered. "Maybe, but your chances are improving again; the curve is swinging up. Anyhow, remember you are just one statistic; the curve applies to the group. Some girls get married every year."

"Don't call me a statistic," she repeated firmly.

"Sorry. And marriages match up with acreage planted to wheat, with wheat cresting ahead. You could almost say that planting wheat makes people get married."

"Sounds silly."

"It *is* silly. The whole notion of cause-and-effect is probably superstition. But the same cycle shows a peak in house-building right after a peak in marriages."

"Now that makes sense."

"Does it? How many newlyweds do you know who can afford to build a house? You might as well blame it on wheat acreage. We don't know *why;* it just *is.*"

"Sunspots, maybe?"

"You can correlate sunspots with stock prices or Columbia River salmon or women's skirts. And you are just as much justified in blaming short skirts for sunspots as you are in blaming sunspots for salmon. We don't know. But the curves go on just the same."

"But there has to be some *reason* behind it."

"Does there? That's mere assumption. A fact has no 'why.' There it stands, self-demonstrating. Why did you take your clothes off today?"

She frowned. "That's not fair."

"Maybe not. But I want to show you why I'm worried."

He went into the bedroom, came out with a large roll of tracing paper.

"We'll spread it on the floor. Here they are, all of them. The fifty-four-year cycle—see the Civil War there? See how it matches in? The eighteen-and-one-third-year cycle, the nine-plus cycle, the forty-one-month shorty, the three rhythms of sunspots—everything, all combined in one grand chart. Mississippi River floods, fur catches in Canada, stock market prices, marriages, epidemics, freight-car loadings, bank clearings, locust plagues, divorces, tree growth, wars, rainfall, earth magnetism, building construction, patents applied for, murders—you name it; I've got it there."

She stared at the bewildering array of wavy lines. "But, Potty, what does it mean?"

"It means that these things all happen, in regular rhythm, whether we like it or not. It means that when skirts are due to go up, all the stylists in Paris can't make 'em go down. It means that when prices are going down, all the controls and supports and government planning can't make 'em go up." He pointed to a curve. "Take a look at the grocery ads. Then turn to the financial page and read how the Big Brains try to double-talk their way out of it. It means that when an epidemic is due, it happens, despite all the public health efforts. It means we're lemmings."

She pulled her lip. "I don't like it. 'I am the master of my fate,' and so forth. I've got free will, Potty. I know I have—I can feel it."

"I imagine every little neutron in an atom bomb feels the same way. He can go *spung!* or he can sit still, just as he pleases. But statistical mechanics work out all the same, and the bomb goes off—which is what I'm leading up to. See anything odd there, Meade?"

She studied the chart, trying not to let the curving lines confuse her.

"They sort of bunch up over at the right end."

"You're dern tootin' they do! See that dotted vertical line? That's right now—and things are bad enough. But take a look at that solid vertical; that's about six months from now—and that's when we get it. Look at the cycles —the long ones, the short ones, all of them. Every single last one of them reaches either a trough or a crest exactly on—or almost on—that line."

"That's bad?"

"What do you think? Three of the big ones troughed back in nineteen-twenty-nine and the depression almost ruined us . . . even with the big fifty-four-year cycle supporting things. Now we've got the big one troughing—and the few crests are not things that help. I mean to say, tent caterpillars and influenza don't do us any good. Meade, if statistics mean anything, this tired old planet hasn't seen a trend like this since Eve went into the apple business. I'm scared."

She searched his face. "Potty, you're not simply having fun with me? You know I can't check up on you."

"I wish to heaven I were. No, Meade, I can't fool about numbers; I wouldn't know how. This is it—the Year of the Jackpot."

Meade was very silent as he drove her home. When they approached West Los Angeles she said, "Potty?"

"Yes, Meade?"

"What do we *do* about it?"

"What do you do about a hurricane? You pull in your ears. What can you do about an atom bomb? You try to outguess it, not be there when it goes off. What else can you do?"

"Oh." She was silent for a few moments, then added, "Potty, will you tell me which way to jump?"

"Huh? Oh, sure! If I can figure it out."

He took her to her door, turned to go.

She said, "Potty!"

He faced her. "Yes, Meade?"

She grabbed his head, shook it—then kissed him fiercely on the mouth. "There, is that just a statistic?"

"Uh, no."

"It had better not be," she said dangerously. "Potty, I think I'm going to have to change your curve."

II

RUSSIANS REJECT UN NOTE

MISSOURI FLOOD DAMAGE EXCEEDS RECORD

MISSISSIPPI MESSIAH DEFIES COURT

NUDIST CONVENTION STORMS BAILEY'S BEACH

BRITISH-IRAN TALKS STILL DEADLOCKED

FASTER-THAN-LIGHT WEAPON PROMISED

TYPHOON DOUBLING BACK ON MANILA

MARRIAGE SOLEMNIZED ON FLOOR OF HUDSON

New York, 13 July—In a specially constructed diving suit built for two, Merydith Smithe, cafe society headline girl, and Prince Augie Schleswieg of New York and the Riviera were united today by Bishop Dalton in a service televised with the aid of the Navy's ultra-new—

As the Year of the Jackpot progressed, Breen took melancholy pleasure in adding to the data which proved that the curve was sagging as predicted. The undeclared world war continued its bloody, blundering way at half a dozen spots around a tortured globe. Breen did not chart it; the headlines were there for anyone to read. He concentrated on the odd facts in the other pages of the papers, facts which, taken singly, meant nothing, but taken together showed a disastrous trend.

He listed stock market prices, rainfall, wheat futures, but the "silly season" items were what fascinated him. To be sure, some humans were always doing silly things—but at what point had prime damfoolishness become commonplace? When, for example, had the zombielike professional models become accepted ideals of American womanhood? What were the gradations between National Cancer Week and National Athlete's Foot Week? On what day had the American people finally taken leave of horse sense?

Take transvestism. Male-and-female dress customs were arbitrary, but they had seemed to be deeply rooted in the culture. When did the breakdown start? With Marlene Dietrich's tailored suits? By the late nineteen-forties, there was no "male" article of clothing that a woman could not wear in public—but when had men started to slip over the line? Should he count the psychological cripples who had made the word "drag" a byword in Greenwich Village and Hollywood long before this outbreak? Or were they "wild shots" not belonging on the curve? Did it start with some unknown normal man attending a masquerade and there discovering that skirts actually were more comfortable and practical than trousers? Or had it started with the resurgence of Scottish nationalism reflected in the wearing of kilts by many Scottish-Americans?

Ask a lemming to state his motives! The outcome was in front of him, a news story. Transvestism by draft dodgers had at last resulted in a mass arrest in Chicago which was to have ended in a giant joint trial—only to have the deputy prosecutor show up in a pinafore and defy the judge to submit to an examination to determine the judge's true sex. The judge suffered a stroke and died, and the trial was postponed—postponed forever, in Breen's opinion; he doubted that this particular blue law would ever again be enforced.

Or the laws about indecent exposure, for that matter. The attempt to limit the Gypsy Rose syndrome by ignoring it had taken the starch out of enforcement. Now here was a report about the All Souls Community Church of Springfield; the pastor had reinstituted ceremonial nudity. Probably the first time this thousand years, Breen thought, aside from some screwball cults in Los Angeles. The reverend gentleman claimed that the ceremony was identical with the "dance of the high priestess" in the ancient temple of Karnak.

Could be, but Breen had private information that the "priestess" had been working the burlesque and nightclub circuit before her present engagement. In any case, the holy leader was packing them in and had not been arrested.

Two weeks later a hundred and nine churches in thirty-three states offered equivalent attractions. Breen entered them on his curves.

This queasy oddity seemed to him to have no relation to the startling rise in the dissident evangelical cults throughout the country. These churches were sincere, earnest, and poor—but growing, ever since the war. Now they were multiplying like yeast.

It seemed a statistical cinch that the United States was about to become godstruck again. He correlated it with transcendentalism and the trek of the Latter Day Saints. Hmm, yes, it fitted. And the curve was pushing toward a crest.

Billions in war bonds were now falling due; wartime marriages were reflected in the swollen peak of the Los Angeles school population. The Colorado River was at a record low, and the towers in Lake Mead stood high out of the water. But the Angelenos committed communal suicide by watering lawns as usual. The Metropolitan Water District commissioners tried to stop it. It fell between the stools of the police powers of fifty "sovereign" cities. The taps remained open, trickling away the life blood of the desert paradise.

The four regular party conventions—Dixiecrats, Regular Republicans, the Regular Regular Republicans, and the Democrats—attracted scant attention, because the Know-Nothings had not yet met. The fact that the "American Rally," as the Know-Nothings preferred to be called, claimed not to be a party but an educational society did not detract from their strength. But what was their strength? Their beginnings had been so obscure that Breen had had to go back and dig into the files; yet he had been approached twice this very week to join them, right inside his own office—once by his boss, once by the janitor.

He hadn't been able to chart the Know-Nothings. They gave him chills in his spine. He kept column-inches on them, found that their publicity was shrinking while their numbers were obviously zooming.

Krakatoa blew up on July 18th. It provided the first important transpacific TV-cast. Its effect on sunsets, on solar constant, on mean temperature, and on rainfall would not be felt until later in the year.

The San Andreas fault, its stresses unrelieved since the Long Beach disaster of 1933, continued to build up imbalance—an unhealed wound running the full length of the West Coast.

Pelee and Etna erupted. Mauna Loa was still quiet.

Flying saucers seemed to be landing daily in every state. Nobody had exhibited one on the ground—or had the Department of Defense sat on them? Breen was unsatisfied with the off-the-record reports he had been able to get; the alcoholic content of some of them had been high. But the sea serpent on Ventura Beach was real; he had seen it. The troglodyte in Tennessee he was not in a position to verify.

Thirty-one domestic air crashes the last week in July . . . was it sabotage or was it a sagging curve on a chart? And that neopolio epidemic that skipped from Seattle to New York? Time for a big epidemic? Breen's chart said it was. But how about bacteriological warfare? Could a chart *know* that a Slav biochemist would perfect an efficient virus-and-vector at the right time?

Nonsense!

But the curves, if they meant anything at all, included "free will"; they averaged in all the individual "wills" of a statistical universe—and came out as a smooth function. Every morning, three million "free wills" flowed toward the center of the New York megapolis; every evening, they flowed out again—all by "free will" and on a smooth and predictable curve.

Ask a lemming! Ask *all* the lemmings, dead and alive. Let them take a vote on it!

Breen tossed his notebook aside and phoned Meade. "Is this my favorite statistic?"

"Potty! I was thinking about you."

"Naturally. This is your night off."

"Yes, but another reason, too. Potiphar, have you ever taken a look at the Great Pyramid?"

"I haven't even been to Niagara Falls. I'm looking for a rich woman, so I can travel."

"I'll let you know when I get my first million, but—"

"That's the first time you've proposed to me this week."

"Shut up. Have you ever looked into the prophecies they found inside the pyramid?"

"Look, Meade, that's in the same class with astrology—strictly for the squirrels. Grow up."

"Yes, of course. But, Potty, I thought you were interested in anything odd. This is odd."

"Oh. Sorry. If it's 'silly season' stuff, let's see it."

"All right. Am I cooking for you tonight?"

"It's Wednesday, isn't it?"

"How soon will you get here?"

He glanced at his watch. "Pick you up in eleven minutes." He felt his whiskers. "No, twelve and a half."

"I'll be ready. Mrs. Megeath says these regular dates mean that you're going to marry me."

"Pay no attention to her. She's just a statistic, and I'm a wild datum."

"Oh, well, I've got two hundred and forty-seven dollars toward that million. 'By."

Meade's prize to show him was the usual Rosicrucian come-on, elaborately printed, and including a photograph (retouched, he was sure) of the much disputed line on the corridor wall which was alleged to prophesy, by its various discontinuities, the entire future. This one had an unusual time scale, but the major events were all marked on it—

the fall of Rome, the Norman invasion, the discovery of America, Napoleon, the world wars.

What made it interesting was that it suddenly stopped—now.

"What about it, Potty?"

"I guess the stonecutter got tired. Or got fired. Or they hired a new head priest with new ideas." He tucked it into his desk. "Thanks. I'll think about how to list it."

But he got it out again, applied dividers and a magnifying glass.

"It says here," he announced, "that the end comes late in August—unless that's a fly speck."

"Morning or afternoon? I have to know how to dress."

"Shoes will be worn. All God's chilluns got shoes." He put it away.

She was silent for a moment, then said, "Potty, isn't it about time to jump?"

"Huh? Girl, don't let *that* thing affect you! That's 'silly season' stuff."

"Yes. But take a look at *your* chart."

Nevertheless, he took the next afternoon off, spent it in the reference room of the main library, confirmed his opinion of soothsayers. Nostradamus was pretentiously silly; Mother Shippey was worse. In any of them you could find whatever you looked for.

He did find one item in Nostradamus that he liked: "The Oriental shall come forth from his seat . . . he shall pass through the sky, through the waters and the snow, and he shall strike each one with his weapon."

That sounded like what the Department of Defense expected the commies to try to do to the Western Allies.

But it was also a description of every invasion that had come out of the "heartland" in the memory of mankind. Nuts!

When he got home he found himself taking down his father's Bible and turning to Revelations. He could not find anything he could understand, but he got fascinated by the recurring use of precise numbers. Presently he thumbed through the Book at random; his eye lit on: "Boast not thyself of tomorrow; for thou knowest not what a day may bring forth." He put the Book away, feeling humbled but not cheered.

The rains started the next morning.

The master plumbers elected Miss Star Morning "Miss Sanitary Engineering" on the same day that the morticians designated her as "The Body I Would Like Best to Prepare," and her option was dropped by Fragrant Features.

Congress voted $1.37 to compensate Thomas Jefferson Meeks for losses incurred while an emergency postman for the Christmas rush of 1936, approved the appointment of five lieutenant generals and one ambassador, and adjourned in less than eight minutes.

The fire extinguishers in a midwest orphange turned out to be filled with nothing but air.

The chancellor of the leading football institution sponsored a fund to send peace messages and vitamins to the Politburo.

The stock market slumped nineteen points, and the tickers ran two hours late.

Wichita, Kansas, remained flooded while Phoenix, Arizona, cut off drinking water to areas outside city limits.

And Potiphar Breen found that he had left his raincoat at Meade Barstow's rooming house.

He phoned her landlady, but Mrs. Megeath turned him over to Meade.

"What are you doing home on a Friday?" he demanded.

"The theater manager laid me off. Now you'll have to marry me."

"You can't afford me. Meade—seriously, baby, what happened?"

"I was ready to leave the dump anyway. For the last six weeks the popcorn machine has been carrying the place. Today I sat through *The Lana Turner Story* twice. Nothing to do."

"I'll be along."

"Eleven minutes?"

"It's raining. Twenty—with luck."

It was more nearly sixty. Santa Monica Boulevard was a navigable stream; Sunset Boulevard was a subway jam. When he tried to ford the streams leading to Mrs. Megeath's house, he found that changing tires with the wheel wedged against a storm drain presented problems.

"Potty!" she exclaimed when he squished in. "You look like a drowned rat."

He found himself suddenly wrapped in a blanket robe belonging to the late Mr. Megeath and sipping hot cocoa while Mrs. Megeath dried his clothing in the kitchen.

"Meade, I'm 'at liberty' too."

"Huh? You quit your job?"

"Not exactly. Old Man Wiley and I have been having differences of opinion about my answers for months—too much 'Jackpot factor' in the figures I give him to turn over to clients. Not that I call it that, but he has felt that I was unduly pessimistic."

"But you were right!"

"Since when has being right endeared a man to his boss? But that wasn't why he fired me; it was just the excuse. He wants a man willing to back up the Know-Nothing program with scientific double-talk, and I wouldn't join." He went to the window. "It's raining harder."

"But the Know-Nothings haven't got any program."

"I know that."

"Potty, you should have joined. It doesn't mean anything. I joined three months ago."

"The hell you did!"

She shrugged. "You pay your dollar, and you turn up for two meetings, and they leave you alone. It kept my job for another three months. What of it?"

"Well, I'm sorry you did it; that's all. Forget it. Meade, the water is over the curbs out there."

"You had better stay here overnight."

"Mmm . . . I don't like to leave *Entropy* parked out in this stuff all night. Meade?"

"Yes, Potty?"

"We're both out of jobs. How would you like to duck north into the Mojave and find a dry spot?"

"I'd love it. But look, Potty, is this a proposal or just a proposition?"

"Don't pull that 'either-or' stuff on me. It's just a suggestion for a vacation. Do you want to take a chaperone?"

"No."

"Then pack a bag."

"Right away. But pack a bag *how?* Are you trying to tell me it's *time to jump?*"

He faced her, then looked back at the window.

"I don't know," he said slowly, "but this rain might go on quite a while. Don't take anything you don't have to have—but don't leave anything behind you can't get along without."

He repossessed his clothing from Mrs. Megeath while Meade was upstairs. She came down dressed in slacks and carrying two large bags; under one arm was a battered and rakish teddy bear.

"This is Winnie," she said.

"Winnie the Pooh?"

"No, Winnie Churchill. When I feel bad, he promises me blood, sweat, and tears; then I feel better. You did say to bring anything I couldn't do without, didn't you?" She looked at him anxiously.

"Right."

He took the bags. Mrs. Megeath had seemed satisfied with his explanation that they were going to visit his (mythical) aunt in Bakersfield before looking for jobs. Nevertheless, she embarrassed him by kissing him goodbye and telling him to "take care of my little girl."

Santa Monica Boulevard was blocked off from use. While stalled in traffic in Beverly Hills, he fiddled with the car radio, getting squawks and crackling noises, then finally one station nearby: "—in effect," a harsh, high, staccato voice was saying, "the Kremlin has given us till sundown to get out of town. This is your New York reporter, who thinks that in days like these every American must personally keep his powder dry. And now for a word from—"

Breen switched it off and glanced at her face. "Don't worry," he said. "They've been talking that way for years."

"You think they are bluffing?"

"I didn't say that. I said, 'Don't worry.' "

But his own packing, with her help, was clearly on a "survival kit" basis—canned goods, all his warm clothing, a sporting rifle he had not fired in over two years, a first-aid kit, and the contents of his medicine chest. He dumped the stuff from his desk into a carton, shoved it into the back seat along with cans and books and coats, and covered the plunder with all the blankets in the house. They went back up the rickety stairs for a last check.

"Potty, where's your chart?"

"Rolled up on the back seat shelf. I guess that's all— hey, wait a minute!" He went to a shelf over his desk and began taking down small, sober-looking magazines. "I dern near left behind my file of *The Western Astronomer* and the *Proceedings of the Variable Star Association*."

"Why take them?"

"I must be nearly a year behind on both of them. Now maybe I'll have time to read."

"Hmm . . . Potty, watching you read professional journals is not my notion of a vacation."

"Quiet, woman! You took Winnie; I take these."

She shut up and helped him. He cast a longing eye at his electric calculator, but decided it was too much like the White Knight's mousetrap. He could get by with his slide rule.

As the car splashed out into the street, she said, "Potty, how are you fixed for cash?"

"Huh? OK, I guess."

"I mean, leaving while the banks are closed and everything." She held up her purse. "Here's my bank. It isn't much, but we can use it."

He smiled and patted her knee. "Good gal! I'm sitting on my bank; I started turning everything to cash about the first of the year."

"Oh. I closed out my bank account right after we met."

"You did? You must have taken my maunderings seriously."

"I always take you seriously."

Mint Canyon was a five-mile-an-hour nightmare, with visibility limited to the tail lights of the truck ahead. When they stopped for coffee at Halfway, they confirmed what seemed evident: Cajon Pass was closed and long-haul traffic for Route 66 was being detoured through the secondary pass.

At long, long last they reached the Victorville cutoff and lost some of the traffic—a good thing, because the windshield wiper on his side had quit working, and they were driving by the committee system.

Just short of Lancaster, she said suddenly, "Potty, is this buggy equipped with a snorkel?"

"Nope."

"Then we had better stop. I see a light off the road."

The light was an auto court. Meade settled the matter of economy versus convention by signing the book herself; they were placed in one cabin. He saw that it had twin beds and let the matter ride. Meade went to bed with her teddy bear without even asking to be kissed good night. It was already gray, wet dawn.

They got up in the late afternoon and decided to stay over one more night, then push north toward Bakersfield. A high pressure area was alleged to be moving south, crowding the warm, wet mass that smothered southern California. They wanted to get into it. Breen had the wiper repaired and bought two new tires to replace his ruined spare, added some camping items to his cargo, and bought for Meade a .32 automatic, a lady's social-purpose gun.

"What's this for?" she wanted to know.

"Well, you're carrying quite a bit of cash."

"Oh. I thought maybe I was to use it to fight you off."

"Now, Meade—"

"Never mind. Thanks, Potty."

They had finished supper and were packing the car with their afternoon's purchases when the quake struck. Five inches of rain in twenty-four hours, more than three billion tons of mass suddenly loaded on a fault already overstrained, all cut loose in one subsonic, stomach-twisting rumble.

Meade sat down on the wet ground very suddenly; Breen stayed upright by dancing like a logroller. When the ground quieted down somewhat, thirty seconds later, he helped her up.

"You all right?"

"My slacks are soaked." She added pettishly, "But, Potty, it never quakes in wet weather. *Never.* You said so yourself."

"Keep quiet, can't you?" He opened the car door and switched on the radio, waited impatiently for it to warm up.

"—your Sunshine Station in Riverside, California. Keep tuned to this station for the latest developments. As of now it is impossible to tell the size of this disaster. The Colorado River aqueduct is broken; nothing is known of the extent of the damage or how long it will take to repair it. So far as we know, the Owens River Valley aqueduct may be intact, but all persons in the Los Angeles area are advised to conserve water. My personal advice is to stick your washtubs out into this rain.

"I now read from the standard disaster instructions, quote: 'Boil all water. Remain quietly in your homes, and do not panic. Stay off the highways. Cooperate with the police, and render—' Joe! Catch that phone! '—render aid where necessary. Do not use the telephone except for—' Flash! An unconfirmed report from Long Beach states that the Wilmington and San Pedro waterfront is under five feet of water. I repeat, this is unconfirmed. Here's a message from the commanding general, March Field: 'Official, all military personnel will report—' "

Breen switched it off. "Get in the car."

He stopped in the town, managed to buy six five-gallon tins and a jeep tank. He filled them with gasoline and packed them with blankets in the back seat, topping off the mess with a dozen cans of oil. Then they started rolling.

"Where are we going, Potiphar?"

"I want to get west of the valley highway."

"Any particular place west?"

"I think so. We'll see. You work the radio, but keep an

eye on the road, too. That gas back there makes me nervous."

Through the town of Mojave and northwest on 466 into the Tehachapi Mountains—

Reception was poor in the pass, but what Meade could pick up confirmed the first impression—worse than the quake of '06, worse than San Francisco, Managua, and Long Beach lumped together.

When they got down out of the mountains, the weather was clearing locally; a few stars appeared. Breen swung left off the highway and ducked south of Bakersfield by the county road, reached the Route 99 superhighway just south of Greenfield. It was, as he had feared, already jammed with refugees. He was forced to go along with the flow for a couple of miles before he could cut west at Greenfield toward Taft. They stopped on the western outskirts of the town and ate at an all-night joint.

They were about to climb back into the car when there was suddenly "sunrise" due south. The rosy light swelled almost instantaneously, filled the sky, and died. Where it had been, a red-and-purple pillar of cloud was spreading to a mushroom top.

Breen stared at it, glanced at his watch, then said harshly, "Get in the car."

"Potty! That was—"

"That used to be Los Angeles. Get in the car!"

He drove silently for several minutes. Meade seemed to be in a state of shock, unable to speak. When the sound reached them, he again glanced at his watch.

"Six minutes and nineteen seconds. That's about right."

"Potty, *we should have brought Mrs. Megeath.*"

"How was I to know?" he said angrily. "Anyhow, you can't transplant an old tree. If she got it, she never knew it."

"Oh, I hope so!"

"We're going to have all we can do to take care of ourselves. Take the flashlight, and check the map. I want to turn north at Taft and over toward the coast."

"Yes, Potiphar."

She quieted down and did as she was told. The radio gave nothing, not even the Riverside station; the whole broadcast range was covered by a curious static, like rain on a window.

He slowed down as they approached Taft, let her spot the turn north onto the state road, and turned into it. Almost at once a figure jumped out into the road in front of them, waved his arms violently. Breen tromped on the brake.

The man came up on the left side of the car, rapped on the window. Breen ran the glass down. Then he stared stupidly at the gun in the man's left hand.

"Out of the car," the stranger said sharply. "I've got to have it."

Meade reached across Breen, stuck her little lady's gun in the man's face, and pulled the trigger. Breen could feel the flash on his own face, never noticed the report. The man looked puzzled, with a neat, not-yet-bloody hole in his upper lip—then slowly sagged away from the car.

"Drive on!" Meade said in a high voice.

Breen caught his breath. "But you—"

"Drive on! *Get rolling!*"

They followed the state road through Los Padres National Forest, stopping once to fill the tank from their cans. They turned off onto a dirt road. Meade kept trying the radio, got San Francisco once, but it was too jammed with static to read. Then she got Salt Lake City, faint but clear.

"—since there are no reports of anything passing our radar screen, the Kansas City bomb must be assumed to have been planted rather than delivered. This is a tentative theory, but—"

They passed into a deep cut and lost the rest.

When the squawk box again came to life it was a crisp new voice: "Air Defense Command, coming to you over the combined networks. The rumor that Los Angeles has been hit by an atom bomb is totally unfounded. It is true that the western metropolis has suffered a severe earthquake shock, but that is all. Government officials and the Red Cross are on the spot to care for the victims, but—"

and I repeat—there has *been no atomic bombing*. So relax and stay in your homes. Such wild rumors can damage the United States quite as much as enemy bombs. Stay off the highways and listen for—"

Breen snapped it off. "Somebody," he said bitterly, "has again decided that 'Mama knows best.' They won't tell us any bad news."

"Potiphar," Meade said sharply, "that was an atom bomb, wasn't it?"

"It was. And now we don't know whether it was just Los Angeles—and Kansas City—or every big city in the country. All we know is that they are lying to us."

He concentrated on driving. The road was very bad.

As it began to get light she said, "Potty, do you know where we're going? Are we just keeping out of cities?"

"I think I know. If I'm not lost." He stared around them. "Nope, it's all right. See that hill up forward with the triple gendarmes on its profile?"

"Gendarmes?"

"Big rock pillars. That's a sure landmark. I'm looking for a private road now. It leads to a hunting lodge belonging to two of my friends—an old ranch house actually, but as a ranch it didn't pay."

"They won't mind us using it?"

He shrugged. "If they show up, we'll ask them. *If* they show up. They lived in Los Angeles."

The private road had once been a poor grade of wagon trail; now it was almost impassable. But they finally topped a hogback from which they could see almost to the Pacific, then dropped down into a sheltered bowl where the cabin was.

"All out, girl. End of the line."

Meade sighed. "It looks heavenly."

"Think you can rustle breakfast while I unload? There's probably wood in the shed. Or can you manage a wood range?"

"Just try me."

Two hours later Breen was standing on the hogback, smoking a cigarette and staring off down to the west. He wondered if that was a mushroom cloud up San Francisco way. Probably his imagination, he decided, in view of the distance. Certainly there was nothing to be seen to the south.

Meade came out of the cabin. "Potty!"

"Up here."

She joined him, took his hand, and smiled, then snitched his cigarette and took a deep drag. She exhaled it and said, "I know it's sinful of me, but I feel more peaceful than I have in months."

"I know."

"Did you see the canned goods in that pantry? We could pull through a hard winter here."

"We might have to."

"I suppose. I wish we had a cow."

"What would you do with a cow?"

"I used to milk four of them before I caught the school bus every morning. I can butcher a hog, too."

"I'll try to find you a hog."

"You do and I'll manage to smoke it." She yawned. "I'm suddenly terribly sleepy."

"So am I. And small wonder."

"Let's go to bed."

"Uh, yes. Meade?"

"Yes, Potty?"

"We may be here quite a while. You know that, don't you?"

"Yes, Potty."

"In fact, it might be smart to stay put until those curves all start turning up again. They should, you know."

"Yes. I had figured that out."

He hesitated, then went on, "Meade, will you marry me?"

"Yes." She moved up to him.

After a time he pushed her gently away and said, "My dear, my very dear—uh—we could drive down and find a minister in some little town."

She looked at him steadily. "That wouldn't be very bright, would it? I mean, nobody knows we're here, and that's the way we want it. Besides, your car might not make it back up that road."

"No, it wouldn't be very bright. But I want to do the right thing."

"It's all right, Potty. It's all *right*."

"Well, then . . . kneel down here with me. We'll say them together."

"Yes, Potiphar." She knelt, and he took her hand. He closed his eyes and prayed wordlessly.

When he opened them he said, "What's the matter?"

"The gravel hurts my knees."

"We'll stand up, then."

"No. Look, Potty, why don't we just go in the house and say them there?"

"Huh? Hell's bells, woman, we might forget to say them entirely. Now repeat after me: I, Potiphar, take thee, Meade—"

III

OFFICIAL: STATIONS WITHIN RANGE RELAY TWICE. EXECUTIVE BULLETIN NUMBER NINE—ROAD LAWS PREVIOUSLY PUBLISHED HAVE BEEN IGNORED IN MANY INSTANCES. PATROLS ARE ORDERED TO SHOOT WITHOUT WARNING AND PROVOST MARSHALS ARE DIRECTED TO USE DEATH PENALTY FOR UNAUTHORIZED POSSESSION OF GASOLINE. BIOLOGICAL WARFARE AND RADIATION QUARANTINE REGULATIONS PREVIOUSLY ISSUED WILL BE RIGIDLY ENFORCED. LONG LIVE THE UNITED STATES! HARLEY J. NEAL, LIEUTENANT GENERAL, ACTING CHIEF OF GOVERNMENT. ALL STATIONS RELAY TWICE.

THIS IS THE FREE RADIO AMERICA RELAY NETWORK. PASS THIS ALONG, BOYS! GOVERNOR BRANDLEY WAS SWORN IN TODAY AS PRESIDENT BY ACTING CHIEF JUSTICE ROBERTS UNDER THE RULE-OF-SUCCESSION. THE PRESIDENT NAMED THOMAS DEWEY AS SECRETARY OF STATE AND PAUL DOUGLAS AS SECRETARY OF DEFENSE. HIS SECOND OFFICIAL ACT WAS TO STRIP THE RENEGADE NEAL OF RANK AND TO

DIRECT HIS ARREST BY ANY CITIZEN OR OFFICIAL. MORE
LATER. PASS THE WORD ALONG.

HELLO, CQ, CQ, CQ. THIS IS W5KMR, FREEPORT. QRR,
QRR! ANYBODY READ ME? ANYBODY? WE'RE DYING LIKE
FLIES DOWN HERE. WHAT'S HAPPENED? STARTS WITH
FEVER AND A BURNING THIRST, BUT YOU CAN'T SWALLOW.
WE NEED HELP. ANYBODY READ ME? HELLO, CQ 75, CQ 75
THIS IS W5 KING MIKE ROGER CALLING QRR AND CQ75.
BY FOR SOMEBODY . . . ANYBODY!

THIS IS THE LORD'S TIME, SPONSORED BY SWAN'S ELIXIR,
THE TONIC THAT MAKES WAITING FOR THE KINGDOM OF
GOD WORTHWHILE. YOU ARE ABOUT TO HEAR A MESSAGE
OF CHEER FROM JUDGE BROOMFIELD, ANOINTED VICAR
OF THE KINGDOM ON EARTH. BUT FIRST A BULLETIN—
SEND YOUR CONTRIBUTIONS TO MESSIAH, CLINT, TEXAS.
DON'T TRY TO MAIL THEM—SEND THEM BY A KINGDOM
MESSENGER OR BY SOME PILGRIM JOURNEYING THIS WAY.
AND NOW THE TABERNACLE CHOIR FOLLOWED BY THE
VOICE OF THE VICAR ON EARTH—

—THE FIRST SYMPTOM IS LITTLE RED SPOTS IN THE
ARMPITS. THEY ITCH. PUT PATIENTS TO BED AT ONCE, AND
KEEP 'EM COVERED UP WARM. THEN GO SCRUB YOURSELF
AND WEAR A MASK, WE DON'T KNOW YET HOW YOU CATCH
IT. PASS IT ALONG, ED.

—NO NEW LANDINGS REPORTED ANYWHERE ON THIS
CONTINENT. THE FEW PARATROOPERS WHO ESCAPED THE
ORIGINAL SLAUGHTER ARE THOUGHT TO BE HIDING OUT
IN THE POCONOS. SHOOT—BUT BE CAREFUL; IT MIGHT
BE AUNT TESSIE. OFF AND CLEAR. UNTIL NOON TOMOR-
ROW—

The statistical curves were turning up again. There was
no longer doubt in Breen's mind about that. It might not
even be necessary to stay up here in the Sierra Madres
through the winter, though he rather thought they would.
It would be silly to be mowed down by the tail of a dying

epidemic, or be shot by a nervous vigilante, when a few months' wait would take care of everything.

He was headed out to the hogback to wait for sunset and do an hour's reading. He glanced at his car as he passed it, thinking that he would like to try the radio. He suppressed the yen; two-thirds of his reserve gasoline was gone already just from keeping the battery charged for the radio—and here it was only December. He really ought to cut it down to twice a week. But it meant a lot to catch the noon bulletin of Free America and then twiddle the dial a few minutes to see what else he could pick up.

But for the past three days Free America had not been on the air—solar static maybe, or perhaps just a power failure. But that rumor that President Brandley had been assassinated—it hadn't come from the Free radio, and it hadn't been denied by them, either, which was a good sign.

Still, it worried him.

And that other story that lost Atlantis had pushed up during the quake period and that the Azores were now a little continent—almost certainly a hangover of the "silly season"—but it would be nice to hear a followup.

Rather sheepishly, he let his feet carry him to the car. It wasn't fair to listen when Meade wasn't around. He warmed it up, slowly spun the dial, once around and back. Not a peep at full gain, nothing but a terrible amount of static.

He climbed the hogback, sat down on the bench he had dragged up there—their "memorial bench," sacred to the memory of the time Meade had bruised her knees on the gravel—sat down, and sighed. His lean belly was stuffed with venison and corn fritters; he lacked only tobacco to make him completely happy.

The evening cloud colors were spectacularly beautiful, and the weather was extremely balmy for December; both, he thought, caused by volcanic dust, with perhaps an assist from atom bombs.

Surprising how fast things went to pieces when they started to skid! And surprising how quickly they were going back together, judging by the signs. A curve reaches trough and then starts right back up.

World War III was the shortest big war on record—
forty cities gone, counting Moscow and the other slave
cities as well as the American ones—and then *whoosh!*
neither side fit to fight.

Of course, the fact that both sides had thrown their
Sunday punch over the North Pole through the most
freakish arctic weather since Peary invented the place had
a lot to do with it, he supposed.

It was amazing that any of the Russian paratroop trans-
ports had gotten through at all.

Breen sighed and pulled a copy of *The Western Astronomer* out of his pocket. Where was he? Oh, yes, *Some
Notes on the Stability of G-Type Stars with Especial
Reference to Sol,* by A.G.M. Dynkowski, Lenin Institute,
translated by Heinrich Ley, F.R.A.S.

Good boy, Ski—sound mathematician. Very clever
application of harmonic series and tightly reasoned.

Breen started to thumb for his place when he noticed a
footnote that he had missed. Dynkowski's own name
carried down to it: "This monograph was denounced by
Pravda as 'romantic reactionaryism' shortly after it was
published. Professor Dynkowski has been unreported since
and must be presumed to be liquidated."

The poor geek! Well, he probably would have been
atomized by now anyway, along with the goons who did
him in. He wondered if the army really had gotten all the
Russki paratroopers. He had killed his own quota; if he
hadn't gotten that doe within a quarter-mile of the cabin
and headed right back, Meade would have had a bad time.
He had shot them in the back and buried them beyond the
woodpile.

He settled down to some solid pleasure. Dynkowski was
a treat. Of course, it was old stuff that a G-type star, such
as the sun, was potentially unstable; a G-O star could
explode, slide right off the Russell diagram, and end up as
a white dwarf. But no one before Dynkowski had defined
the exact conditions for such a catastrophe, nor had anyone
else devised mathematical means of diagnosing the in-
stability and describing its progress.

He looked up to rest his eyes from the fine print and saw that the sun was obscured by a thin low cloud—one of those unusual conditions where the filtering effect is just right to permit a man to view the sun clearly with the naked eye. Probably volcanic dust in the air, he decided, acting almost like smoked glass.

He looked again. Either he had spots before his eyes or that was one fancy big sunspot. He had heard of being able to see them with the naked eye, but it had never happened to him.

He longed for a telescope.

He blinked. Yep, it was still there, about three o'clock. A *big* spot—no wonder the car radio sounded like a Hitler speech.

He turned back and continued on to the end of the article, being anxious to finish before the light failed.

At first his mood was sheerest intellectual pleasure at the man's tight mathematical reasoning. A 3 percent imbalance in the solar constant—yes, that was standard stuff; the sun would nova with that much change. But Dynkowski went further. By means of a novel mathematical operator which he had dubbed "yokes," he bracketed the period in a star's history when this could happen and tied it down with secondary, tertiary, and quaternary yokes, showing exactly the time of highest probability.

Beautiful! Dynkowski even assigned dates to the extreme limit of his primary yoke, as a good statistician should.

But as Breen went back and reviewed the equations his mood changed from intellectual to personal. Dynkowski was not talking about just any G-O star. In the latter part, he meant old Sol himself, Breen's personal sun—the big boy out there with the oversize freckle on his face.

That was one hell of a big freckle! It was a hole you could chuck Jupiter into and not make a splash. He could see it very clearly now.

Everybody talks about "when the stars grow old and the sun grows cold," but it's an impersonal concept, like one's own death.

Breen started thinking about it very personally. How long would it take, from the instant the imbalance was triggered until the expanding wave front engulfed earth? The mechanics couldn't be solved without a calculator; even though they were implicit in the equations in front of him. Half an hour, for a horseback guess, from incitement until the earth went *phutt!*

It hit him with gentle melancholy. No more? Never again? Colorado on a cool morning . . . the Boston Post Road with autumn wood smoke tanging the air . . . Bucks County bursting with color in the spring. The wet smells of the Fulton Fish Market—no, that was gone already. Coffee at the *Morning Call*. No more wild strawberries on a hillside in Jersey, hot and sweet as lips. Dawn in the South Pacific with the light airs cool velvet under your shirt and never a sound but the chuckling of the water against the sides of the old rust bucket—what was her name? That was a long time ago—the S. S. *Mary Brewster*.

No more moon if the earth was gone. Stars, but no one to gaze at them.

He looked back at the dates bracketing Dynkowski's probability yoke.

He suddenly felt the need for Meade and stood up.

She was coming out to meet him. "Hello, Potty! Safe to come in now—I've finished the dishes."

"I should help."

"You do the man's work; I'll do the woman's work. That's fair." She shaded her eyes. "What a sunset! We ought to have volcanoes blowing their tops every year."

"Sit down, and we'll watch it."

She sat beside him.

"Notice the sunspot? You can see it with your naked eye."

She stared. "Is that a sunspot? It looks as if somebody had taken a bite out of it."

He squinted his eyes at it again. Damned if it didn't look bigger!

Meade shivered. "I'm chilly. Put your arm around me."

He did so with his free arm, continuing to hold hands with the other.

It *was* bigger. The spot was growing.

What good is the race of man? Monkeys, he thought,

monkeys with a touch of poetry in them, cluttering and wasting a second-string planet near a third-string star. But sometimes they finish in style.

She snuggled to him. "Keep me warm."

"It will be warmer soon—I mean I'll keep you warm."

"Dear Potty." She looked up. "Potty, something funny is happening to the sunset."

"No, darling—to the sun."

He glanced down at the journal, still open beside him. He did not need to add up the two dates and divide by two to reach the answer. Instead he clutched fiercely at her hand, knowing with an unexpected and overpowering burst of sorrow that this was

THE END